# 'Til
# Death Do
# Us Part

**Jayne Ann Krentz** is the critically-acclaimed creator of the Arcane Society world, Dark Legacy series and Rainshadow series. She also writes as **Amanda Quick** and **Jayne Castle**. Jayne has written more than fifty *New York Times* bestsellers under various pseudonyms and lives in the Pacific Northwest.

The historical novels she writes as Amanda Quick all feature her customary irresistible mix of passion and mystery, and also have a strong psychic/paranormal twist.

Visit her online:
www.jayneannkrentz.com
www.facebook.com/JayneAnnKrentz
www.twitter.com/JayneAnnKrentz

*A Ladies of Lantern Street Novel*:
Crystal Gardens
The Mystery Woman

*Arcane Society Novels*:
*By Jayne Ann Krentz*
*writing as Amanda Quick*
Second Sight
The Third Circle
The Perfect Poison
Burning Lamp
Quicksilver

*By Jayne Ann Krentz*
White Lies
Sizzle and Burn
Running Hot
Fired Up
In Too Deep

*By Jayne Ann Krentz*
*writing as Jayne Castle*
Dark Light
Obsidian Prey
Midnight Crystal
Canyons of Night

*Dark Legacy Novels*:
*By Jayne Ann Krentz*
Copper Beach
Dream Eyes

*Rainshadow Island Novels*:
*By Jayne Ann Krentz*
*writing as Jayne Castle*
The Lost Night
Deception Cove
The Hot Zone

*Other titles by Jayne Ann Krentz*
*writing as Amanda Quick*:
With This Ring
I Thee Wed
Wicked Widow
Lie By Moonlight
The Paid Companion
Wait Until Midnight
The River Knows
Affair
Mischief
Slightly Shady
Otherwise Engaged
Garden of Lies
'Til Death Do Us Part

*Other titles by Jayne Ann Krentz*
Light in Shadow
Truth or Dare
Falling Awake
All Night Long
River Road
Trust No One

# 'Til Death Do Us Part

## AMANDA QUICK

piatkus

PIATKUS

First published in the US in 2016 by Berkley,
an imprint of Penguin Random House
First published in Great Britain in 2016 by Piatkus

3 5 7 9 10 8 6 4 2

A CIP catalogue record for this book
is available from the British Library.

ISBN 978-0-349-40942-9 [TPB]

Printed and bound by CPI Group (UK) Ltd, Croydon, CR0 4YY

Papers used by Piatkus are from well-managed forests
and other responsible sources.

MIX
Paper from
responsible sources
FSC
www.fsc.org  FSC® C104740

Piatkus
An imprint of
Little, Brown Book Group
Carmelite House
50 Victoria Embankment
London EC4Y 0DZ

An Hachette UK Company
www.hachette.co.uk

www.piatkus.co.uk

*For Frank: always and forever*

" I 've got to get rid of her, Birch." Nestor Kettering reached for the brandy bottle and refilled his glass. "I can't abide the sight of my wife. You have no idea what it's like living with her in the same house."

Dolan Birch shifted a little in his chair and stretched out his legs toward the fire. "You are not the first man to marry for money and find himself dissatisfied with the bargain. Most husbands in your situation would find a way to coexist. It is quite common for couples in Society to lead separate lives."

Nestor contemplated the fire. Dolan had invited him for a late-night brandy following another evening of cards at their club. The result was that they were now sitting together in the small but quite elegant library of Dolan's town house. Anything to avoid going back to Number Five Lark Street, Nestor thought.

They had considered stopping at a brothel but Nestor had not felt any great enthusiasm for the notion. The truth was, he did not like brothels. He worried that the women carried disease. Furthermore, it was no secret that the prostitutes frequently stole their clients' watches, tiepins, and money.

He preferred his women to be respectable, virginal, and, above all, devoid of close family connections. The last thing he wanted was to be confronted by an irate father or brother. He chose his mistresses from London's spinster class—innocent, well-bred women who were grateful for a gentleman's attentions.

Thanks to Dolan Birch, for the past year he'd had access to a steady supply of young, attractive governesses who met his criteria. He lost interest once the conquest had been made, but that was not a problem. The women were easy to discard. No one cared what happened to them.

Dolan's town house was not nearly as large as his own mansion, Nestor reflected, but it was a good deal more comfortable because there was no wife hanging about. Dolan had inherited the house upon the death of his wife, a wealthy widow. The woman had expired in her sleep soon after the wedding—and shortly after she had redrafted her will leaving the house and her handsome fortune to her new husband.

Some men had all the luck, Nestor thought.

"I do not know how much longer I can abide Anna's presence," he said. He swallowed more brandy and lowered the glass. "I swear, she drifts through the house like some faded ghost. She actually believes in spirits, you know. Attends a séance at least once a week, regular as clockwork. She seeks out a new medium every month or so."

"Who is she trying to contact?"

"Her father." Nestor grimaced. "The bastard who trapped me with the terms of his will."

"Why does she want to contact him?"

"I have no idea and I don't give a bloody damn." Nestor set the brandy glass down hard on the table. "I thought it would be so easy back at the beginning. A beautiful bride and a fortune to go with her."

Dolan contemplated the fire. "There is always a catch."

"So I have discovered."

"Your wife is quite beautiful. Most men would say that you are extremely fortunate to have such a woman in your bed."

"Bah. Anna bears a striking resemblance to a corpse in bed. Cold as hell. I haven't been with her since I cut short the honeymoon."

"The chaste ones sometimes are quite cold. One must seduce them."

Nestor snorted. "Anna was no virgin when I married her. Another reason why her father was so eager to marry her off, I suppose."

Dolan set his glass aside and propped his elbows on the arms of his chair. He put his fingertips together. "There's an old saying to the effect that if you marry for money, you will earn every penny."

"I cannot escape her. If she dies, the money goes to distant relatives in Canada, and believe me, they will be waiting to pounce on the inheritance."

"Some in your position would have her committed to an asylum," Dolan mused. "If she is declared insane, she will lose control of her fortune."

Nestor groaned. "Unfortunately, her father considered that possibility. If I have her committed, the result is the same as if she dies— the money goes to Canada."

"Have you considered renting or buying a house in the country and sending her there to live?"

"Of course," Nestor said. "The problem is that she won't obey me and there is no way to force her to do so. She says she does not want to live in the country."

"But she does not go out into Society."

"No, but London is where most of the mediums are located."

"A good thrashing might change her mind."

Nestor grunted. "I doubt it." He tightened one hand into a fist. "As I told you, she controls her own inheritance. If she leaves me, she can take the fortune with her. Damn it, there must be a way out."

Dolan was silent for a long moment.

"Perhaps there is," he said at last.

Nestor went still. "Do you have a suggestion?"

"Yes, but there is a price."

"Money is not a problem," Nestor said.

Dolan drank some brandy and lowered the glass. "As it happens, it is not money that I require in exchange for my services."

A shiver of unease gave Nestor pause. "What do you want?"

"I am, as you know, a businessman. I wish to expand one of my enterprises, and you are in a unique position to be of assistance to me."

"I can't imagine how," Nestor said. "I don't have a head for business."

"Fortunately, I do, so I don't require your business skills. It is your other talent that I wish to utilize."

"What other talent?"

"You have a gift for charm and seduction," Dolan said. "Your skills in that department are really quite extraordinary."

Nestor waved that aside. It was the truth. He did have a talent for seduction.

"What do you want from me?" he asked.

Dolan explained.

Nestor relaxed. He smiled.

"Shouldn't be any problem," he said. "That's all the payment you require in exchange for getting Anna out of my life?"

"Yes. If you are successful, I will consider your account settled."

"Then we have a bargain," Nestor said.

For the first time since his wedding night, he glimpsed a spark of hope.

2

S HE BELONGED TO him.

He was locked inside a cage the size and shape of a coffin. A dark thrill heated his blood like a powerful, intoxicating drug.

When the time came he would purify the woman and cleanse himself with her blood. But tonight was not the time. The ritual had to be followed correctly. The woman must be made to comprehend and acknowledge the great wrong that she had done. There was no finer instructor than fear.

He huddled inside the concealed lift, listening to the sounds of someone moving about in the bedroom on the other side of the wall. There was a narrow crack in the paneling. Excitement sparked through him when he caught a glimpse of the woman. She was at her dressing table, adjusting the pins in her dark brown hair. It was as if she knew he was watching and was deliberately taunting him.

She was passable in appearance, but he had seen her on the street and had not been particularly impressed with her looks. She was overly tall for a woman and her forceful character was etched on her face. She was dangerous. It was all there in her unnerving eyes.

No wonder he had been sent to purify her. He would save her from herself—and save himself in the process.

She was not the first woman he had saved. Perhaps this time he would finally be cleansed.

The lift had been installed inside the thick walls of the old mansion for the purpose of conveying an elderly, infirm lady from one floor to another. But the woman had died a few years ago, leaving the big house to her granddaughter and grandson. He had been told that neither of them made use of the device. Having been locked inside the cage for what felt like an eternity, he understood why. The air was close and still and the darkness was almost as absolute as that of the grave. *Almost.*

He was free to descend in the lift at any time. It was operated by an arrangement of ropes and pulleys that could be controlled from either inside or outside the compartment. He knew how it functioned because he'd had a helpful chat with one of the many tradesmen who came and went from the mansion on the days when the woman held the outrageous parties she was pleased to call *salons*. The truth was that the only difference between her business and a brothel was the pretense of respectability that she succeeded in giving the social gatherings.

The tradesman had informed him of the usefulness of the lift for conveying heavy items between floors. The man had also mentioned that the woman never made use of the lift. Evidently she had a fear of being trapped inside the cage.

The woman rose from the dressing table chair and moved out of sight. A moment later he heard the muffled sound of the bedroom door opening and closing.

Silence.

He slid the cage door aside and opened the wooden panel. The wall sconce had been turned down low but he could make out the bed, the dressing table, and the wardrobe.

He moved out of the lift. The heady exhilaration he always experienced at such moments roared through him. With every step of the ritual he came closer to achieving his own purification.

For a precious few seconds he debated where to leave his gift. The bed or the dressing table?

The bed, he decided. So much more intimate.

He crossed the room, not concerned with the soft thud of his footsteps. The guests had begun to arrive. There was a fair amount of traffic in the long drive that led to the front steps of Cranleigh Hall. The rattle of carriage wheels and the clatter of hooves created a great deal of noise.

When he reached the bed he took the velvet pouch and the black-bordered envelope out of the pocket of his overcoat. He opened the pouch and removed the jet-and-crystal ring. A fashionable item of memento mori jewelry, the stone was engraved with the gilded image of a skull. The woman's initials were inscribed in gold on the black enameled sides: *C. L.* When the time came a small twist of her hair would be tucked into the locket concealed beneath the skull stone. He would add it to his collection.

He admired the ring for a moment and then slipped it back into the pouch. He placed the gift on the pillow where she could not fail to notice it.

Satisfied, he stood still for a time, savoring the intense intimacy of the experience. He was in her most personal space, the room where she slept—the room where she believed herself to be alone; the room where she no doubt felt safe.

That sense of safety would soon be destroyed. She belonged to him. She simply did not know it; not yet.

He started to go back to the concealed lift but paused when he saw the framed photograph on the wall. It showed the woman as she had been some ten years earlier, a girl of sixteen or seventeen. She stood on the brink of womanhood, still innocent and unknowing, but already there was something disturbing about her eyes.

Her brother was also in the picture. He appeared to be about ten years of age. The two adults in the photograph were no doubt the children's parents. He could see something of the man in the boy.

He took the picture down from the hook and hurried to the lift. Stepping inside, he closed the panel and then the cage door. Darkness as deep as the jet stone in the ring enveloped him. He dared not light a candle.

He groped for the cables and breathed a sigh of relief when they worked. He lowered the lift to the ground floor.

When he emerged he found himself back in the small antechamber behind the rear stairs. There was no one about. The elderly housekeeper and her equally aged husband, the butler, were busy with the social gathering in the library.

In the old days when the mansion had housed a large family and a dozen or more servants it would have been nearly impossible to slip in and out of the place unnoticed. But now there was only the woman, her brother, and the old housekeeper and butler in residence.

He made his way out through the tradesmen's entrance and moved, unseen, into the gardens. The gate was still unlocked, just as he had left it.

A few minutes later he was lost in the fog. He clutched the framed photograph very tightly in his gloved hand. The weight of the knife in its sheath beneath his greatcoat was reassuring.

The ritual was almost complete.

The woman with the unnerving eyes would soon understand that she belonged to him. It was her destiny to be the one to cleanse him. He was certain of it. The connection between them was a bond that could be shattered only by death.

3

"YOU CAN'T BE serious," Nestor Kettering said with the cold arrogance of a man who was accustomed to getting whatever he desired. "I know that deep in your heart you still love me. You cannot have forgotten the passion we felt for each other. Emotions that powerful cannot die."

Calista watched him from behind the barricade of her mahogany desk. A mix of anger and disbelief crackled through her. "You are wrong. You destroyed the feelings I had for you over a year ago when you ended our association."

"I was forced to end things when I discovered that you had deceived me."

"I never lied to you, Nestor. You believed me to be a wealthy heiress. When I disabused you of that notion you disappeared overnight."

"You gave me the impression that you were well situated." Nestor swept out a hand to indicate the great house and gardens around them. "You not only deceived me, you continue to deceive respectable Society and your clients. The truth is you are in trade, Calista. You cannot deny it."

"I don't. Just as you cannot deny that you are married now. You found your heiress. Go home to her. I have no interest whatsoever in becoming your mistress."

It had been a mistake to agree to speak privately with Nestor, she thought. Three weeks ago he had sent her a bouquet of flowers and a note asking to meet with her. She had been startled because she had not heard from him in nearly a year. She had immediately instructed Mrs. Sykes to get rid of the flowers. Not for a moment had she considered acknowledging the floral gift.

The second bouquet had arrived a few days later. Once again she had told the housekeeper to toss the flowers into the rubbish.

She had not expected Nestor to show up on her doorstep because she had given him no encouragement. He was a wealthy man now. If he wanted a mistress, there were plenty to be had in London.

When he had arrived, unannounced, a short time ago, Mr. Sykes had mistaken him for a potential client. That was not entirely his fault, Calista reflected. Nestor had a great talent for convincing others to believe what he wanted them to believe.

He was a breathtakingly handsome man with an elegantly sculpted profile, silver-blond hair, and eyes as warm and blue as a summer sky. When he smiled it was almost impossible to look away. But it wasn't his polished good looks that made him so dangerous—it was his gift for charm and deception.

Indeed, Calista thought, he was a magician of sorts, one who specialized in breaking hearts and destroying other people's dreams.

The thing about a magician, however, was that once one knew the secret behind the tricks, the fascination with the performance was shattered forever. Seeing Nestor again after a little more than a year apart, she could only give thanks for her narrow escape. *To think she had once considered marrying him.*

Now she had to find a way to get rid of him. She had a legitimate prospective client due to arrive in a few minutes. She did not want Trent Hastings to overhear the quarrel that was taking place in her study. She had it on good authority that the author was a recluse who might easily be put off by such a scene.

Evidently perceiving that he could not induce her to take the blame for their parting, Nestor switched to another tactic.

"Leaving you was the hardest thing I've ever done, Calista." He raked his fingers through his hair and began to pace the small study with a languid, catlike stride. "You must understand my situation. I had to marry a fortune for the sake of my family. You must see that I had no choice."

At one time she had viewed Nestor's dramatic gestures and intense moods as evidence of a romantic spirit. She had believed him to be a man of strong passions; a man who sought a true metaphysical and intellectual bond with her. But today it was clear that what she had once mistaken for passion and great depth of feeling was, instead, nothing but shallow melodrama. There was better acting to be found in the theater.

What had she ever seen in him? she wondered—aside from his smoldering gaze and poetic good looks, of course.

"I do comprehend the situation you were in," she said. She glanced at the clock and saw that her next appointment was due in less than five minutes. It was past time to get rid of Nestor. "I comprehend precisely why you wanted to marry me. You were under the impression that my grandmother had left a fortune to me and my brother. When you discovered that all we got was her monstrosity of a mansion, you did not walk away from me—you ran."

Nestor stopped at the window, clasped his hands behind his back, and bowed his head. "You will admit that this grand house gives an impression of wealth."

"I find that impression useful in my business," she said briskly.

11

He shook his head. "Do not tell me that you have not thought of me this past year. I dream of you every night."

"I do not think about you often, Nestor, but when I do I give thanks that you ended our association when you did. I dread to imagine what my life would have been like if we had married."

He turned to look at her with a beseeching expression.

"You may be content with your spinsterhood, but I am married to a coldhearted bitch who thinks it is amusing to have affairs with my friends," he said.

"Probably because she suspects you are having affairs with her friends."

Nestor exhaled a long, heartfelt sigh. "I will not deny that I have occasionally sought comfort where I could find it. I am lonely, Calista. I remember how we used to laugh together and share our impressions of books and art and poetry. As far as I can determine, my wife's only serious intellectual pursuits are shopping and séances."

"As she evidently has the money to pursue both, I fail to see the problem."

"I have endured nearly a year of a marriage made in hell," Nestor said through his teeth. "The least you can do is spare me your sarcasm."

She got to her feet. "This meeting is finished. You appear to be under the mistaken assumption that I would be eager to resume our relationship. But that is not the case. It has been over a year since you revealed your true nature to me, and now that I am aware of it, I am no longer interested in pursuing any sort of association with you."

"I don't believe that." He stopped in front of her desk and flattened his palms on the polished surface. "You are afraid to trust your heart again. I understand. But I remember your passionate spirit very well."

"Whatever I once felt for you evaporated long ago, Nestor."

"Nothing could vanquish that burning flame. You and I are not like other people. We are possessed of a deep appreciation of the metaphysical. We comprehend the meaning of a true marriage of the souls. We do not need the legal trappings. We are meant to be together until death do us part."

"Under the circumstances I'd rather you didn't quote the old lines in the wedding vows to me. You are wasting your time, Nestor."

"You must give me a chance. You owe me that much."

"I owe you nothing," she said. "I insist that you leave. I have an appointment in a few minutes."

"Do not tell me that you no longer have feelings for me. I refuse to believe that. You and I were privileged to know a rare sort of love, one that will once again transport us to a higher plane on the wings of passion. I promise that I will rekindle the emotions you once felt for me."

"Sorry. Not possible."

She had been in the introductions business for some time now, and if there was one thing she had learned, it was that friendship—not passion—provided the only solid foundation for an enduring relationship. All she promised her clients was an opportunity to meet like-minded people and perhaps develop friendships. If some of those associations were transformed into marriages, that was all well and good. But her agency made no guarantees. And her clientele, spinsters and men of a certain age who found themselves alone in the world, were usually as clear-eyed as she was on the subject.

Although she was not about to tell Nestor, the truth was that now, safely ensconced in the spinsterhood that she had once feared, she had serious reservations about the value of marriage, at least for women. It was a stacked deck of cards in favor of men, as far as she was concerned.

The Married Woman's Property Act a few years earlier had provided a measure of legal relief for females—they could now own and control property in their own names after marriage. But given how difficult it was for a woman to earn a respectable living and actually *acquire* property, the reality was that the act did little for a vast number of females, many of whom were trapped in dreadful marriages. Divorce was still extremely difficult and expensive to obtain. It often left a woman facing life on the streets.

She no longer held any romantic illusions about the institution of marriage. It was Nestor who had helped teach her that lesson. And for that, she could not forgive him.

The clatter of hooves and carriage wheels drew her attention to the scene outside her study window. A hansom was coming up the drive. Her next appointment, no doubt. She really had to get rid of Nestor.

The cab halted at the front steps of Cranleigh Hall. A man in a long gray coat got out. The high collar of the coat was pulled up around his face, partially concealing his profile. The hat pulled down low over his eyes obscured even more of his features. He carried an elegant walking stick with a curved handle in one leather-gloved hand but he did not use it to make his way up the steps to the front door. He moved with a long, purposeful stride. A very determined man, she thought.

Anticipation flickered through her. So this was Trent Hastings.

She did not know what she had been expecting, but this whisper of excitement was certainly not it. *He's here on business,* she reminded herself.

She tried to get a better look at him but he was out of sight on the top step now.

"Are you listening to me, Calista?" Nestor asked. Anger and impatience flared in his tone.

"Hmm? No, actually, I'm not listening to you. Kindly do me the great favor of leaving. I am very busy today."

"Bloody hell." Nestor visibly seethed. "I'm not here to apply to become one of your clients. I am here because I cannot live without you."

"You appear to be doing very nicely without me. And I have absolutely no desire to become your mistress."

"I have money now. I will take care of you. We will be lovers."

"Sorry, otherwise employed at the moment. You do not love me. You never loved me. I think the only person you are capable of loving is yourself. Admit it, you are here because you have grown bored with your marriage."

"You're damn right, I'm bored."

"That is your problem, not mine. Leave, Nestor. Now."

"Damn it, you're too old to play the silly, naïve virgin," he hissed. "What are you now? Twenty-seven? I'm sure you've taken any number of lovers from your list of so-called clients."

For the first time, her temper blazed.

*"How dare you?"*

"I merely put the obvious into words," Nestor said. He smirked, pleased to have drawn blood. "There is no need to put a respectable face on your business. An introductions agency, indeed." He snorted. "I must say I admire your ingenuity. You have proven to be a remarkable businesswoman, Calista. But let's be clear. You are nothing but the madam of a high-class brothel."

Anger and a whisper of panic flashed through her. She was very careful about how she operated her business. She worked only by referral. She made certain that her brother, Andrew, researched all of her potential clients before she accepted them. The salons and teas she hosted were elegant, eminently respectable affairs.

But she was keenly aware of the dangers of malicious gossip. Nestor was not the first man who had concluded that her agency provided something other than respectable introductions.

"I do not care to listen to your insults." She reached for the bellpull. "Leave now or I will summon my butler to escort you out."

"That doddering old man who met me at the door? He can barely hold a visitor's hat and gloves. He would faint dead away if you demanded that he try to forcibly remove me."

She hoisted her skirts a few inches above her ankles, whisked around the side of her desk, and crossed the study.

She yanked open the door. "Get out of here now or I will scream."

"Have you gone mad?"

"It's certainly a possibility. My nerves have been badly frayed of late."

That was no less than the truth. She had found the second memento mori object on her pillow last night. After the discovery, she and Andrew and Mr. Sykes had gone through every room on every floor of the big house, checking the locks on windows and doors. She had not slept much at all.

"Calista, you must listen to me," Nestor snarled.

"No," she said. "The last thing I need is a professional fortune hunter trying to make me believe that he is still in love with me after he abandoned me to marry another woman. I would remind you that I am not alone in this house. My housekeeper and butler may be elderly, but I assure you they are still quite capable of whistling for a constable if necessary. Yes, Nestor, I will scream bloody murder if that's what it takes to remove you from the premises."

It was the startled look on his face that made her realize they were no longer alone.

*"Can I be of any assistance?"*

The dark, masculine voice came from directly behind her. The words were spoken in a chillingly polite manner that could have been mistaken for aloof disinterest if not for the razor-sharp steel edge just below the surface.

She spun around and saw Mrs. Sykes, wide-eyed with shock, in the hall. The housekeeper was accompanied by the man who had just alighted from the hansom.

Her heart sank. This was not an auspicious start to what she had hoped would prove to be an excellent business relationship.

Her first thought was that, fine clothes aside, the caller bore a striking resemblance to the sort of individual one might expect to encounter in a dark alley on a moonless night.

It was not the ragged web of scars on the left side of his cheek and jaw that made him appear dangerous—it was something about his eyes. They were a startling blend of green and gold and infused with an implacable will.

Nestor was at last stunned into silence.

It was Mrs. Sykes who, no doubt calling upon years of professional training, shattered the crystalline atmosphere.

"Your ten o'clock appointment is here, Miss Langley," she said. "Mr. Hastings." Then she immediately spoiled the effect by lowering her voice to a conspiratorial whisper. "The *author*, miss."

"Yes, of course." Calista collected herself and gave Trent her best client smile. "You must be Eudora Hastings's brother. A pleasure to meet you, sir."

"I apologize for the interruption," Trent said. He continued to watch Nestor with a detached curiosity that was more ominous than anything he might have said. "I trust my arrival is not a problem for you."

"Not at all." Calista stepped back, and motioned with her hand to invite him to enter the study. "Do come in. Mr. Kettering was just leaving. Isn't that right, Mr. Kettering?"

Nestor shot her a furious glare, but it was obvious to all of them that he was trapped. Nevertheless, he rallied for one last strike.

"You're Trent Hastings, the author of the Clive Stone detective novels?" he asked with a deceptively lazy air.

"That is correct," Trent said.

"Pity about those scars. No wonder you felt the need to seek out the services of an *introductions* agency. It must be rather difficult to meet respectable ladies with that face."

"*Nestor,*" Calista gasped, horrified.

Mrs. Sykes stared at Nestor, appalled.

Satisfied, Nestor gave Calista a thin smile.

"You must excuse me, Calista," he said. "I'm a busy man."

He brushed past her and moved out into the hall where he paused with a dramatic flourish and looked back at Trent.

"Read the latest chapter of your new book in the *Flying Intelligencer*, Hastings. This one isn't shaping up to be your best work, is it? The plot is quite weak. I already know the identity of the villain and you're only halfway through the story. I do hope you're going to kill off Wilhelmina Preston. Can't abide that character."

Nestor did not wait for a response. He went down the hall, his footsteps ringing on the hardwood floor.

"I'll see him out," Mrs. Sykes said.

She hurried after Nestor.

Very deliberately, Trent removed his leather gloves, revealing more scars on the back of his left hand.

"I do apologize," Calista said.

"There's no need," Trent said. "I have been a writer for several years now. I learned long ago that everyone's a critic."

4

"EVERYONE HAS SCARS, Mr. Hastings." Calista looked up from her notebook and gave Trent a reassuring smile. "Some are more visible than others, but that need not present any great problem."

Much to her relief, Trent had not attempted to invade her privacy by inquiring about Nestor's presence. Instead he had surveyed her study with the same detached curiosity he had applied to Nestor and then he had accepted her invitation to sit down.

Relieved that the unfortunate scene was concluded, she had hurried back behind her desk, sat down, and opened her notebook. She was prepared to conduct a standard client interview. But it was Trent who had asked the first question and it had caught her off guard. *Do you think my scars will be an issue?*

Trent leaned back in his chair and fixed her with a considering look. "You don't think my face will get in the way of finding me a wife?"

"You appear to be under a misapprehension concerning the nature of my business," she said. "I do not promise that my introductions will end in matrimony, sir. I endeavor to promote associations between like-minded individuals who find themselves single for one reason or another—*respectable*, like-minded people. Not everyone seeks marriage. Some hope for friendship and companionship."

"Why do I have the impression that you are one of those who doesn't seek marriage?"

Her day was not improving, she reflected. First, Nestor had stormed back into her life expecting to take up where they had left off, and now the excellent prospective client she had hoped to attract was proving difficult.

She reminded herself to be patient. Trent Hastings was certainly not the first wary individual she had dealt with. In spite of the fact that she conducted her business strictly on the basis of word of mouth and confidential referrals, more than one person had entered her office with some trepidation. Few arrived knowing exactly what to expect from an introductions agency.

None, however, had referred, even obliquely, to the fact that she was not married. At her age, her status was clear to one and all—she was a spinster.

"If we might return to the subject at hand," she said. "I can assure you that I have several very respectable ladies among my clients who are possessed of the sort of discerning intelligence that enables them to look beyond the superficial. Their first and most important requirement in a friend—or a husband, for that matter—is strength of character."

"And just how do you go about ascertaining a client's character?"

She tapped the tip of the pencil against the blank page of her notebook. She was supposed to be conducting the interview, but Trent was the one asking the questions.

Earlier that morning she had looked forward to the prospect of meeting him. She had recognized the name that Mrs. Sykes had written in the appointment book for two reasons. The first was that Trent's sister, Eudora Hastings, was a client. The second reason was that, until approximately five minutes ago, she had considered herself a great fan of his mystery series.

The prospect of adding the highly successful but notoriously reclusive author to her roster of satisfied customers had elevated her spirits for a time. But now she was starting to have second thoughts—and not because of the scars that marred his striking face.

"I have discovered that one can determine a great deal about character by conducting an extensive interview," she said. "My father was an engineer and my mother was a botanist. I learned the techniques of research from them."

Trent glanced at her bookshelves again. "Yes, I can see their influence. I am honored to have my books shelved between Mrs. Loudon's *Botany for Ladies* and the *Building News and Engineering Journal*."

She cleared her throat. "Yes, well, I am a great fan of your novels, sir. So is my brother, my housekeeper, and my butler. Indeed, you are quite popular in this household." She paused. "Actually, now that I think about it, I do have a question for you concerning the story that is currently being serialized in the *Flying Intelligencer*."

Trent exhaled deeply. "I was afraid of that."

She ignored the comment.

"My question concerns the introduction of Miss Wilhelmina Preston. She is a most interesting character in part because of her many scientific interests. I can see where she might prove quite helpful to Clive Stone in his investigations. Indeed, I am wondering if you are about to introduce a romantic relationship between Clive and Wilhelmina."

"I never discuss a story in progress."

"I see." Chagrined, she returned to her notes. "In that case—"

"My sister tells me that you have tried to adapt scientific methods to your matrimonial business," he said.

"That is true." She tightened her grip on the pencil. It was time to take control of the interview. "Today I propose to ask you a few general questions. I will also explain the process I employ to match my clients. If we are both satisfied with this initial discussion I will schedule another, more lengthy appointment. During that session we will prepare a comprehensive list of the qualities you seek in a relationship, whether that be companionship or matrimony, and itemize what you have to offer."

"Money," Trent said.

Calista paused, her pencil poised above the blank page. "Excuse me?"

"My single, most sterling quality is that I possess a rather comfortable income. I have done rather well by investing the money from my books in properties. The question is, do I have enough money to persuade one of those intelligent, discerning lady clients you mentioned to overlook my scars?"

Another man might have tried to grow whiskers or a beard to camouflage the scars in question, but Trent Hastings made little effort to conceal the damage that had been done to the left side of his face.

The marks looked as if they had been etched into the skin by acid or flames. They ran down the side of his jaw, disappearing beneath the high, crisp collar of his white shirt. She had no idea what had happened to brand him in such a manner but she was certain that it had been horribly painful. Mercifully his eyes had been spared.

Some might pity him or avert their gazes, she thought. But a person who possessed any degree of insight would surely conclude that a man who had survived the experience that had scarred him, and learned to deal with its effect on others, was a man of strong character.

Such a man would make a very good friend or a very dangerous enemy. She was starting to think that such a man also would be very difficult to match. It was not his scars that would complicate the process, she decided. The challenge would be finding a lady who could stand up to such a strong-willed male.

"Finances, of course, must necessarily be a consideration for both parties when it comes to marriage," she said.

"According to my observations, it is usually the primary consideration."

"Forgive me, sir, but I am gaining the impression that you are somewhat cynical when it comes to the matter of marriage."

"I am realistic, Miss Langley."

She put down her pencil, closed the notebook, and clasped her hands together on the desktop.

"I don't deny that when it comes to marriage, there is an element of practicality that cannot be overlooked," she said. "But if I know that a client is seeking marriage, I take precautions to verify the finances of both individuals."

For the first time, Trent actually looked interested in her matchmaking process.

"How the devil do you do that?" he asked.

"I employ an assistant who conducts a bit of very discreet background research to ascertain the truth regarding the financial status of the clients. Not everyone is forthright about that aspect of their personal life."

"Huh. Interesting. Who is this assistant?"

"My brother."

"I see. I find your emphasis on financial matters intriguing."

"You are the one who raised the subject," she said.

"Probably because I made this appointment to discover whether or not you are attempting to defraud my sister."

*"What?"*

"Eudora is one of your clients. Naturally I have some concerns."

For a few seconds Calista was speechless. She finally managed to pull herself together.

"Yes, Miss Hastings is a client. But I assure you, sir, she is in no danger from me. Indeed, she appears to be enjoying my weekly salons. She is a very intelligent, well-read lady."

"My sister may be intelligent and well-read, but she is a spinster of a certain age who has very little experience of men. She is also quite comfortably positioned in terms of her finances."

"Thanks to your fortune?"

"Yes. That makes her vulnerable to the sort of unscrupulous men who prey on single women who possess a good income or a healthy inheritance."

For the first time she glimpsed some fierce emotion stirring beneath the surface of the man. A shiver went through her. He wasn't angry at her—not yet, merely suspicious—but she was willing to wager that at some time in his past he'd very likely encountered a fortune hunter who had taken advantage of someone he cared about.

"I thought I made it clear," she said, striving for a calming tone, "I am alert to the type of person who might attempt to take advantage of my clients. I would not dream of introducing your sister to a gentleman who was anything but respectable and entirely honest about his finances."

"It strikes me, Miss Langley, that there might be a financial incentive for you to provide certain clients with introductions to other clients who are wealthy or well-connected."

"That is quite enough." For the second time that morning she found herself on her feet and furious. "You insult both your sister and me, sir. I must ask you to leave at once."

For a heart-stopping moment she was afraid he would not allow himself to be kicked out of her office. She reached for the bellpull behind her and prepared to tug on it.

To her overwhelming relief, Trent got to his feet. He went toward the door without a word. She released the bellpull, gripped the back of her chair, and held her breath.

Trent opened the door and paused. He turned to face her.

"One more question before I leave, Miss Langley," he said.

She swallowed hard. "I am not in the mood to answer your questions, sir."

"I understand, but curiosity compels me. Do you really think you could have found me a suitable wife?"

"I very much doubt it, Mr. Hastings. I'm afraid you just failed the interview."

He inclined his head a scant half inch. "Yes, I can see that."

He let himself out into the hall and closed the door in a deliberate manner that said more than words.

He did not intend to return.

Just as well, Calista thought. But the atmosphere in the study suddenly felt several degrees colder than it had a moment ago.

5

THE INTERVIEW WITH Calista Langley had not gone well.
Trent walked into the front hall of the town house braced for
a controlled display of sorrowful disappointment, hurt, resentment,
and a few accusatory tears from his sister.

But for the first time in a very long while, Eudora managed to take
him completely by surprise.

She stormed down the stairs in a cloud of outraged fury.

"You went to see Miss Langley, didn't you?" she demanded. "How
dare you? My business with her is just that—my business. It is none
of your concern."

Eudora was in her midtwenties, perhaps a year or two younger than
Calista, Trent thought, but she gave the impression of being the older
of the two.

Today Calista had made a fashionable impression in an elegant
blue gown. Her chestnut-brown hair had been caught up in a delightful confection on top of her head and anchored with several handsome
hairpins. The style served to underscore her striking profile and intel-

ligent hazel eyes. There was something bright, vivid, and dynamic about her. He had found himself oddly fascinated. She was an interesting, intriguing woman and he was quite sure she would be interesting and intriguing at seventy or eighty. Some qualities never aged.

Eudora, on the other hand, had, until recently, appeared to be fading before his eyes. Determined to play the role of the devoted sister who had sacrificed herself to the task of managing her brother's household, she wore her bright blond hair parted in the center and scraped back in a tight knot. Her gowns were fashioned of dull, dark, practical fabrics.

She pursued her self-assigned career with a vengeance. The house they shared functioned like a finely tuned machine. From dawn until bedtime there was a serene, orderly cadence to life. The staff went about their duties with flawless precision. The gardens were maintained with exquisite attention to detail.

But over the years the spirited, vivacious girl who had once insisted on learning how to ride a bicycle and playing croquet had vanished. In her place had emerged a woman who appeared to have locked herself in perpetual mourning. Eudora did not go about in widow's weeds or wear a veil, but she might as well have done so in Trent's opinion.

Nevertheless, she had appeared to be going through some changes lately, and he had been pleased, at least at first. She was certainly paying more attention to style and she had even gone shopping for some new earrings.

He knew he would have been relieved by the transformation had he not realized that it was linked to Calista Langley's weekly salons.

"Calm yourself," he said. He handed his hat and gloves to Guthrie, the butler, but he kept his grip on the cane. "I made the appointment with Miss Langley because I was curious about her and her services."

"I don't believe that for a moment," Eudora snapped. "You called on her to try to intimidate her. Admit it. You could not persuade me that she was a fraud and a con artist or worse, so you attempted to frighten her into severing our association."

"If that was my plan I can assure you it failed," Trent said. "Approximately three minutes into the conversation it became clear that it would take someone far more ferocious than a mere author to throw a scare into Miss Langley."

Eudora halted on the last step, startled. Then she appeared pleased. Triumph gleamed in her blue eyes.

"So Miss Langley gave you a proper setdown, did she? I am delighted to hear that."

"I comprehend that you are angry that I went to see her," he said. "But I felt it necessary to investigate Miss Langley's rather unusual business."

"She arranges salons where respectable people can meet. What is so dangerous about that?"

"We have discussed this," Trent said. He went down the hall toward the refuge of his study. "Miss Langley undertakes to introduce complete strangers to each other."

"*Single* strangers," Eudora said.

"It would be one thing if she was well-acquainted with all of the parties involved, but that is hardly the case. The people who attend her salons are not personal friends, they are her clients. You possess a sizeable inheritance. That makes you vulnerable to the worst sort of predators."

Eudora hurried after him.

"Miss Langley insists on references from every client," she said. "In addition, she conducts detailed interviews with each one to make certain that there are no fortune hunters or married men hoping to prey on the ladies on her guest list."

He paused in the doorway of the study. "They're not guests, Eudora. She is not a Society hostess entertaining respectable acquaintances with teas and musicales. She's a businesswoman and that means money is her chief consideration."

He went into the room. Eudora pursued him.

"You have no right to interfere in my private affairs," she said.

"I'm your brother." He hooked the cane over the back of his chair and went to stand at the window. "I have a responsibility to protect you."

"I don't need to be protected from Miss Langley."

He looked out at the vibrant garden and the glass-and-iron conservatory. Gardening and reading were Eudora's only pleasures these days. At least, they had been until she had begun attending Miss Langley's weekly salons. Lately she had returned from the events talking of the latest news in a wide variety of subjects—art, travel, books, the theater.

"I know you feel I'm being overcautious," he said. "Nevertheless—"

"Do you really believe that I'm in danger of falling for a fortune hunter's lies? Please give me some credit for common sense."

"I don't doubt your intelligence or your common sense," Trent said quietly. "But I am concerned about this connection with Miss Langley."

There was a short silence behind him.

"What did you think of her?" Eudora asked after a moment.

Her tone of voice was suspiciously neutral. He realized he had been trying to sort out his chaotic impressions of Miss Langley since leaving her very impressive mansion.

"What?" he said, trying to buy time to assemble his thoughts.

"You heard me. Now that you have met her, what is your opinion of Miss Langley?"

He attempted to formulate a response but for some reason he could not find the right words. *Attractive* but not in the ordinary sense of the word. *Unconventional* would be a more accurate description. But for some reason he kept coming back to *fascinating*.

He was a naturally curious man with wide-ranging interests that had led him to investigate any number of odd subjects and skills. The research involved in each new Clive Stone novel routinely led him down unusual, sometimes bizarre paths. But Calista Langley aroused his curiosity in new and unsettling ways.

He had known immediately that Calista was a woman who was willing to fight for what she wanted; a woman who would do whatever it took to protect what was hers. And if she loved, he thought, she would be quite fierce about the business. There was something in her person that hinted at a capacity for passion.

He had known some intelligent, independent, strong-willed women in his life—he was attracted to the species—but Calista Langley was unique in her appeal.

"I found her . . . interesting," he said. He turned around and gripped the back of his desk chair with both hands. "I admit she was not what I had expected."

"Interesting?" Eudora looked startled. Then her eyes narrowed a little. "I think I understand. You find her *interesting* because she did not allow you to intimidate her."

"I doubt that a medium-sized army could intimidate Miss Langley. But that only makes me all the more cautious about both her and the way she makes her living."

"I am not going to stop attending her salons, Trent—not unless she strikes me off her guest list. And if she does, I will know that you are to blame."

"Are these gatherings really so important to you?"

"Yes. Trent, please try to understand. I find the salons stimulating. There are so many new people to meet and the lectures are always on intriguing topics. Last week Professor MacPherson gave a talk about the Roman antiquities that can be found right here in Britain. The week before, Mr. Harper discussed his travels in the American West. The next salon will feature a lecture on the latest advances in photography."

"Tell me, has Miss Langley introduced you to any man in particular?"

Eudora stiffened. "A guest is introduced to everyone at the salons. That is the purpose of the gatherings."

"Let me be more specific. Have any of Miss Langley's male clients made an attempt to deepen his acquaintance with you?"

Eudora's jaw tightened in a stubborn line. "None of the gentlemen to whom I have been introduced has behaved in any way that could be termed improper or objectionable. But I can tell that nothing I say will convince you of that. Why don't you see for yourself?"

"That was exactly what I attempted to do today, if you will recall."

"I'm not talking about your failed effort to intimidate Miss Langley." Eudora smiled a brittle smile. "I suggest that you apply to become one of her clients."

"Don't be ridiculous."

"I realize that after today she may not be disposed to add you to her guest list, but I might be able to prevail upon her to take you on a trial basis. After all, she is a fan of your novels. Perhaps I can persuade her to allow you to attend a couple of salons with me and form your own conclusions about her business."

"Are you serious?"

"Give it some consideration, dear brother." Eudora spun around and went toward the door. "Because I assure you, I have every intention of continuing to accept her invitations."

She let herself out into the hall and closed the door with considerably more force than was necessary.

Trent lowered himself into the chair. For a time he contemplated his private realm. His study was the one place where he could be assured of being alone and uninterrupted. The entire household understood that when the door was closed he was not to be disturbed except in case of fire or the end of the world.

31

He should get back to his writing, he thought. The visit to Calista Langley had been a disaster, not to mention a waste of time. In any event, the next installment of *Clive Stone and the Affair of the Missing Bride* was due to the editor of the *Flying Intelligencer*.

But he pondered the closed door for a long time. He was quite sure now that one of Calista's male clients had, indeed, taken a particular interest in Eudora. It did not require the devious mind of an author of mystery novels to deduce that Eudora returned that interest.

He had always hoped that Eudora would encounter a good man whom she could love, one who would appreciate her clever mind and organizational talents. A man who could give her what she needed most—a home of her own to manage.

In the past few years it had become increasingly evident that might not happen.

His intelligent, lovely little sister had become a spinster. That would not have been such a bad fate if she had been happy. But he was quite sure that was not the case. For some time there had been a certain wistfulness about her that had tugged at his heart. He wanted to protect her but he did not think it was in his power to make her happy.

Now things appeared to be changing for her, thanks to the mysterious Calista Langley. She was providing Eudora with the one thing he could not give her.

He ought to be grateful that his sister was at long last emerging from her self-imposed martyrdom. Nevertheless, he was concerned. Calista Langley was an unknown quantity. His intuition told him that she had the power to disrupt his quiet, well-ordered, and extremely predictable life.

He could not decide exactly how he felt about that but he was certain of one thing: he felt *something*—and the sensation was remarkably intense. Calista was the first woman in a very long time who had intrigued him more than the characters in his imagination.

6

"I'LL BE GOING out tonight after dinner," Andrew announced. "No point waiting up for me. I'm meeting some friends. I won't be home until quite late."

His tone was laced with the familiar touch of defiance. Calista forked up a bite of stewed chicken while she considered how to deal with her brother's announcement. The truth was there was very little she could do or say to stop him from going out on the town, and the last thing she wanted was a quarrel. You must choose your battles, she thought.

Andrew was seated at the far end of the long dining table, hurrying to finish the meal so that he could leave the house to meet his friends. It might have been easier to talk in the more intimate confines of the morning room but Mrs. Sykes insisted on serving dinner in the gloomy, darkly paneled dining room.

The housekeeper and her husband had lived and worked in Cranleigh Hall since taking up their first posts as maid and footman several decades earlier. They had grown old along with their grim, depressed employer,

Roberta Langley. Roberta had left the mansion to her grandchildren but Calista privately considered that the Sykeses had a better claim on the moldering pile of wood and stone than she and Andrew did.

She knew that she and her brother should be grateful to have such a distinguished roof over their heads. There was no denying that Cranleigh Hall had proved extremely useful as a business prop. Prospective clients were reassured and greatly impressed by the imposing residence and the elegant address in Cranleigh Square. But in Calista's opinion, the great house would never be a warm and welcoming home to Andrew or to her.

She had a number of concerns about Andrew's new habit of staying out late into the night, but one of them was very personal and quite selfish. She did not want to be alone in the mansion. True, the Sykeses were always present, but they retired to their quarters promptly at nine o'clock, every night. Once they were abed, the loneliness that seemed to be infused into the very walls of the mansion emerged to haunt her.

The anxiety that had been icing her nerves ever since someone had pushed the dreadful little tear-catcher through the letter box in the door two weeks ago had intensified thanks to the visit from Nestor Kettering that morning. For days she had felt as if her every move was being watched. And now she faced another night alone.

She had to grow accustomed to the sensation, she told herself. Soon Andrew would announce that he wished to move into lodgings of his own. It was inevitable. Every young man needed to be free to discover his own path in life. She had no right to make him feel guilty for abandoning her.

"Will you go to the theater?" she asked, trying to sound pleasant and politely interested.

"Maybe." Andrew wolfed down some green beans. "Probably play some cards afterward."

Calista tightened her grip on her fork and tried not to show her concern. Of all the myriad vices available to a young man in London, she most feared the gambling hells. There was no faster path to ruin.

The small inheritance that had come to them along with Cranleigh Hall had gone to pay for the establishment of her introductions agency. Presenting a gracious, refined image to clients had required the purchase of fashionable furnishings for the first-floor rooms. She had known from the outset that she would be walking a tightrope of respectability. Appearances were everything in her business.

And fortunately, business had been brisk. She and Andrew were doing quite nicely on the income from her introductions agency but they could not afford to take risks.

She put the fork down very carefully on her plate. "Andrew—you are not in trouble, are you? Financially, I mean?"

"Why must every dinner table conversation between us end with you implying that I cannot take care of myself? I am no longer a boy. I do not need my older sister hovering over me at every step."

Andrew was most certainly not a boy, she thought. Not anymore. He was nineteen, lean and fit and infused with the vitality of a young man coming into his prime. He had the additional advantages of their father's strong, distinguished profile and intelligent hazel eyes.

He was no longer the frightened little nine-year-old to whom she'd had to explain that their parents had been lost at sea and were never coming home. He did not need her now to protect him from the bleak moods of a grandmother consumed with bitterness. He was ready to step out into the world.

Nevertheless, the thought of losing Andrew to the dark streets of London filled her with a special kind of panic. It was obvious that there was no point berating him. It would only drive him away all the faster. And she would be truly alone all the sooner.

Best to change the subject.

"Today I had a rather disturbing interview with a gentleman I had hoped would become an excellent client," she said.

Andrew looked wary for a moment, then his eyes tightened a little in genuine concern. "Anything to do with those nasty little memento mori objects that you received recently?"

"No. This is an entirely different matter. My visitor was Trent Hastings."

She had no intention of mentioning the unpleasant scene with Nestor Kettering. She feared Andrew's reaction.

Andrew's brows shot up in astonishment. "Trent Hastings, the author?"

"Precisely."

"But surely that is good news." Andrew's eyes lit with enthusiasm. "Just think what securing a well-known client such as Mr. Hastings would do for your business."

"You know very well I do not advertise the names of my clients. Many would be quite embarrassed."

"Yes, I know. But you depend on word of mouth, and the right words from Trent Hastings's mouth would send a number of excellent clients your way."

"Unfortunately, I don't think there will be any helpful recommendations coming from Mr. Hastings. He seems to think that I am in the business of taking advantage of some of my female clients who enjoy a respectable income—specifically his sister."

"That's utter nonsense. How dare he insult you and impugn your reputation?" Andrew crumpled his napkin on the table. "I'll have a word with him."

"No, you will not." The thought of Andrew confronting a man as intimidating as Hastings was enough to send another bolt of panic through her. She should never have mentioned the interview with

Hastings to him, she thought. Frantically she searched for a diplomatic way to head off disaster. "Really, there's no need for you to speak to him. I set him straight, I assure you. It was all a simple misunderstanding. Keep in mind that his sister is an excellent client. We don't want to do anything to make her cancel her arrangements with my agency."

"Hastings apologized?"

"Not exactly, however—"

"That bastard. Do you have his address? Never mind. I'll find him."

"Andrew, please, listen to what I'm saying. It was all a mistake." She summoned up a reassuring smile. "I was just somewhat taken aback at the time, that's all."

"He owes you an apology."

"I think he will come to understand that in time." Not much chance of that happening, she thought, but she kept the opinion to herself. "Meanwhile, I don't want to do anything that might put Eudora Hastings in a position that forces her to choose sides, as it were. If she were to sever our business connection it would only give rise to unfortunate rumors."

"Huh."

Andrew was still angry but common sense was winning out.

"It's all right," she said quietly. "I promise you, Mr. Hastings will not be a problem. His sister is a very strong-willed lady and she enjoys my salons. She told me that she had a delightful time at last week's event and she accepted the invitation to the next one. I doubt very much that her brother will be able to keep her away."

Andrew did not appear to be entirely convinced but curiosity got the better of him.

"What's he like?"

"Mr. Hastings? He is quite—" Calista paused, trying to find the right word. "Formidable."

"I meant what does he look like?"

"Oh." She summoned up a mental image of Trent. "Well, as to that, he is endowed with a very manly build. Dark hair. Arresting eyes."

Andrew frowned. "A *manly* build?"

"Mmm, yes, I think that is how one would describe it."

Andrew watched her with a speculative expression. "Would you say that he was the sort of man women would describe as handsome?"

"Not exactly. But quite gratifying to look upon, if you know what I mean."

"No, I don't know what you mean."

Calista ignored the interruption. "He seems to think the scars will be a problem if he were to come to me as a client but I assured him that he was wrong."

"Scars?"

"On the left side of his jaw. Rather dramatic, I'm afraid. There are some on one of his hands, too. He must have been the victim of an accident at some point in the past."

"But the scars didn't frighten you?"

"Not at all," Calista said. "He was rather annoying, to be sure, but I did not feel threatened."

Andrew went very still. "Do you think it's possible he might be the person who is responsible for the memento mori objects?"

"*What?* Good heavens, no. Whatever gave you that idea? I'm sure Mr. Hastings is not the one who gave me those horrid objects."

"Why are you so positive of his innocence?"

She thought about that for a few seconds, trying to put her intuitive certainty into words.

"From what I observed today, Mr. Hastings is nothing if not direct," she said. "He would not torment a woman from the shadows."

"How can you be sure?"

She considered the question for a moment and then waved it aside. "I don't know. Something about the way he looks at one, I suppose."

"Not much to go on."

"No. But you know very well that my intuition has generally been quite accurate when it comes to judging people."

"Not when it came to that bastard who left you standing at the altar."

It was a very good thing that she hadn't mentioned Nestor's visit today, she decided.

"Mr. Kettering and I were about to become engaged," she said patiently. "I wasn't quite at the altar."

"Very little difference."

Some of the old anger that she had experienced because she had allowed herself to be deceived by Nestor resurfaced. She had been such a naïve fool. She strove to keep her voice lowered to a level that would not alarm Mr. and Mrs. Sykes, who were eating in the kitchen.

"Trust me," she said, "there is a great deal of difference."

"Sorry," Andrew said brusquely. "Didn't mean to bring up the subject of Kettering."

"My nerves have been somewhat strained of late."

And that was putting it mildly, she thought.

"I know." Andrew's mouth tightened in a grim line. "Bloody hell, I can't believe the person who is sending you the memento mori gifts actually gained access to this house, unnoticed. He was in your *bedroom*, Calista."

"There is no need to remind me. We've been through this several times. There were a great many people coming and going yesterday afternoon because of the preparations being made for the next salon. Tradesmen and delivery people were in and out all day long."

"He must have got in disguised as a deliveryman. The thing is, who could have known about the existence of that old lift?"

"Anyone who ever worked in this house or in the gardens, for starters," Calista said.

"None of them has any reason to try to frighten you."

"Whatever the case, I'm quite certain it wasn't Mr. Hastings who sent the tear-catcher to me and left the ring on my bed. Please believe me when I tell you that he did not come to see me today because he is feeling vengeful. In his view, he was simply attempting to protect his sister. You would no doubt have done the same in his place."

"He must be a suspicious man by nature."

"That is only to be expected. He writes novels with plots that revolve around dark secrets and murder. One can only imagine how dwelling on such matters day in and day out might affect a person's view of human nature."

"I certainly have formed a very dark view of Trent Hastings now that you've told me about your meeting with him."

"I must admit I won't be rushing out to purchase his next book," Calista said. "Which is a pity. I quite enjoyed his last novel."

"Very clever plot and the final scenes with the villain were riveting." Andrew's brows scrunched together. "Not sure I care for the character of Miss Wilhelmina Preston in this new story, however."

"What's wrong with Wilhelmina Preston? I rather like her."

"It's all very well to insert a woman into the plot but we don't want Clive Stone to get sidetracked with a romance. It will ruin the series."

"That is a matter of opinion."

7

H ER HUSBAND WAS a very dangerous man. She was terrified of him.

Anna Kettering was intensely aware of her racing pulse. Her heart was pounding. Her breath seemed to be trapped in her throat. She was certain now that the only thing keeping her alive was her inheritance.

The terms her father had insisted on incorporating into his will were strict and quite clear. If anything happened to her—a fall down the stairs, a fever, *anything*—the money would go to distant relatives in Canada.

Papa must have had some suspicions about Nestor, she thought. Her husband had appeared to be the ideal husband. Her father must have feared that Nestor was too perfect.

Her fingers were shaking so badly it was all she could do to insert the key into the lock. She finally managed to get the door open. One last glance down the long hall assured her that there was no one about to observe her. It was the servants' afternoon off and Nestor was supposedly attending a sporting event but she knew she had to be very careful.

Satisfied that she was alone in the big town house, she entered the shadowed chamber and quickly closed and locked the door. She lit a candle and looked around the small space.

The room was decorated in the somber hues of deep mourning. An elaborate arrangement of white flowers was displayed on a wrought-iron stand. The heavy scent of the dead and dying blooms was almost overpowering. The gilt mirror had been covered with black velvet as was the custom. It was nonsense to think that it was bad luck for the mourners to see their own reflections in the house of the recently deceased but some of the old superstitions still informed the rituals associated with death.

The clock on the mantel had been stopped at five minutes to midnight—the time of death.

She crossed the small space and looked down at the silver tray lined with white velvet. The tear-catcher and the jet ring were gone. The only item left was a black enameled bell inscribed with the initials *C. L.* The bell was attached to a metal chain. There was a ring at the end of the chain.

A photograph of the deceased hung on the wall. A pair of scissors had been applied to it in order to remove everyone except the dead woman from the scene. Black lace was draped around the frame.

Below the photograph was a funeral announcement card. The name of the deceased was written in an elegant hand: *Calista Langley.* The line where the date of death was to be inserted had not yet been completed.

Calista Langley was not the first woman whose portrait had hung in the chamber.

Anna hurried back across the room and let herself out into the hallway, relocking the door behind her. She did not breathe a sigh of relief until she was downstairs.

There was no question but that her husband was obsessed to the point of madness. She had to find a way out of the nightmarish marriage. But who would believe her?

It was all too easy for a husband to convince the authorities that his wife was insane, but it would be next to impossible for a wife to have her husband committed.

8

CALISTA WALKED INTO Masterson's Bookshop with a sense of relief. The bells over the door tinkled cheerfully in welcome. There was something about the very atmosphere of the place that calmed her strained nerves. The tranquility of the cozy shop was infused with the comforting smell of the volumes, old and new, that were shelved in the bookcases.

It was as if she had stepped into a different dimension. Outside, the fog drifted ominously in the street. The clatter of hooves and carriage wheels echoed eerily in the mist. Strangers appeared and disappeared into the gray, featureless landscape. With each step she had been uncomfortably aware that any one of the people she had passed could have been the intruder who had left the memento mori ring in her bedroom.

But inside Masterson's all was calm and serene. It was only when she took a few deep breaths that she realized just how unnerved she had become in the past several days.

The middle-aged woman behind the counter was in the midst of ringing up a sale but she smiled warmly.

"Miss Langley," she said. "How nice to see you. I'll be with you in a moment."

"Good day to you, Mrs. Masterson," Calista said. "Please don't rush on my account. I always enjoy a browse through your shop."

"Right, then, take your time."

Martha Masterson went back to her customer, a young man who looked to be about the same age as Andrew.

"There you are, sir," she said briskly. "Enjoy *Clive Stone and the Affair of the Murder Machine*. It's been very popular since it came out as a book."

"Read it when it was serialized in the *Flying Intelligencer* of course, but I wanted a copy for my personal library," the customer said. "I'm reading Mr. Hastings's latest in the newspaper now. Not sure about the character of Wilhelmina Preston, though. Don't know why the author had to bring in a lady who appears to be more or less in the same line of work as Clive Stone."

"Miss Preston is a scientist," Martha said. "Not a detective."

"But Stone is asking her for assistance on his new case," the customer grumbled.

"Not to worry," Martha said. She gave the young man a reassuring wink. "Perhaps Wilhelmina Preston will prove to be the villainess. You know Mr. Hastings likes to conceal the criminal in plain sight in his stories."

"The villainess." The customer was clearly cheered by that news. "Now, that would be a very clever twist. Good day to you, Mrs. Masterson."

"Good day, sir."

Martha waited until the door closed behind the young man and then she made a *tsk-tsk*ing sound.

"I do hope Mr. Hastings hasn't made a serious blunder with the character of Wilhelmina Preston," she said. "My female customers are thrilled by her appearance but my gentlemen customers are a bit alarmed, to say the least."

"Speaking of Mr. Hastings," Calista said. "He is the reason why I am here today. First, I wish to thank you for sending his sister to my agency."

Martha's eyes gleamed with satisfaction. She was a comfortably rounded woman with a friendly, outgoing manner. "So Eudora Hastings took my advice, did she? I do hope you will be able to find a match for her. That poor woman is growing old long before her time. Such a pity."

"She has attended some of my salons and appears to be enjoying herself." Calista hesitated, choosing her words carefully. "I am wondering if you or Miss Ripley have recommended my services to any of your gentlemen customers recently?"

"No," Martha said, surprised. "Why do you ask?"

"Merely curious," Calista said, somewhat untruthfully. "Thank you, again."

She did not realize until that moment just how much she had hoped to find some connection between Martha Masterson and whoever was sending the memento mori items. The odds of identifying the person who seemed determined to make her life miserable had been poor from the outset, she reminded herself. Nevertheless, there had been a faint possibility that the bookshop proprietor and her friend had unintentionally sent some mentally unhinged individual to the agency. Martha was the one former client who came into contact with a wide variety of people due to the nature of her business.

So much for that notion. She would have to go back to her client files and look for someone else who might have been less than discreet with the wrong person.

She was about to make some excuse to depart without making a purchase when a voice spoke from the back room.

"Is that you, Miss Langley?"

A woman of approximately the same age as Martha appeared. Slim, tall, and angular, Arabella Ripley was the physical opposite of the proprietor. Her narrow, sharp-featured face was transformed by a bright smile when she saw Calista.

"I thought I heard you out here, dear," Arabella said. "I was just unpacking a new shipment of books. So nice to see you again. What was it I heard you asking Martha?"

"Miss Langley wanted to know if we had sent any gentlemen to her agency," Martha explained.

"Oh, my, no," Arabella said. "Just that very nice Miss Hastings. Was that all you wanted to know?"

"Yes, thank you," Calista said. A thought struck her. It seemed like a shot in the dark but she was desperate. "On second thought, have you, by any chance, mentioned my agency to any other ladies besides Miss Hastings?" she ventured.

Martha and Arabella exchanged questioning glances and then each shook her head.

"No, no one else," Martha said. "We are very discreet about your agency."

"Thank you," Calista said. "I appreciate that."

Arabella's brows rose in concern. "Do you need more business, dear? We could certainly sit down with our list of regular customers and see if there might be some other prospective clients."

"No, no," Calista said quickly. "Business is quite brisk, thank you. Just curious. I'm, ah, attempting to determine the most useful ways to attract new, respectable clients. As you know, I work only by referral, so my promotional possibilities are somewhat limited."

"Yes, we understand, dear," Martha said. "One can hardly put an advertisement in the newspapers, can one? Can't have just anyone turning up on your doorstep demanding to be introduced to other people. Discretion is the key to your business."

"We are extremely careful about discussing your services." Arabella smiled at Martha and then turned back to Calista. "You changed both our lives by introducing us last year. I can't imagine how lonely we would be now if it hadn't been for your agency. We don't want to see your business ruined by the wrong sort of rumors."

Calista drew a deep breath. "As I said, I'm just doing a bit of research. If you will excuse me, I must be on my way."

The shop door opened with considerable force, sending the delicate bells into a discordant cacophony. Nestor loomed on the threshold. Calista stopped breathing.

"Thought I saw you come in here, Calista," Nestor said.

He gave her what he no doubt considered his most devastating smile but his eyes were cold and sharp. An icy shudder swept through Calista but she managed what she hoped was a cool, unruffled expression.

"Mr. Kettering," she said. "I had no idea you were a customer of this shop."

"Never stepped foot in it until today," he said. He did not bother to glance at Martha and Arabella. "But when I saw you enter, I thought it might be a good time to catch you. Allow me to buy you a cup at the tea shop on the corner."

"Sorry," she said. She adjusted her gloves and headed for the door, hoping that Nestor would step aside. "I have a number of appointments to keep."

She advanced on him with such determination that he was left with no choice but to move. Behind her, Martha spoke in uncharacteristically unwelcoming tones.

"May I help you, sir?" she asked.

Nestor's response was short and curt. "Not today."

He pursued Calista out onto the street.

"Calista, I must speak with you. The least you can do is give me a moment of your time."

It was a command, not a request. She did her best to ignore him but when he fell into step beside her she knew she had no choice but to confront him. She came to a halt and turned to face him.

"Whatever you wish to say to me, do me the favor of saying it quickly," she said. "I have a great many things to do today."

"How did your appointment with Hastings go yesterday?" Nestor growled.

"That is none of your affair."

"Did you take him on as a client?"

"I refuse to discuss my business with you. Now, if that is all you wish to say, you must excuse me."

She started to turn away. Nestor grabbed her arm. Shocked that he would be so bold on a busy street, she looked down at his hand wrapped around her upper arm and then she met his eyes.

"Do you wish me to summon a constable?" she asked softly.

He released her as if she had sent a jolt of electricity through him.

"I insist that you give me a chance to prove that my feelings for you have not changed over the past year," he said.

"The thing is, I don't care whether or not your feelings have changed. Even if you were not married, it wouldn't matter because my feelings for you burned to ashes long ago. You set the fire."

"I can rekindle the flame."

"No," she said, "you can't."

"Bloody hell, Calista—"

She started to turn away again but paused. She would never get a better opportunity to ask the one question that had been disturbing her since Nestor had reappeared in her life.

"Why have you decided to come back into my life now?" she asked.

"What?"

"You heard me. You've been married for nearly a year. What made you call on me after all this time?"

Nestor frowned, clearly surprised by the unexpected query. Then he appeared to realize that he now possessed something she wanted—an answer.

"Give me another chance to prove my love for you and I will tell you," he said.

So much for the direct approach, she thought. Disgusted, she turned away, searching for a cab, but the fog was so thick she could scarcely see any vehicles at all until they were almost in front of her.

In desperation she started walking, hoping to lose Nestor in the mist.

But he spoke again and this time she froze.

"If you do not allow me to try to resurrect the passion we once shared, I shall feel free to discuss the rather unusual nature of your business with certain parties in Society," he warned. "A word dropped in the right ears at my club might do considerable damage to your professional reputation—"

"You really are a bastard, aren't you?" She whirled around to face him, trembling with rage. "Clearly I had a narrow escape a year ago. Your wife has my deepest sympathies. But let me assure you that if you attempt to compromise my professional reputation, I shall drag you down with me. I will go straight to the press."

"What are you talking about?"

"Just imagine the gossip in the papers if it gets out that a former fortune hunter who married well is now hunting another wealthy bride through an introductions agency. One wonders what the current Mrs. Kettering thinks of this plan. Et cetera, et cetera, et cetera. You'll be ruined, Nestor."

Nestor stared at her, his mouth falling open in shock. "You're mad."

"We both know where that sort of talk would lead, don't we?" she said. "People would question the stability of your finances. You cannot survive in Society with chatter like that swirling around you. At the very least you and your wife would likely be forced to retire to the country. You'd hate that, Nestor. You're a shark who thrives in Society."

His face turned a blotchy red.

"You stupid little bitch," he said.

He said it very, very softly.

"Did you really think that I would not strike back if you tried to blackmail me? You don't know me very well, Nestor. One of the great advantages of spinsterhood is that it allows a woman an opportunity to learn how to sharpen her claws."

A cab appeared miraculously out of the fog. She whisked up her skirts and went swiftly toward it. The driver jumped down and opened the door with a flourish.

"Your destination, ma'am?" he asked.

"Cranleigh Square."

"Aye, ma'am."

He handed her up into the cab, put up the steps, and closed the door. A moment later the carriage lumbered off down the street.

She looked back only once. Nestor had disappeared into the fog. She took a few more deep breaths in an effort to calm her skittering pulse and regain control of her roiling emotions.

Only then did she notice the box wrapped in black silk and tied up with black satin ribbon sitting on the opposite seat.

It might as well have been a cobra. Her pulse and her breathing certainly reacted as though the box contained a venomous snake.

The envelope tucked under the black ribbon was bordered in black.

9

FOR A FEW seconds she stared at the horrid package, willing it to disappear. Perhaps the events of recent days had affected her nerves so badly that she was starting to hallucinate.

She shook off the dazed sensation and steeled herself to pick up the box. It was surprisingly heavy. She had to use both hands to get a firm grip on it.

She slipped the envelope out from under the ribbon. Her name was written on it in an elegant hand. *Miss Calista Langley.* There was no return address.

She tried to summon up the faces of the people who had been on the street just before she got into the cab. But in her anger she had been focused entirely on Nestor. She had paid very little attention to passers-by. Traffic had been heavy, as usual in the middle of the afternoon, but the fog had obscured much of the scene.

It dawned on her that she had experienced no difficulty hailing a cab. That was unusual on such a damp, fogbound day. It was as if the carriage in which she was riding had been waiting for her.

She reached up with one gloved hand and rapped smartly on the roof of the vehicle. The trapdoor opened immediately. The driver looked down at her, squinting a little.

"Aye, ma'am?" he asked. "Change your mind about yer destination?"

"No," she said. "But there seems to be a problem. Your previous fare left a package behind on the seat. It is wrapped in black silk. A mourning gift, I suspect."

"Right y'are. It's for you, ma'am. My condolences on your sad loss." The driver touched the brim of his low-crowned hat and started to close the trap.

"A moment, please. There is some mistake. I have not suffered any loss."

"I was told the package is for you, ma'am. The gentleman tipped me well to make certain that I picked you up when you came out of the bookshop. Described you very accurately, he did. Said you'd be wearing a fashionable dark red gown and a little hat with a red feather."

She seized on the one bit of potentially useful information. "A gentleman, you say? I must know him. Was it the man I was speaking with just before you handed me up into your cab?"

"No, ma'am."

That would have been too easy, she thought. But it was possible that Nestor had employed someone else to put the box into the cab.

"Please tell me what the other man looked like," she said. "It's very important that I thank him for his gift."

"There wasn't anything in particular about him. Wore a very nice black overcoat, hat, and scarf. Expensive. Early thirties, I'd say."

"Any jewelry? A stickpin or a ring, perhaps?"

"None that caught my eye. Very good leather gloves, though. Sorry, ma'am, but that's about all I can tell you."

The spare description fit several of the gentlemen who had signed up for her services and a few whom she had rejected.

The driver closed the trapdoor. She looked down at the box in her lap. She did not want to open it, not while she was alone. She would wait until she was home and safe in familiar surroundings with Mr. and Mrs. Sykes and Andrew.

She set the box on the opposite seat and sat looking at it, trying to think of what to do next. She needed a plan, some logical course of action. But her thoughts kept chasing each other in hopeless circles that seemed to grow tighter and tighter with each passing day.

This was what it had come to—a life lived on the razor edge of fear. The sense of being watched all the time and the ghastly gifts were playing havoc with her nerves. She could not ignore the situation any longer or tell herself that her tormentor would grow bored with the dreadful game. Her intuition was screaming at her, warning her that whoever was sending her the gifts was growing more obsessed and more dangerous with each passing day.

But how did one fight a demon that lurked in the shadows?

She sat very still, mesmerized by her troubling thoughts, for the remainder of the journey back to Cranleigh Square. Somehow she was certain that whatever was inside the box would prove to be even more frightening than the tear-catcher and the jet-and-crystal ring.

No, she did not want to be alone when she opened the box wrapped in black silk.

10

TRENT WAS AT the library window watching the fog that seethed in the gardens of Cranleigh Hall and drinking the tea that had been thrust upon him by the housekeeper when the cab came up the drive.

Footsteps echoed in the front hall. He heard the door open. The elderly butler appeared on the front steps and made his way to the carriage with a stiff, halting stride.

The housekeeper spoke from the doorway of the library. "I expect that will be Miss Langley. I told you she would be home in time for tea, sir. She'll be so pleased when she discovers that you are here."

Trent was not at all certain that Calista was going to greet the news of his presence with any enthusiasm. He watched through the window as the butler handed her down from the cab.

There was something shadowed and grim about her. She held a package wrapped in black fabric and black ribbon in her hands. When the butler attempted to relieve her of her burden she shook her head.

The butler escorted her up the steps and into the front hall. The cab clattered off down the drive.

Out in the hall there was some low-voiced conversation.

A moment later Calista appeared in the doorway, still clutching the black box. She looked at him with a mix of wariness and thinly veiled anxiety. It was, he thought, the expression of a woman who has just received some bad news and is anticipating more of the same.

"Mr. Hastings," she said. "I was not expecting you today."

"Which would be an excellent reason for declining to see me," he said. "I apologize. I took the chance of finding you at home because I wished to tell you that I have decided not to stand in my sister's way."

"I see. You will allow her to remain a client of my agency?"

"As she has taken pains to remind me, she is an adult. She has the right to make her own choices. I can tell that she enjoys your salons. It is just that I fear—"

"You fear she will be hurt if some heartless gentleman takes advantage of her. I quite understand. In your place I would have similar qualms. And I will be the first to admit that I cannot guarantee that Eudora will not suffer such a fate. It is a risk every woman confronts."

Spoken like a lady who had, indeed, confronted just such a fate, he thought.

"I am keenly aware of that, Miss Langley." He paused for emphasis. "Might I add that men are not immune from the same sort of misfortune."

"No, of course not, but generally speaking they have more options when they find themselves in a bad marriage. All I can tell you is that I give you my word that I will do my best to provide Miss Hastings with only the most suitable introductions. In fact, I think I can promise you that she will be safer at any of my salons than she would be in most ballrooms in Society."

He smiled a little. "Forgive me, Miss Langley, but you are not setting the bar very high."

She winced. "I suppose that is all too true. But I assure you that I go to great lengths to make certain that I do not inadvertently accept cads and fortune hunters as clients."

"You refer to those investigations that your brother conducts."

"Andrew has a knack for uncovering the truth about my clients' finances and marital status."

For a short time he could not think of anything else to say. She watched him as if she had no idea what to do with him now that he had delivered his message. He ought to take his leave, he thought. But instead of heading for the door he found himself searching for an excuse to linger in her company.

He glanced at the black box in her hands. "Perhaps I should offer my condolences? I apologize again for the interruption. I was not aware of a death in the family."

She shuddered and took a sharp breath.

"No," she whispered. She straightened her shoulders. In the next breath her voice sharpened. "No one has died." She moved to the nearest table and slammed the box down with considerable force. "But I vow I would not be at all averse to seeing a certain individual dead."

It was as if he'd shattered some spell that had bound her. A moment earlier the atmosphere in the drawing room had been still and quiet. Now it was charged with the energy of Calista's rage and frustration.

"Do you mind if I ask who it is you wouldn't mind seeing in a coffin?" he said, intrigued.

"I have no idea. But when I find out—" She broke off, visibly fighting to compose herself. "I'm sorry, Mr. Hastings. You caught me at a bad time. I have just sustained a shock. I am not myself."

"I take it that it is the contents of that box that is distressing you?"

"Yes."

"What is inside?"

"I don't know. I haven't opened it yet. But I'm sure that it will be just as unpleasant as the two previous memento mori gifts have been."

An edgy flicker of alarm raised the fine hair on the back of his neck. He moved closer to the table and looked at the name on the black-bordered envelope.

"Someone is sending you gifts suitable for those in deepest mourning?" he asked.

"I suppose it's possible that the sender considers them cruel jokes." Calista tightened one hand into a fist at her side. "But whoever it is, he has gone too far. I swear, I can feel him watching me from the shadows. He is out there, somewhere, circling, prowling around me, waiting to pounce."

He touched the envelope. "May I?"

She hesitated. "I did not mean to burden you with my personal concerns."

"You haven't done anything of the kind. I am a curious man by nature and you have made me very, very curious." He glanced at the blob of black wax. There was no impression on it. "You have not broken the seal."

"I'm sure the note will be similar to the others. Go ahead, read it."

He broke the seal and removed a card from the envelope. The black border was very wide indicating deep mourning. He read the short note aloud.

*"Only death can part us."* He looked up. "There is no signature."

"There was none on the cards that accompanied the previous two gifts, either," Calista said.

"The stationery is of very good quality," Trent said. "Your correspondent is a person of some means."

Calista shot him a fierce glare. "He is not my correspondent."

"Forgive me. A poor choice of words, especially in light of the fact that I am an author. I was simply making an observation about the social status of the individual who is tormenting you."

"I know. It's my turn to apologize. Forgive my temper, sir. This entire matter has put my nerves on edge."

"Understandable." He looked at the box. "Why don't you unwrap it? The nature of the object inside might provide us with more information about the person who sent it."

"I doubt it." But she began to untie the ribbon. "I'm sure it will be similar to the others—some dreadful object intended for someone who is grieving. And it will no doubt have my initials on it."

That information elicited another whisper of dread.

"The objects are marked with your initials?" he asked, wanting to be certain.

"I have received two gifts thus far, a tear-catcher and a ring designed to hold a lock of hair from the deceased. Both were inscribed with the initials *C* and *L*."

She undid the ribbon, tossed it aside, and then yanked off the expensive black silk wrapping to reveal a plain wooden box. Trent could tell that she was holding her breath.

She raised the lid of the box as if expecting to find a dangerous trap inside.

For a moment they both simply stared at the object in the box.

"A bell," Calista said without inflection.

It was some eight or ten inches high, cast in some heavy metal and covered in gleaming black enamel. The initials *C* and *L* were inscribed in flowing gilt script on the outside.

A long chain of metal links extended from the clapper inside the bell to a finger ring. Trent picked up the gift to examine it more closely.

Calista contemplated the bell with a mix of horror and loathing.

"Dear heaven." She took a step back.

There was no point trying to soothe her fears by denying the obvious, Trent thought.

"It's a safety coffin bell," he said. "I've seen advertisements in the press for similar items. At the time of burial the bell is installed above the grave. The chain is attached to the inside of the coffin. The ring goes around one of the fingers of the deceased. The idea is that if the dead person is buried alive by accident and awakens inside the coffin, he or she can ring the bell and summon help."

Calista turned away, folded her arms very tightly beneath her breasts, and began to pace the room. "He is threatening to bury me, perhaps while I am still alive. I don't understand. Who could possibly hate me with so much passion?"

A dark fury heated Trent's blood. It had been a long time since he had experienced such a surge of raw emotion. It caught him by surprise. He wanted to hurl the bell against the nearest wall.

But such a loss of control would not do Calista any good. He suppressed the flash of rage and concentrated on his examination of the coffin bell.

"What are you looking for?" she asked.

"Anyone who goes to the trouble of designing such an expensive bell—to say nothing of the chain and the finger ring—will have no doubt patented it and very likely made certain that each device is stamped with some identification."

"Hmm." Calista unfolded her arms. "I never thought of that. Then again, I have not been thinking at all clearly of late."

He turned the bell upside down and studied the interior—and very nearly smiled with satisfaction when he saw the mark. "*J. P. Fulton, London.*"

Calista held out her hands. "Let me see that."

He gave her the bell and watched her peer into the interior, marveling at the sudden shift in her mood. A moment ago she had been cast into the abyss. Now she was flushed with excitement.

"Do you think that if I am able to locate this J. P. Fulton I might be able to find out who bought the coffin bell from him?" she asked.

"What I think," Trent said carefully, not wanting to raise her hopes unrealistically high, "is that finding J. P. Fulton would be an excellent place for us to start our investigation."

Calista stilled. "*Our* investigation?"

"You surely don't believe that I am going to let you pursue this matter alone, do you? Whoever sent you this bell has as good as threatened your life, and I doubt very much that the police would be of much assistance, at least not at this point."

"No." Her jaw tightened. "My brother and I considered going to the police, but what good would that do? There is nothing to be done unless or until the person who is haunting me perpetrates some act of violence."

"By then it may be too late."

She looked at him, mute and appalled.

"I'm sorry," he said. "That was far too blunt. But your situation is dire. It does not allow for social graces."

She swallowed hard. "I am well aware of that. Please understand. I appreciate your offer to help but this is not your problem, sir." She set the coffin bell on the desk. "Given the horrid nature of this new gift, I am afraid that there may be considerable risk involved for anyone who attempts to assist me."

He looked at her. "I am most certainly not the hero of my novels. But I have been told that I have a talent for logical thinking. In addition, thanks to the research that I have done for several of my books, I have acquired a few useful skills and some connections in certain quarters that may prove helpful."

"I don't understand."

"Never mind, it doesn't matter now. Let us return to your immediate situation. What precautions have you taken?"

She hesitated. "After the tear-catcher arrived we all assumed that there had been some mistake and that it had been sent to the wrong address. But when the jet-and-crystal-locket ring appeared on my bed—"

"Your *bed*?" He was shocked, in spite of himself. "This is worse than I thought. Whoever is doing this to you was actually able to acquire access to your bedroom?"

"Yes." She crossed her arms again as though she had felt a cold draft of air. "As I was saying, since that incident, Mr. Sykes and Andrew have been very careful to check the locks on the windows and doors throughout the entire house each night. I have begun to do the same."

"How did someone get into your bedroom without being seen?"

"We believe he came in disguised as one of the tradesmen who brought in supplies for the weekly salon," Calista said. "We suspect he used the old lift concealed in the wall to gain access to my bedroom."

He thought about that. "Did the intruder take anything?"

"Yes, as a matter of fact." She appeared surprised by the question. "A framed photograph that hung on the wall of my bedroom. It was a picture of Andrew and me and our parents. How did you know?"

"It just seemed likely that he might have wanted some token to mark his bold move into your private space. He was no doubt consumed with an unwholesome excitement at that moment. After all, he had taken a great risk."

"I hadn't thought of it that way." She shook her head in dismay. "That is very insightful of you, sir. Your theory has a terrible kind of logic."

"Miss Langley, what you are telling me is beyond unnerving. No wonder you are on edge. Any idea of how the intruder might have learned of the concealed lift?"

"I have no notion, but it is hardly a great secret. Mr. and Mrs. Sykes are aware of it, of course, and so is anyone who ever worked in Cranleigh Hall. Over the years there have been a number of maids and tradesmen who have made use of the lift to move heavy items to various floors."

"Do you make use of the lift?"

"No, never." Calista shuddered. "I hate the thing. The interior is quite close and dark and the thought of getting trapped inside is enough to keep me out of it, I assure you. It bears a striking resemblance to a coffin."

"I assume you have taken steps to secure access to it?"

"Yes, of course. The little room on the ground floor where the lift door is located is kept locked at all times now."

He moved to the window, clasped his hands behind his back, and studied the elegant gardens that surrounded the big house.

"When you consider the matter closely," he said after a time, "we do have some information about this person who has fixed his attention on you. Given a few more details, we should be able to come up with a list of suspects who can then be investigated individually."

There was a short, tense silence behind him. Then he heard Calista's skirts and petticoats rustle softly. He turned around and saw that she had taken a step closer to him.

"Do you really think so?" she said.

"Yes," he said.

He should not make promises he was not certain that he could keep, he told himself. But he could not bear to dash the wary hope he saw in her eyes.

"One of the many things that concerns me is what to do with the villain if I do manage to learn his identity," she said. "It is hardly a crime to send memento mori gifts and there is no way to prove that someone intruded into my bedroom, let alone stole a photograph."

"We will deal with that problem after we find the individual who is playing this wicked game."

"I do have a theory," she admitted with some hesitation.

"What is that?"

"I have begun to wonder if one of the gentlemen I have rejected as a client might have decided to take revenge."

He considered that briefly and nodded. "That is definitely a possibility we must consider."

"The box containing the coffin bell was inside the cab that I hailed this afternoon. It turns out the driver was paid a special gratuity to pick me up."

"The driver saw the man who put the box in the cab?"

"Yes. But he did not get a close look at his face. Trust me, I demanded a description. All I got was the information that the individual appeared to be in his early thirties, was well dressed, and wore expensive gloves."

"But the driver was certain that it was a man?"

"Quite certain," Calista said. "I intend to sort through my files of rejected male clients. I have Andrew's notes and my own to examine. I shall draw up a list of men who might want revenge."

Trent thought about that for a moment. "How many men have you rejected?"

"It will not be a long list. I have always been very careful when it comes to clients. Because of that I have not had to reject many. But there have certainly been a few. I may be able to eliminate some of them now that I have the cab driver's description."

Trent contemplated the coffin bell. "Your plan is a good one, but I believe the first step is to find the shop where that bell was purchased."

She watched him with a mix of hope and uncertainty.

"You are determined to help me discover the identity of the person who is doing this?"

"If you will allow me to do so," Trent said.

"I must admit, I am quite desperate. My nerves are starting to fray. I would be very grateful for some assistance."

"I wish to help you, Miss Langley. But let me be clear—I do not want your gratitude."

She smiled for the first time since she had walked into the drawing room. It was a rather tremulous smile but it was warm and genuine.

"Then I will repay you in kind, sir," she said.

"In kind?"

"Your sister mentioned in passing that you are something of a recluse."

"Eudora told you that?" Trent said. He would have a word with her when he got home.

"I understand that as a writer you must spend a great deal of time alone. That would, of course, make it difficult to meet people."

"I assure you, I am not keen to meet great numbers of people."

She paid no attention. "In exchange for your assistance in identifying the person who is sending me these objects, I will endeavor to introduce you to a suitable female companion. I'm sure there is someone on my roster of clients who will be just perfect for you. I perceive that you would appreciate a lady who can provide stimulating, intellectual conversation. One who can share your interests."

Reflexively he touched the scars on his jaw. "Promise me that she will not feel obliged to share her opinion of my novels."

**11**

"AH, YES, THAT is one of my late husband's patented safety coffin bells," Mrs. Fulton said. "No one should be buried without one. I can only guarantee that it will function properly, however, if one also purchases the special coffin that Mr. Fulton designed to be used with the bell. I cannot recommend attempting to use it with an inferior coffin."

Calista was not sure what she had expected when she and Trent walked into the somber premises of J. P. Fulton Coffins & Mourning Goods. But for some reason it came as a bit of a shock to discover that J. P. Fulton was no longer among the living. His widow was now in charge.

Mrs. Fulton appeared to be in her midforties, attractive in a dignified way that suited her profession. She wore a stylish black gown with a high collar of black lace that framed her throat. Her pale blond hair, lightened with gray, was snugged up into a tight chignon and crowned with an artificial flower. The hair decoration would have appeared almost frivolous if it were not for the fact that it was fashioned of black silk. Her hands glittered with jet-and-crystal rings. A clear crystal brooch decorated in black enamel trimmed the bodice of her gown. Jet earrings dangled from her ears.

"Do you sell a great many of these bells without the coffins?" Trent asked.

"No," Mrs. Fulton said. "As I told you, they are not of much use without the specially designed safety coffin. I offer a wide variety of burial boxes at a range of prices. There is the basic model—the Rest-in-Peace—for those who cannot afford to send their loved ones off in a more fashionable style. But most people prefer either the Eternal Slumber design or the newest model, the Peaceful Dreamer. Cost varies with the materials and decorations, naturally, but all are equipped to accommodate the safety bell. Would you care to view our selection?"

She motioned toward a shadowy doorway.

Calista glanced into the other room and saw a number of coffins on display in the dimly illuminated chamber. She felt a distinct chill on the back of her neck.

"No, thank you," she replied.

"What we would like to know is the identity of the customer who purchased this particular bell," Trent said. He took some money out of his pocket. "And we are happy to compensate you for the time it will take you to answer our questions."

Mrs. Fulton glanced at the coffin bell that Calista had placed on the counter. Her brows snapped together in a sharp frown.

"How did you come by it?" she asked.

"It was given to me," Calista said. "The initials inscribed on it are mine."

"How very odd." Mrs. Fulton gave her a critical appraisal. "You appear quite healthy."

"I am in excellent health."

"You are perhaps enjoying a miraculous recovery from some near-fatal ailment?"

"No," Calista said. "I possess a remarkably sound constitution."

"I see." Mrs. Fulton's frown grew darker. "I'm not sure I understand what this is about."

"We believe the bell was purchased recently," Trent said. "You no doubt have a record of the transaction."

She regarded him with growing suspicion. "Why do you wish to know the identity of my customer?"

Calista sensed Trent's irritation and impatience. She stepped in to respond before he could say anything that would cause the situation to deteriorate further.

"We believe there was some mistake," she said smoothly. "As you have observed, I am not at death's door. Someone purchased this extremely fine and very expensive security device for an individual who, presumably, is dying. We wish to find the customer who purchased it so that he can give it to the intended recipient."

"Very odd." Mrs. Fulton tapped one finger on the counter and contemplated the bell again. She finally appeared to make up her mind. "I suppose there is no harm in giving you the name of my client. If you will wait a moment, I will check my records."

She reached under the counter and took out a heavy journal bound in black leather. Opening the thick volume at a midway point she began to peruse the most recent entries.

There were, Calista noticed, a great many sales recorded in the journal. The business of funerals and mourning was a large and thriving industry. Judging by the premises, Mrs. Fulton catered to a fashionable clientele.

There was a wide assortment of expensive memento mori on display in the shop. One tall case was devoted to jet-and-crystal jewelry. Lockets, bracelets, brooches, and rings—most designed to hold a twist of hair from the deceased—were tastefully exhibited on red velvet. Artificial flowers made of black lace and silk were artfully arranged in vases embellished with depressing scenes of crypts and headstones. An entire shelf was filled with elegant little bottles made to catch and hold the tears of those who grieved.

There was also a great deal of black-bordered funeral stationery arranged according to the various stages of mourning—the wider the borders, the more recent the bereavement.

One wall featured empty picture frames decorated with weeping angels and skulls and skeletons. They were designed for postmortem pictures of the deceased who was often posed with the living. Calista did not care for the modern habit of summoning a photographer to take a picture of the dead. It was, however, a popular practice and more than one photographer made a living with the business of death.

Mrs. Fulton's fingertip stopped halfway down a page. "Ah, here we are. One patented safety coffin bell inscribed with the initials *C* and *L*. Ordered by a Mr. John Smith."

Disappointment splashed through Calista. She glanced at Trent and shook her head ever so slightly. There was no John Smith on her list of rejected clients. The name meant nothing to her.

Nevertheless, she told herself, it was a name; a starting point, perhaps.

"Is there an address?" Trent asked.

"No, I'm afraid not." Mrs. Fulton snapped the journal closed and put it back under the counter. "The bell was paid for in cash so there was no need for an address."

Trent took a card out of a small case and placed it on the counter. "If you think of any other information about Mr. Smith, please feel free to send word to this address. I promise that there will be a large gratuity for further details."

Mrs. Fulton picked up the card and studied it closely. "Are you the author of the Clive Stone novels by any chance?"

"As a matter of fact, yes," Trent said.

"Hmm. I'm reading *The Affair of the Missing Bride* in the *Flying Intelligencer*. I must say, I rather like the character of Wilhelmina Preston."

"Thank you," Trent said.

"I do hope you don't kill her off in the end."

"If I do, I promise you that she will be buried in a J. P. Fulton patented safety coffin with a bell."

Mrs. Fulton flushed with pleasure. "That would be excellent for my business."

"Something to keep in mind should you choose to assist us in our inquiries," Trent said. "One more thing, what about the coffin?"

Mrs. Fulton looked taken aback. Clearly she had not expected the question.

"I beg your pardon?"

"You said the bell Miss Langley received only works with your specially designed safety coffins," Trent said. "I would like to know if this John Smith also purchased one of those."

Mrs. Fulton managed a brittle smile. "As I recall, the customer wanted the bell first so that he could give it to his dying fiancée while she was still on this earthly plane. He thought it would comfort her to know that if she was accidentally buried alive and woke up in her coffin she would be able to ring the bell for rescue. J. P. Fulton bells make a very thoughtful gift for the nearly departed."

Calista could scarcely breathe.

"Has Smith returned to purchase the coffin?" she asked.

"Not yet, but I'm expecting him any day. He assured me that it wouldn't be long now before it was needed."

12

"MRS. FULTON WAS lying," Trent said.
An invigorating sense of anticipation heated his blood.
Something was amiss at the mourning goods shop. He was certain
of it.

Calista had been gazing reflectively out the window as the cab
rolled forward down the street. But at his words she turned quickly to
fix him with an intent expression.

"Do you really think so?" she asked.

"I can't be positive," he admitted. "I was trying to read upside down
because we were on the opposite side of the counter. I couldn't see the
entry she was pointing to clearly but I'm certain that the last letter of
the surname ended in a *Y* or perhaps a *G*. It was definitely a letter that
dipped below the line."

"Why would she lie?"

He considered that briefly. "One reason might be that she simply
wished to protect the identity of a good customer."

"I must admit that I can understand that. In her shoes, I would be strongly inclined to do the same. I am very careful with my client files. But surely we made it clear that there had been a mistake. We told her that the bell had been sent to the wrong address. At the very least one would think that she would have offered to take the bell and return it to her customer herself."

"We need to get a closer look at Mrs. Fulton's financial records."

"How do you propose to do that? I'm quite sure she would never agree—" Calista stopped, mouth parted in sudden shock. "Hang on, surely you don't mean to go into her shop at night when no one is around?"

"A quick look at that journal is all that's required."

"What you are suggesting is quite impossible, sir. You might get arrested."

"Give me some credit, Miss Langley. I am not without experience in this sort of thing."

"Experience? You are an author, sir. How can you possibly claim experience in lock picking?"

He found himself unaccountably offended.

"I do a great deal of research for my novels," he said evenly. "If you will recall, Clive Stone is an expert at picking locks. I don't claim to have his level of expertise but I should be able to manage the old-fashioned lock on the front door of Mrs. Fulton's shop."

"This is not a work of fiction, Mr. Hastings. It is all very well to send Clive Stone out in the middle of the night to investigate a villain's lair, but I cannot allow you to take such a risk on my behalf."

"I won't take the risk on your behalf. I shall do it for myself."

"Have you gone mad?"

"Consider it research."

"Rubbish. Let me make one thing very clear, Mr. Hastings. This is my problem—my case, as it were. If you insist on carrying out this wild scheme, I must insist on accompanying you."

"There is not a chance in hell of that happening, Miss Langley."

She gave him a steely smile. "You will need someone to keep watch. I shall take a whistle and use it to signal you if I see a constable approaching while you are inside the shop."

"Huh. That is a rather clever idea."

"Thank you. I got it from a Clive Stone novel."

13

IRENE FULTON WAITED until the cab had disappeared down the street before she reached under the counter and retrieved the journal of business transactions.

With the volume tucked under her arm, she walked across the shop, turned the sign in the window to Closed, and then went upstairs to her private rooms. She set the journal on the table while she put the kettle on the stove. When the tea was ready she sat down, opened the journal, and studied certain sales she had made during the past year.

There was nothing a shopkeeper liked to encourage more than repeat business, but she'd begun to have a few questions about the customer who bought the same items again and again for various elderly relatives, all of whom were at death's door. And now a dangerous-looking gentleman and a woman who had received the gifts had come around asking questions.

The pattern was always the same—first came the order for a lovely tear-catcher. Next, the order for the hair-locket ring. That was followed by a request for a safety coffin bell and, finally, a coffin. The customer specified that all of the items were to be inscribed with the initials of the soon-to-be deceased. The notes were always accompanied with payment in full. The customer never questioned the price.

With the exception of the earliest purchases, the memento mori and the bells were sent to the customer's address—not the home of the dying relative. The coffins, however, were delivered directly to various funeral parlors. Each of the deceased had been buried by a different funeral director.

Irene closed the journal and sipped her tea while she pondered how to proceed.

After some time she carried the journal back downstairs and placed it neatly in its customary position under the counter. She put on her cloak, went into the elegantly lit coffin display chamber, and made her way to the back door of the shop.

She let herself out into the service lane and set off for the first of the three funeral parlors on her list. She knew the proprietors. They might be willing to talk to her. They trusted her. After all, they were all in the same business—the business of death.

The first stop was a small funeral parlor in an unfashionable section of town. For a small gratuity the middle-aged proprietor was happy to discuss the arrangements.

"The deceased wasn't elderly," he confided. "Not at all. Nineteen or twenty perhaps. And it wasn't a natural death. Murdered she was and that's a fact."

Irene tensed. "Are you certain?"

"Throat was slit. Hard to mistake that sort of thing. The gentleman who brought her to me told me the story. Very sad. She was a governess who had lost her post after her employer caught her in bed with the master of the house. She found herself starving to death and facing a life on the streets. So she started selling whatever she had to sell to anyone who would pay for it."

75

"She became a prostitute?"

"Not an uncommon story. I was told that she was murdered by one of her clients. Naturally the family wanted to keep the details out of the press."

"Yes, of course," Irene said.

"Murder is always awkward for a respectable family, especially a murder like that. The scandal, you know."

14

CALISTA WAS IN her study reviewing her notes in the files of the men she had rejected over the years when Mrs. Sykes appeared in the doorway.

"Sorry to interrupt you, ma'am, but there's a client here to see you," she said.

"A client?" Calista glanced at the clock. It was nearly five. "But I don't have any appointments until tomorrow."

"It's Miss Eudora Hastings, ma'am. She says she is here for personal reasons. She tells me it's quite urgent that she see you immediately."

"Yes, of course." Calista closed the folder she had just opened. "Please show her in, Mrs. Sykes."

Eudora was ushered into the study a short time later. She was dressed in her customary quiet manner. The brown gown would have been more appropriate on a woman twice her age. It did nothing for her pretty eyes.

"Thank you for seeing me on such short notice, Miss Langley," she said.

"Not at all." Calista motioned toward a chair. "Please sit down."

"Thank you." Eudora perched on the edge of the chair. "I give you my word that I won't stay for more than a few minutes, but I felt it necessary to talk to you about my brother."

"I don't understand. Is there a problem?"

"I'm not certain. The thing is, I know that he has called on you twice. I am aware that the first visit concerned me. Afterward, I made it clear to Trent that I intend to remain a client of your agency. I believed that the matter was settled."

"That was my impression."

"But today I understand that he called here again and then went out for a drive with you." Eudora closed her eyes briefly. "Oh, dear, I'm making a dreadful mess of this."

It was obvious that she was flustered and had no idea how to begin the conversation. It was far from the first time that Calista had dealt with a nervous client. She pushed the folder aside, folded her hands on top of her desk, and smiled her most reassuring smile.

"Take your time," she said. "Perhaps I can help you. As I'm sure you're aware, your brother initially had some reservations about your association with my agency. But today he came to tell me that he has withdrawn his objections. I hope you now feel more comfortable with our arrangement."

"Yes, I know you somehow put Trent's concerns to rest. I'm very glad because I had no intention of severing my association with your agency but at the same time I did not want my brother to worry about me."

"If you and Mr. Hastings are now in accord, I must assume that it is some other issue that brought you here today."

"To be quite blunt about it, I am worried about Trent."

Calista stilled. "I see. He mentioned that he is assisting me in a private matter, then?"

"Yes. I'm sorry. I realize that it is none of my affair. Nevertheless—"

"Nevertheless, you are concerned about him."

"Yes, exactly."

"I understand. You fear that he may be arrested," Calista said. "I have the same concerns. Trust me when I tell you that I tried to dissuade him from his plan."

Eudora stared at her, shocked. "What are you talking about? Why on earth would anyone arrest Trent?"

Calista cleared her throat. "What, exactly, has your brother said to you, Miss Hastings?"

"It wasn't what he said, it was what he did."

"I'm afraid I don't follow you."

"I told you, he went for a drive in a cab with you today."

"Yes, he did. Surely you are not alarmed by the knowledge that the two of us were alone together. We both know that I am of an age and station when that sort of thing no longer causes gossip. I do hope you are not about to tell me that you feel that I and my business have somehow been compromised by your brother. That would be going too far."

"I am not afraid that you will be compromised, Miss Langley. My brother would never do anything to harm a woman. He is the one I am concerned about."

"I see." Calista nodded. "Then it is his safety that concerns you?"

"His safety? No, of course I'm not worried about his physical safety. It is the safety of his heart that concerns me."

"I find myself utterly bewildered, Miss Hastings."

"Trent appears to have developed a rather keen interest in you."

The light began to dawn.

"Oh, dear," Calista said. "I'm afraid there has been a serious misunderstanding."

"I know my brother very well. His mood underwent a dramatic change after he returned from his first visit here to Cranleigh Hall yesterday. Mind you, he didn't seem particularly happy or pleased."

"I see."

"But he appeared to be more—I'm not sure how to put this—more energized. *Aroused* might be a more accurate word."

"No," Calista said quickly, "it wouldn't. Not accurate. Not at all."

Eudora ignored her. "In recent years he has retreated more and more from daily life. He has always spent long hours in his study, writing, but lately it is as if he lives inside that room. He seems to be watching his own life pass by as though it were a rather dull play."

I know the feeling, Calista thought.

"Just the other day my brother Harry suggested that Trent might be sinking into depression. But when Trent returned from that first interview with you, it was as though he had been given a strong tonic," Eudora concluded. "I took it as a good sign."

"Of what?"

"I wasn't sure at first. Trent was definitely in a fine temper. We had a great quarrel. It was quite refreshing—for both of us. We haven't argued in years. Nevertheless I confess I was bewildered. Today, however, when he made an excuse to call upon you again I realized that something odd had, indeed, happened between the two of you. And then I discovered that he actually invited you to go out for a drive. I can't recall the last time he went out for a drive with a lady."

"That is not what happened. Well, not exactly."

"I will be blunt," Eudora said. "My brother is a healthy man. From time to time he has engaged in discreet liaisons with the odd widow. But that is the thing, you see. He is always discreet."

"I see."

"Generally speaking, the women he becomes involved with do not expect or even desire marriage. They are invariably ladies who enjoy their widowhood and their financial independence."

"I see," Calista repeated, for lack of anything more intelligent. She tried to think of some way to put a halt to the conversation but she was mesmerized by Eudora's words.

"Trent's affairs tend to stagger along for a few months and then they simply collapse," Eudora continued. "Either the lady grows bored or Trent loses interest. I have always told myself that I would be thrilled if he developed truly strong feelings for a woman. But now that it may be happening, I am uneasy."

Calista tightened her clasped hands. With an effort she managed to keep her expression calm and reassuring.

"So that is what this is about," she said briskly. "You have been plain with me, Miss Hastings. I shall be equally honest with you. When I was young I dreamed of marriage and a family as most women do. But that was not to be and I have directed my energies and my passions into my profession. I am beyond the age when I must be acutely concerned with my personal reputation. I have come to savor my freedom. I do not answer to any man and I consider that a great blessing, I assure you."

Eudora appeared briefly distracted. "I do understand. The older one gets, the less one is willing to be ordered about by a man."

"That is certainly true in my case. I am far from wealthy but my business provides me with a good measure of financial security. I do not need a man to support me. In short, Miss Hastings, I have no designs on your brother. He is quite safe with me."

*Except for his plan to commit a small burglary on my behalf,* she amended silently.

Eudora's mouth quivered. "That is what I'm afraid of, Miss Langley."

"I don't understand."

But Eudora was no longer paying attention. Tears were leaking from her eyes and she was fumbling for a hankie in her handbag.

Calista grabbed a clean handkerchief from her desk drawer, leaped to her feet, and hurried around the desk. She thrust the linen square into Eudora's hand.

"What on earth is the matter, Miss Hastings?"

Eudora seized the handkerchief and blotted her eyes.

"I apologize for making a fool of myself," she whispered. "I do not know what I hoped to accomplish by coming here today. It is just that I felt compelled to do something, you see, because it is all my fault."

Calista took a step back. "I am quite lost now. What is your fault?"

"The fact that my brother has never married and never had a family of his own. Because of me, Trent's life has been ruined."

## 15

IRENE RETURNED TO her shop with the information she needed to confirm her suspicions. None of the three women who had been buried in the J. P. Fulton patented Safety Coffins had been elderly. They had all been young, attractive governesses with little in the way of family except the well-dressed man who brought in the bodies.

None of the women had died of natural causes. All had been murdered in the same manner. Their throats had been slit. In each case the bodies had been discovered by a male relative who told the funeral directors that he had not summoned the police because of a fear of scandal.

The memento mori items and the bells had all been ordered by the customer while the women were still alive. The coffins had been ordered after the deaths.

The description of the man who had delivered the bodies and paid the funeral directors for their discretion was always the same—a fine-looking, respectable gentleman, well-spoken and fashionably dressed. He claimed to be a distant relative of the victim who was willing to pay well for the funeral directors' discretion. But he had used a different name on each occasion.

She opened a drawer and took out a sheet of black-bordered notepaper. She was not personally in mourning—her elderly husband had succumbed to a stroke over a decade earlier and she did not miss him in the slightest. But she always used black-bordered stationery for the same reason that she wore stylish black gowns. It was simply sound business to take advantage of every opportunity to advertise her wares.

She wrote a quick message and inserted the notepaper into a black-bordered envelope. Then she went to the rear door of her shop and summoned one of the boys who slept in a nearby doorway. She did not want to risk sending her message by the post.

She gave the envelope and a coin to the street urchin.

"See that this is delivered immediately. Wait for a reply. There will be another coin when you return."

"Yes, ma'am."

The boy, excited by the prospect of being able to afford a meal that night, took off at a run.

Irene went back upstairs to wait for the response to her note. If there was one thing she had learned from J. P. Fulton, it was that there were a number of creative ways to increase one's income if one remained alert to opportunities.

Those engaged in the funeral and mourning goods trade were often in a position to learn dark family secrets. After all, nothing hinted at the truth like death. An unmarried daughter who died in childbirth? A woman beaten to death by a brutal husband? A husband who succumbed to an accidental dose of rat poison? All such secrets could be quietly interred with the body by an accommodating funeral director, assuming someone was willing to pay for the silence.

Discretion was the key to a successful business.

16

"I'M NOT SURE what to say," Calista said.

Eudora crumpled the hankie in one hand. "Something happened a few years ago—something quite dreadful. My brother saved me but in the process he was scarred for life. Because of those terrible marks on his face, the woman he loved ended their association."

"Really?" Calista frowned. "That seems rather unlikely."

"It's the truth. Trent has never loved another woman, not the way he loved Althea. As I said, there have been occasional, discreet liaisons in the past few years. But after Althea broke his heart, he never loved again."

"And you blame yourself."

"Yes. Suffice it to say that the damage that was done to his face was intended to be inflicted on me."

"Good heavens. I had no idea."

Eudora mopped her eyes. "We never talk about it, not even within the family. But it's always there, somehow, if you know what I mean."

"I understand family secrets. May I ask how old you were at the time of the . . . incident?"

"Fifteen. There are three of us but I'm the youngest. Our father died when I was twelve. Mother remarried when I was fourteen. Our stepfather proved to be a brute of a man. Mama was dreadfully unhappy. When she drowned in the pond many said she had suffered from lingering melancholia. But that wasn't true. And then came the incident that scarred Trent for life. I won't trouble you with the details. Suffice it to say that it all ended with him losing Althea."

"Who, exactly, was Althea?"

"The daughter of a family that lived in the same village. Althea and Trent knew each other from childhood. They fell in love when Althea was eighteen and Trent was twenty-one. But Trent wanted to see the world before they got engaged. Althea promised to wait for him and she did. But shortly after he returned the incident occurred. She could no longer abide the sight of his face.

"All these years Harry and I have worried because Trent seemed unable to love again. But now I find myself in a dreadful panic because he has taken a keen interest in you."

"For heaven's sake, your brother and I shared a cab," Calista said. "There is no great love affair blossoming here, Miss Hastings."

"I know my brother. He would not have paid another call on you today, let alone gone out driving with you, if he were not very interested—not when he has another chapter in his latest novel due at the publisher's." Eudora's eyes narrowed. "Are you telling me that you cannot return his interest?"

"There are no affections to be returned."

"He would never have met you if it hadn't been for me. I cannot bear the thought of being once again responsible for Trent enduring another doomed love affair."

It was time to take command of the situation, Calista thought. Exasperated, she went back behind her desk but she did not sit down.

"For heaven's sake, Miss Hastings, calm yourself," she said. "You have allowed your imagination to run riot in this matter. I assure you, there is nothing of a romantic nature about my relationship with your brother. He has kindly offered to lend me the benefit of his expertise and advice regarding a certain situation in which I find myself. That is all there is to it."

Eudora stared at her. "You require the expertise and advice of an author of detective fiction?"

"It is not his writing skills that I need. It is his investigative talents."

"But he doesn't have any. Trent is not a real detective. He only writes stories that feature one."

"I understand, but he has volunteered his services and, to be frank, it is not as if I have a great many alternatives. None, actually. I am attempting to identify a person who seems to have focused his attentions on me. I do not want those attentions and I have done nothing to encourage them. He sends nasty little gifts and notes that have lately become quite threatening."

"How horrible." Eudora paused to absorb that information. "It must be very unnerving."

"I will be the first to admit that the situation has started to affect my nerves."

"You have no idea who is doing this?"

"None." Calista glanced at the folders on her desk. "Although I have a theory that he may be one of the men I rejected as a client."

"Someone who wishes to exact revenge, perhaps?"

"That would seem to be a distinct possibility."

"You say my brother is investigating this matter for you?"

"We are investigating it *together*," Calista said. She wanted to get that point quite clear. "Mr. Hastings believes he can be of some assistance to me. In fact he more or less insisted on giving me the benefit of his expertise. Rest assured you can attribute any improvement in his mood to the simple fact that he is intrigued by the prospect of conducting a real investigation."

Eudora considered that briefly and then she visibly brightened. "Yes, I see what you mean. Perhaps he views it as an opportunity to conduct research for his next novel. He is very keen on that sort of thing."

"Precisely. In fact, I believe he employed that very word when we discussed the subject. *Research*."

"Well, in that case, perhaps I ought to take an entirely different view of the situation. It is clear from Trent's improved mood that this research project is doing him a world of good. At the very least it will get him out of the house."

"You're pleased that he might be persuaded to get out more on my account?"

"I told you, my brother has become a recluse, Miss Langley. Make no mistake, from time to time, he does associate with certain individuals he refers to as friends, but I fear that, for the most part, they are not the sort that one can invite for tea, if you see what I mean."

"No," Calista said. "I'm afraid I don't."

"Let's just say that he enjoys an odd array of associates. My point is that anything that encourages him to socialize with normal, respectable people is a very good thing." Eudora paused. "Unless there is some danger involved?"

"As to that, I cannot say. I am also new to the investigation business."

"Oh, dear. Now I am quite torn. I don't know what to think."

"Save yourself some time and energy because it is highly unlikely that your opinion will change your brother's mind in any way. Trust me when I tell you that I tried to talk him out of the idea."

"He can be quite stubborn." A gleam of curiosity lit Eudora's eyes. "Perhaps I can assist you both in the project?"

"Thank you for the offer but I have no idea what you could do."

Calista picked up one of the files. "For that matter I'm not sure what I should be doing."

Eudora rose and walked to the desk. "Those are the files of the potential clients you rejected?"

"Yes."

"How many?"

"Only about a dozen. I have been able to narrow the list by removing a few who seem to be too elderly."

"What were your reasons for rejecting them?"

"The reasons varied. Several were attempting to conceal their marital status. Others I suspected were fortune hunters. And then there are those who simply made me uneasy for no particular reason. I never argue with my intuition when it comes to selecting my clients."

"Perhaps you should start by sorting the files into specific categories."

"What do you mean? One way or another, I believe that all of the applicants lied to me."

"I understand," Eudora said. "But it sounds like you are looking for someone who has developed an obsession with revenge. Knowing precisely why each was rejected might help you narrow the field."

"You appear to be very knowledgeable on the subject."

"As it happens, my other brother, Harry, is a doctor. He is quite taken with the new science of psychology. He talks a great deal about the work being done in the field in Germany and America. He's sure it will change the way certain areas of medicine are practiced." Eudora contemplated the pile of folders. "May I take a look at your notes?"

Calista thought about that. "Would you, by any chance, be interested in accepting a temporary position as my assistant?"

Eudora's eyes brightened with enthusiasm. "I would be delighted to accept such an interesting position."

Calista smiled. "In that capacity it would be entirely proper for you to help me review and organize my notes."

Eudora flipped open a file. "These are excellent. Quite detailed. Harry would approve."

"Thank you."

Eudora turned a page in the file. "This one appears to have lied about his inheritance."

"A rather common problem in my business." Calista paused. "You say you know something about psychology?"

"Harry is the expert, not me, but I have learned a few things from him."

"I don't suppose you would be interested in giving me your opinion on some of the people in those files?"

"I will see what I can do," Eudora said.

Belatedly another thought occurred to Calista. "Your brother might not be pleased."

"I make my own decisions, Miss Langley."

"If you're certain you feel comfortable about doing this—"

Eudora tightened her grip on the file she was holding.

"Yes," she said. "Quite comfortable. In fact, I will look forward to it."

It occurred to Calista that Trent might not be the only member of the Hastings family who had been drifting through life of late.

17

TRENT OPENED THE door of the cab and kicked down the steps. He got out and reached back to assist Calista. It was the second time he had touched her. This time she thought she had braced herself for the strange little thrill that had whispered through her a half hour earlier when he had handed her up into the carriage.

She was wrong. When his powerful hand closed around her gloved fingers, another rush of sensation swept across her senses. It reminded her of the energy one felt in the atmosphere just before a summer storm struck. The promise of lightning was enough to make her pulse quicken.

Judging by his broad shoulders and the lithe, coordinated way he moved, she had known that Trent was a man in his prime. But when she experienced the masculine strength in him as she did when he handed her down from the carriage, she was even more intensely aware of him. That awareness reached deep into the very core of her being.

They were both maintaining a façade of cool control but she knew that Trent was tense with anticipation. So was she—which was no doubt the reason for her heightened sense of awareness, she decided.

They were here because of the note from Mrs. Fulton that Trent had received three hours ago. At last they were about to take positive action. She was fed up with not being able to do anything except wait for the next memento mori gift to arrive. Now, thanks to Trent deducing the source of the coffin bell, they appeared to be on the verge of a revelation.

They stood quietly for a moment, studying the fog-drenched scene. All of the shops, including J. P. Fulton's, were closed for the night. The rooms above the businesses were also dark. It was a quiet, respectable neighborhood that went to bed at an early hour. There were no taverns or music halls in the vicinity to draw an unsavory or boisterous crowd. No prostitutes congregated beneath the streetlamps. No pickpockets or drunkards hovered in the shadows.

"I shouldn't have let you come with me," Trent said. "I don't know what the devil made me think this was a sound idea."

"Common sense is what made you see reason," Calista said. "Mrs. Fulton is a widow who no doubt lives alone. Furthermore, she is in the sort of business that demands an aura of dignity. If she is seen entertaining a single man in the middle of the night her livelihood might well be in jeopardy. My presence will reassure her and no doubt induce her to be more forthcoming."

"She sent the note to me, not you. If she wants money she had better be prepared to be very forthcoming."

"I would remind you yet again, Mr. Hastings, that this investigation is my affair. I appreciate your offer to assist me but I will not allow you to take control of it. I do hope that is clear."

"I should not have sent word to you that I had received the note."

"If you hadn't told me about it, I would have been furious."

"I was afraid of that."

"Afraid of my wrath?" She smiled, rather pleased. "That is good to know."

He tightened his grip on his walking stick.

"Please don't make me regret my decision," he said.

She glanced at him but the collar of his coat was pulled up, concealing much of his face. In the fog-and-gaslight shadows it was impossible to read his expression. He offered no more arguments, however. There was nothing additional to say on the subject and they both knew it. She was the reason he was involved in the affair in the first place. She had every right to be at his side.

He instructed the cab to wait and then clamped a hand around Calista's arm to steer her across the street.

They stopped at the entrance of the shop. The shades in the windows had all been lowered but a faint, ghostly light seeped out at the edges. The lamps inside had been turned down very low but they burned.

Trent knocked quietly.

"She's in there," Calista said. "I wouldn't be surprised if she has grown anxious at the thought of meeting you alone."

"Perhaps."

Trent tested the knob with his gloved hand. It turned easily. He used his walking stick to ease the door open.

"Mrs. Fulton," he said into the silence. "Miss Langley and I are here to speak with you."

Calista moved into the salesroom. The dim light was coming from the coffin chamber at the rear of the shop.

"Mrs. Fulton?" Calista moved to the foot of the narrow stairs and raised her voice. "I do hope you don't mind that I accompanied Mr. Hastings tonight. I thought you might be more comfortable if there was a woman present."

Somewhere in the darkness a floorboard creaked.

"This is not good," Trent said quietly. "We need to leave. Now."

"No," Calista said quickly. "We can't leave, not yet. We must find out what she has to tell us."

"Out." Trent seized Calista's upper arm and yanked her away from the bottom of the stairs.

He started to give her a push toward the door. She hoisted her skirts so that she could run.

A tall figure exploded out of the shadows behind the counter and blocked the path to the front door. The spectral light from the coffin chamber glinted on the blade in his hand.

He did not hesitate for even an instant. He lunged toward Trent, the wicked knife outstretched for a killing thrust.

Trent swung his stout walking stick in a short, slicing arc aimed at the knife in the man's hand. Startled by the unexpected counterattack, the intruder reacted with a quick sideways movement and managed to retreat just out of range.

Calista knew there was little hope of escaping through the front door as long as the man with the knife was in the way, not unless Trent got lucky with the walking stick. And to do that, he would have to get closer to his opponent and risk the long blade.

Trent evidently came to the same conclusion. He hauled Calista back through the doorway of the coffin chamber. The man who was attacking them followed but more cautiously this time, wary of the walking stick.

The heel of Calista's high-button shoe caught on the hem of her petticoats. Frantically she struggled with her skirts but it was too late. She was off balance.

Trent released her abruptly, putting himself between her and the assailant. Helplessly entangled with her gown and underclothes, she reeled sideways and fetched up hard against an elaborately decorated coffin. The lid was open. She landed on her knees and grasped one edge of the ornate burial box for support.

She was about to push herself upright when she saw the body in the coffin. Mrs. Fulton gazed up at her with eyes that were blank with the shock of death. Her throat was a bloody sash. The white satin interior of the box was stained a terrible crimson.

A primal roar of rage from the assailant made Calista whirl around. She saw that Trent had grabbed an urn off a pedestal. He used his free hand to heave the heavy object at the attacker.

Hemmed in by the closely spaced coffins, the attacker could not dodge out of the way. He threw up an arm to ward off the urn but it struck him with enough force to drive him back a couple of paces.

The big vase crashed to the floor, shattering into dozens of jagged shards. Both men ignored the debris.

The attacker recovered and surged forward again but he was careful not to get too close to Trent's walking stick. The situation would have been a standoff, Calista thought, if not for her.

The attacker seemed to realize that at the same instant that she did. He switched directions and lunged toward her. But she was already on her feet, skirts and petticoats hauled up to her knees. The assailant was fast and quite athletic but Calista had one singular advantage—she had anticipated that he might try to use her as a hostage a few seconds before the same notion occurred to him.

She slipped between two coffins and rushed down an aisle created by twin rows of burial boxes. She could hear the attacker behind her. She glanced back and saw that he was in the process of climbing over the coffin that contained Mrs. Fulton's body.

She raised her skirts higher and sidestepped between another pair of coffins.

Behind her she heard a soft, sickening thud. The unnerving sound was followed by an anguished howl of rage and pain. The attacker, Calista thought. Not Trent.

She reached the end of the row of coffins and grabbed an urn off a pedestal. It was similar to the one that Trent had employed. She had not expected it to be so heavy. She could barely hold on to it using both hands.

She swung around and saw that Trent had abandoned the walking stick in favor of a tall, ornamental iron stand designed to display a funeral wreath. It was long enough to be used against the attacker without making it necessary for Trent to get within striking range of the blade.

She realized that he had just employed the floral stand to reach across a row of coffins and strike the assailant.

Blood spurted from the intruder's head, some of it cascading down his face. He howled again and dashed the back of one gloved hand against his eyes. Simultaneously he tried to retreat out of range but he was hampered by the coffins that hemmed him in on either side.

Trent moved between two coffins. He was now in the same aisle as the intruder, blocking the path to Calista. He readied the iron stand for another savage blow.

The assailant abandoned the attack. He clambered over the nearest coffin and ran toward the door.

He rushed out of the display chamber, across the salesroom, and disappeared into the night. The blood from his wound marked his path.

18

TRENT LOOKED AT Calista.

"Are you all right?" he said.

His voice sounded harsh and fierce, even to his own ears. The energy of the recent violence was still heating his blood. His heart was pounding and he was breathing hard from exertion and the gut-twisting knowledge of what had almost happened. My fault, he thought. *I should never have let her come with me tonight. I was almost too late.*

Another moment and the bastard would have had his hands on her. *I was almost too late.*

"Yes. Yes, I'm all right." She glanced out the display chamber doorway toward the front entrance of the shop. "Do you think he will return?"

"We are not going to remain here to find out." He tossed the heavy iron stand aside and moved into the next aisle of coffins to retrieve his walking stick. "Come. There is one thing I want to do before we leave."

"He killed Mrs. Fulton."

"What?"

"She's in that coffin." Calista motioned toward a white coffin fitted with white satin. "See for yourself."

"What in blazes?" Distracted, he went to the open coffin and looked down. Mrs. Fulton was, indeed, in the coffin. Her blood had soaked the satin lining. "It seems she will not require one of her husband's patented safety coffin bells."

"That villain who tried to kill you must have been a burglar who broke in shortly before we arrived. He murdered Mrs. Fulton. We no doubt interrupted him while he was searching for valuables."

"That's a possibility, but a rather remote one, I think."

Calista moved down the aisle of coffins, careful not to look into the white, satin-lined box.

"Why do you say that?" she asked.

She wanted a logical answer but he could tell from the shock in her eyes that she suspected the same thing he did.

"I can't be positive but I find it difficult to believe that, by sheer coincidence, someone murdered the proprietor of this shop within hours of me receiving the note that brought us here."

"It was a trap." Calista drew a shaky breath.

"It is the only logical assumption under the circumstances. We must leave." He motioned her to go ahead of him down the aisle. "I can only hope the cab waited for us but with our luck the killer will have commandeered it."

"What about Mrs. Fulton? There's been a murder here tonight. We cannot ignore it."

"We do not want to be found at the scene. When you are safely home I will send a message to my acquaintance at the Yard."

"You know someone at Scotland Yard?"

"I thought I made it clear that my research has provided me with a number of connections at various levels of Society. Inspector Wynn is a very capable policeman. More to the point, he can be counted on to respect your privacy. I will give him an account of what happened here tonight and a description of the killer. There is no need for you to become involved."

Calista did not argue. She understood as well as he did that getting caught up in a murder investigation would devastate her business.

He followed her into the salesroom. She went warily toward the door.

"One moment," he said.

Calista paused, her hand on the knob, and glanced back. "What is it?"

"Mrs. Fulton's journal of sales transactions. With luck it's still here."

He went behind the counter and struck a light. The leather-bound volume was precisely where he had watched Mrs. Fulton place it earlier that day. He picked it up and tucked it under his arm.

"Right," he said. "Now we can leave."

Outside, the fog still seethed in the streets but a great hush had fallen over the neighborhood. No ominous footsteps rang in the mist.

There was no cab, either.

"No surprise," Trent said, "given the way our luck is running tonight."

19

"I DON'T THINK THE assailant took our cab," Calista said. "I suspect the driver fled the scene when he became aware of the commotion inside the shop. The last thing he would have wanted was a passenger covered in blood. Damnation."

For some obscure reason Trent found her unladylike language amusing.

"J. P. Fulton's is a shop that sells coffins and mourning goods," he said. "Perhaps the driver concluded that the fleeing man was a spirit from the Other Side."

"It's more likely he realized that there was violence afoot and he did not wish to become involved. He certainly did not make any effort to come to our rescue. He didn't even send for a constable. If he had, one would have arrived by now."

"Just as well for us. Your business does not need the scandal that will surely accompany the discovery of Mrs. Fulton's body."

"But what of the man with the knife?" Calista said.

He looked at her, trying to read her face in the glare of the streetlamp. "You're sure you didn't recognize him?" he asked.

"Quite sure." She shuddered. "He is most certainly not one of the men I rejected as a client. I don't know whether to be relieved or even more alarmed by that fact."

"As I said, I will give a description to Inspector Wynn." Trent paused, considering possibilities. "I will give it to another acquaintance of mine as well. Perhaps one or both of them will be able to identify the intruder."

"He did fit the description the cab driver gave me yesterday," Calista said, very thoughtful now. "A well-dressed gentleman who appears to be in his early thirties. Now we have a few more details. Light-colored hair. If it weren't for his murderous eyes I might even describe him as handsome."

"A gentleman who is skilled in the use of a knife," Trent added. "That is not a common talent among the upper classes."

"I expect that he will likely be needing stitches, assuming he survives the wound you gave him. At the very least he'll no doubt be wearing a large bandage for a while."

"Head wounds tend to bleed freely. Unfortunately, I didn't hit him hard enough to take him down the first time and I didn't get a second strike." He remembered the journal and held it out to her. "Would you please carry this for me? Under the circumstances I would prefer to keep my hands free."

"Yes, of course," she said.

She tucked the journal under her arm. He tightened his grip on the curved handle of his cane.

"Sooner or later we will come across a cab," he said.

They walked in silence for a time. He was intensely aware of her beside him. The heels of her high-button boots echoed faintly in the night. The sound stirred his senses. But then, everything about Calista seemed to have that effect.

"It was very clever of you to realize that the killer was going to try to use you as a hostage," he said. "You moved quickly."

He did not want to think about what might have happened if the assailant had gotten his arm around Calista's throat.

"I could not think of anything else to do," she said. "But you were the one who saved us."

"We saved each other."

Calista seemed cheered by that observation.

"It appears that we are an excellent team," she said. "I must say, your skill with the walking stick is quite impressive. Where did you learn to use it as a weapon?"

"I took lessons from an instructor who studied under Colonel Monstery at one of Monstery's fencing and boxing academies in America. Monstery is a great proponent of the walking stick or the cane as a weapon because it is readily available for use yet is very nearly invisible. No one pays much attention to it."

"Because so many gentlemen carry one," Calista concluded. "It is considered a fashionable accessory, not a weapon." She gave him a sidelong glance. "Now I know why Clive Stone carries a walking stick."

"I'm not fond of guns. The results tend to be very permanent, assuming one hits the target. Alternatively, they frequently jam just when one needs them the most."

"I see." She was silent for a moment before adding, "In hindsight you will admit that it was a good thing that I accompanied you this evening."

"In hindsight, I will admit that we got very, very lucky tonight. The evening could just as easily have turned disastrous—as it did for Mrs. Fulton."

Calista fell silent again. He sensed her mood deflating. Should have kept my mouth shut, he thought.

"It was my fault," she said at last, grim and resolute.

"What the devil are you talking about?"

"You would never have been put in harm's way if it were not for the fact that you are assisting me in this strange affair. It is my fault that you were very nearly murdered tonight, Mr. Hastings."

The rush of exasperation and anger came out of nowhere, slamming through him. He halted abruptly and turned to face her.

"No, it was not your fault," he said. "Damnation, woman, I have enough people around me who are convinced that they are somehow responsible for whatever ill fortune befalls me. I do not need another martyr in my life."

She looked startled. "What?"

"I chose to assist you in this matter. It was my decision. Are we clear on that point?"

"You offered to do me a favor, sir."

"It was my decision. Research, remember?"

She looked at him for what seemed like forever. In the weak glare of the streetlamp he could not read her eyes.

"The thing is," she said finally, "this affair has evolved into something far more than mere research. I had hoped to repay you by providing you with my introduction services. But we both know that is quite inadequate now, considering the risk you took tonight."

"I did not ask for repayment."

"Nevertheless, I am indebted to you and becoming more so by the hour. If something terrible were to happen to you, as it almost did a short time ago, I would bear the burden of guilt for the rest of my life."

"Miss Langley, do me the courtesy of respecting my pride and my honor in this matter. I cannot in good conscience allow you to continue this dangerous investigation on your own. If something terrible were to happen to *you*, I would bear the burden of guilt for the rest of *my* life."

"How dare you throw my words back in my face?"

"I dare because I am quite desperate to convince you that I want to assist you."

"I'm not sure what to say," she whispered.

"Then perhaps it would be best if we stopped talking altogether."

"Yes, Mr. Hastings. Perhaps that would be for the best."

"I do have one favor to ask."

"Yes?"

"Would you kindly stop calling me Mr. Hastings? Given what we have just been through together, I think it is in order for you to call me by my given name."

"Trent."

She sounded as if she was trying the name on for size to see how it fit.

"It's not a difficult name," he said. "Only one syllable. I'm sure that with practice you will find that you can manage it."

"Are you teasing me, sir?"

"Perhaps."

He thought he saw a tiny smile come and go at the edge of her mouth but he couldn't be certain.

"I was very frightened tonight, Trent," she said carefully. "Terrified, actually. I am feeling very odd at the moment. Shaky. Rattled."

"I doubt that, Miss Langley. You have nerves of steel."

"Calista."

"Calista," he said. He liked the way the name sounded when he spoke it aloud—resolute, intriguing, and a little mysterious. "Rest assured that feeling shaky and unnerved is not uncommon after one endures a near disaster."

"You're certain?"

"Quite."

"How do you feel?"

"Probably best not to go into that too deeply," he said.

"If we are to be partners in this affair, we must be honest with each other."

"You're sure?"

"Positive."

"What I feel, Calista, is that I would very much like to kiss you."

He realized he was holding his breath as he waited for her response.

"I think I would like it if you kissed me." In the shadows her eyes were sultry; inviting. "The desire to embrace you is probably a result of the recent shock to my nerves."

He stifled a groan. "Probably."

"Perhaps a kiss would be therapeutic—a cathartic experience, as it were."

"You certainly know how to take the romance out of the moment, Calista."

"I am not a romantic woman," she said.

She said it so calmly and with such conviction that he almost laughed.

"Then you have chosen to go into a rather peculiar line of work," he said.

"Perhaps, but it strikes me as a good deal more uplifting than selling coffins and mourning goods."

"I take your point."

"Are you going to kiss me?" she asked. "If not, we should continue on our way. The hour grows late."

"Are you certain that you would like me to kiss you?" he asked.

"Yes."

Another wave of heat heightened all his senses.

"For therapeutic reasons?" he asked. He was a fool to ask but he had to know.

"For any reason."

Not quite the answer he wanted but good enough for now. Then again, any affirmative response would have been good enough—for now. He could not recall the last time he had been so desperate to embrace a woman. Perhaps it was, indeed, nerves that had made Calista say yes, but damned if he cared about the why of it all.

He wrapped his gloved hand very carefully, very gently around the back of Calista's neck. His pulse quickened. Desire was now a swiftly rising tide that threatened to sweep away all the obstacles in its path.

"Trent," she whispered, breathless.

That was all he needed. He drew her close before she could say something else that would ruin the moment and covered her mouth with his own.

The kiss started out the way he had intended—a smoldering fire that he was confident he could control. All he yearned for tonight was some indication that she would respond to him, he thought. A fog-shrouded street at midnight was hardly the time or place to pursue the question in greater depth. He just needed to know that she felt at least some small measure of desire for him.

For a few seconds he thought he was doomed. Calista stood, stiff and still, as though frozen by his touch. A strange sense of despair hovered over him, waiting to descend.

But in the next heartbeat she made a soft, urgent little sound deep in her throat. Clutching the journal in one hand, she put her gloved palm on his shoulder and clenched her fingers very tightly. Her mouth softened under his.

She returned the kiss with the uncertainty of a woman who yearned for passion but did not dare to trust such a powerful emotion. He understood the volatile mix of strong feelings. Knowing that she was as wary as he was gave him confidence as nothing else could have done.

"It's all right," he said against her mouth. "It's only a kiss. Nothing more need come of it."

"Certainly not here in the middle of the street."

The unexpected note of dry, sensual humor in her husky voice caught him off guard and simultaneously fanned the flames of his arousal. A shudder of erotic excitement swept through him.

He was vividly aware of her womanly scent. He could feel the sleek, supple shape of her body through the heavy fabric of her gown. The kiss awakened sensations he had not experienced in a very long time; perhaps never. He was consumed with a surging vitality and a deep, aching hunger.

Calista seemed to be affected just as strongly by the kiss. She trembled under his hand, but not from fear or uncertainty.

He took her mouth again.

The rattle of a harness and the brisk *clip-clop* of hooves on pavement broke the spell. His first impulse was to pull Calista into the nearest doorway and hide from the vehicle. But reality prevailed.

Nevertheless, it took an effort of will to end the kiss. For a few seconds he just looked at her. They were both breathing as hard as they had earlier after the battle in the coffin chamber. He pulled himself together.

"Cab," he said. He was rather proud of the fact that he was not only able to locate the word in his fever-fogged brain, but also utter it aloud.

She, too, made a visible effort to recover her composure. "Right. Cab."

He raised a hand. The vehicle rolled to a halt. Trent handed her up the steps.

There was very little traffic. The driver arrived in Cranleigh Square twenty minutes later and turned into the drive that led to the front steps of the mansion.

The door opened the moment the cab stopped. But it was not the housekeeper or the butler who appeared. It was a young man in shirtsleeves. He looked disheveled and frantic.

"Calista?" he said. He stared at her and then at Trent. "Where have you been? I've been worried to death. My God, what has happened to you?"

"Mr. Hastings," Calista said. "Allow me to introduce you to my brother, Andrew."

One look at Andrew's appalled expression told Trent that the evening's excitement was not yet finished.

Andrew lowered his head and charged down the front steps.

"Bastard," he snarled. "How dare you outrage my sister? I'll kill you for this."

20

HORRIFIED, CALISTA JUMPED down to the ground and stepped in front of Trent. "Andrew, stop. You don't know what you're doing."

She had never seen Andrew in such a state, she realized. Once again she was forced to acknowledge that he was no longer her little brother who needed her comfort and protection. He was a full-grown man with a man's strong body and strong, fierce emotions. In his present mood he was not only shockingly dangerous, he was also in danger.

Andrew's youth might be an asset to him but Trent had experience on his side and, as he had demonstrated earlier that evening, a great deal of strength and expertise in using his walking stick as a weapon.

She was not at all certain how to deal with the situation. She only knew that she could not let the two men come to blows.

Andrew was forced to scramble to a halt to avoid colliding with her. He stared past her at Trent.

"Get out of the way, Calista," he ordered. "Hastings has done something terrible to you and he will pay for it."

"You don't know what you are saying. Mr. Hastings saved my life tonight."

"My God, Calista. What is that stain on your gown?"

"It is the blood of the man who tried to murder Mr. Hastings and me this evening," she said, striving to cut through the violent atmosphere with a calm, brisk tone.

"What?" Andrew was dumbfounded. "I don't understand."

Trent stirred behind her.

"I think it would be best if we continued this conversation inside," he said. "I'm sure you will both agree that it would not do to awaken your neighbors around the square."

Andrew glared at him but Calista could see that the reference to potential scandal was forcing him to come to his senses, at least temporarily. Without a word he stormed back into the house.

Calista handed the journal to Trent, hoisted her skirts, and hurried after her brother.

"Andrew, please listen to me."

Trent followed her into the front hall and closed the door.

"Why don't you go upstairs and refresh yourself, Calista?" he said. It was an order, not a suggestion. "I'll handle this."

Calista started to argue. But at that moment she caught sight of herself in the mirror over the console. Her hair had come free of the pins and now hung in wild, tangled locks. When she glanced down at her gown she saw the crimson stains on the hem of her skirt and petticoats. She realized she had walked through the killer's blood on her way out of J. P. Fulton's. No wonder Andrew was shocked and enraged.

Before she could think of anything to say Mrs. Sykes appeared.

"What's going on here?" she said. She stared, wide-eyed, at Calista. "Dear heaven. What on earth happened to you?" She turned an alarmed gaze on Trent. "Mr. Hastings, surely—"

"I'm all right," Calista said quickly. "Mr. Hastings and I were attacked tonight. Mr. Hastings saved me. If not for him, I would very likely be in a coffin by now, and I mean that quite literally. Now, if you will excuse me, I'm going to change into another gown. I would appreciate your assistance."

"Yes, of course." Mrs. Sykes recovered from her shock and took charge like the professional she was. "We must get you out of those clothes."

Calista cast one last look at Andrew. His face was set in grim, stubborn lines. He did not take his eyes off Trent.

Mr. Sykes materialized. He took in the situation in a single glance.

"Allow me to show you into the library," he said to Andrew and Trent. "From the looks of things, you could both do with a brandy."

Neither man argued. But, then, one rarely argued with a professional butler, Calista thought.

"We must leave the gentlemen to Mr. Sykes," Mrs. Sykes advised from the landing. "When it comes to this sort of thing, men understand each other in ways that women cannot begin to comprehend."

"So I am discovering," Calista said.

She collected her skirts and hurried up the stairs. Just as she entered her bedroom she heard the door of the library close very firmly.

21

"YOU HAVE EVERY right to be concerned about your sister's condition tonight," Trent said. He swallowed some brandy and watched Andrew pace the carpet. "But she told you the truth. I give you my word that I did not hurt her. We were attacked by a man with a knife."

Andrew narrowed his eyes. "The blood."

"As Calista told you, that is the assailant's blood on her gown. I managed to fend him off with an iron stand of the sort that is used to display funeral wreaths."

Andrew came to a halt in the middle of the room. "How in blazes did you happen to come by a wreath stand? And where did this attack take place?"

"The location was the premises of J. P. Fulton's Coffins and Mourning Goods."

Andrew looked suspicious at that news but he resumed his pacing.

"What were you doing there?" he demanded.

"You have not been paying close attention to your sister's problems lately, have you?"

"If you're talking about those nasty memento mori gifts she has been receiving, you're wrong. I have been paying attention. I didn't say anything to Calista, but I have been looking into the backgrounds of some of the men she rejected. I suspect that whoever is sending the funeral objects is a man she rejected as a client."

"That is very insightful. Why didn't you tell her that is what you were doing?"

"Because I thought it would only make her more anxious." Andrew's jaw twitched. "And because I am not getting anywhere with my investigation, damn it. I have not been able to identify a likely suspect."

"That is not your fault. Calista got a good look at the man who attacked us tonight. She assured me she did not recognize him."

Andrew halted again. "He's not one of the men she rejected?"

"No, nor is he a client." Trent sipped some brandy and lowered the glass, thinking about the possibilities. "It doesn't mean there isn't some connection to your sister's business, however."

"She has had dozens of clients since she opened her agency. How on earth are we to find a link to the person sending these death gifts if she did not recognize the bastard tonight?"

"When one hits a wall in a maze, one must look for another way out."

"That sounds like something Clive Stone would say," Andrew muttered. "It is rather annoying in real life."

"So I have been told."

Andrew glowered. "By whom?"

"My sister, among others."

"Yes, well, the point is, this is not one of your stories, sir."

"I am well aware of that. But in this particular instance, we may have another way out of the maze."

"What are you talking about?"

"Mrs. Fulton's journal of transactions." Trent put down his glass, got to his feet, and picked up the leather-bound volume. "As Clive Stone is fond of saying, money leaves a very bright trail."

22

M R. Sykes was waiting at the door of the library when Calista came back downstairs clad in a clean gown, her hair tucked up in a neat knot.

"I can report that the situation is under control," he said. "Common sense and brandy have prevailed."

She gave him a grateful smile. "Thanks to you, Mr. Sykes."

"A short time ago, Mr. Hastings wrote out a note that I have dispatched to an acquaintance of his at the Yard. It is in regard to a case of murder on the premises of J. P. Fulton's Coffins and Mourning Goods. I will confess that this business of the memento mori gifts has become extremely worrisome, miss. From the sound of things, you and Mr. Hastings had a very close call tonight."

"I'm afraid that we can no longer hope that those dreadful gifts are the work of a nasty prankster. A woman was murdered tonight, and had it not been for Mr. Hastings's quick reactions I'm afraid there would have been another death. Perhaps two."

Sykes glanced at the closed door of the library. "May I say that I am very relieved to know that Mr. Hastings is now involved in this affair."

Calista raised her brows. "You are?"

"Yes, indeed. Who would know more about how to track down a murderous villain?"

"Some would say that Mr. Hastings is a writer, not a real detective."

"We don't appear to have a real one at hand, do we?"

"No, Mr. Sykes. We do not. Mr. Hastings is all that is available." She paused. "And I will say that he was quite convincing tonight."

"So I understand, miss. He spoke very highly of your own actions this evening. I believe he employed the words *clever* and *heroic* when he described the scene to your brother."

"Did he?" She was absurdly pleased by that information.

"Indeed." Sykes opened the door a crack and peered through the opening. "I think it is safe for you to enter now."

"Thank you."

She swept past him into the library—only to stop short at the sight of Andrew and Trent. They were standing close together at her desk, their attention fixed on a page in Mrs. Fulton's journal of accounts.

Andrew looked up, his eyes alight with discovery and fresh anger.

"Nestor Kettering," he said.

Shock jolted through Calista with such force she could scarcely catch her breath. She managed to make her way to the nearest chair where she more or less collapsed.

"I don't understand." She forced herself to think. Finally a glimmer of common sense returned. "Believe me, I am not fond of Nestor Kettering, but he is most certainly not the man who attacked us tonight."

"I know that." Trent watched her closely, his eyes tightening at the corners. "But according to this journal, Mrs. Fulton recently sold a coffin bell inscribed with the initials *C* and *L* to a Mr. N. Kettering of Number Five Lark Street," he said. "A few days before that he

116

bought a locket ring of jet and crystal inscribed with the same initials."

"And before that he ordered a tear-catcher," Andrew added. "There's got to be a connection. That bastard is the one who is attempting to frighten you."

She absorbed that information and then shook her head. "It makes no sense. Why would he do that? In the end he married a beautiful heiress. He got everything he wanted."

"But not you," Andrew said. "He didn't get you, Calista."

"He didn't want me, Andrew. When he discovered that I was not the heiress he had believed me to be, he disappeared."

Andrew said nothing but his frustrated fury was once again a palpable force in the atmosphere.

Trent continued to watch Calista. "I think it's time that someone told me more about Nestor Kettering. Was he a client at one time?"

"No." Calista summoned her composure. "Nestor was never a client. Last year I met him in a bookshop. He appeared to be interested in the same authors as me—you, for example, sir—and we struck up a conversation. He was handsome, charming, well-mannered, and well-dressed. And he appeared to be intelligent and thoughtful. In short, he was too good to be true."

"You fell in love with him?" Trent asked. He seemed to be bracing himself for her answer.

"For a time I thought he might be the man I had always hoped to find," she said. "A man who would be a friend, a companion, and, yes, perhaps a man I could love."

"You told him about your business, didn't you?" Trent said.

"Yes," she said. "The subject of money eventually arose. I told him the truth about my finances and that I make my living by engaging in the introductions business. I believed I could trust him. He was . . . quite shocked. It took me a while to realize exactly why."

Andrew grunted. "Kettering saw the house, the fashionable clothes, and the salons and he assumed she had inherited a fortune. He charmed her, claimed he was madly in love with her, and asked her to marry him."

Trent looked at Calista. "Did you agree?"

"I told him I would consider his proposal," Calista said. "Kettering was not the first man to make the mistake of concluding that I was well situated financially. Usually I do not attempt to correct the misunderstanding. Instead I use it as a reason for declining an offer of marriage."

Trent nodded in understanding. "You pretend to be yet another wealthy heiress who does not wish to lose control of her finances."

"Precisely. But for some reason I found myself wanting to test Nestor. I wanted to know how deeply he cared about me. So I told him the truth about my inheritance. When he discovered that the only well-furnished rooms in this house are those on the ground floor and that my income derives entirely from trade, he was horrified. And angry. He said I had deceived him."

"The bastard took off to search elsewhere for a wealthy wife," Andrew concluded. "And he found one."

"Since then I have seen Nestor on only two occasions," Calista said. She looked at Trent. "The first was yesterday, just before you arrived for your appointment. The second time was this afternoon outside a book-shop."

"Damnation." Andrew spun around to glare at her. "You never told me that Kettering had come here to see you."

"I knew you would be upset. I'm sorry."

"Bloody hell, Calista. I've got every right to be upset. I'm your brother. You should have told me."

"No good would have come of it," she said. "I apologize, Andrew. I did what I thought was best."

He groaned. "When will you stop trying to protect me?"

She did not respond to that. She had no answer for him.

"I'll find the bastard," Andrew vowed. "I'll put a stop to this harassment."

"Andrew, please, don't say things like that," Calista said.

"I won't allow him to frighten you," Andrew said.

Trent leaned back against the edge of the desk and crossed his arms. "I would remind both of you that we are very likely dealing with a murderer who is definitely not Nestor Kettering. Let us take this step-by-step."

Andrew eyed him. "What do you mean?"

"We must consider the facts that we know for certain," Trent said. "Kettering has suddenly reappeared in Calista's life after about a year of silence. He seems quite intent on seducing her even though she has made it clear she wants nothing to do with him."

"Absolutely clear," Calista said.

"We also know that although Kettering was the one who purchased the memento mori items and the coffin bell, he was not the person who attacked us tonight. In addition, I think we can safely assume that it was the man with the knife who murdered Mrs. Fulton, not Kettering."

"Where does that leave us?" Andrew asked.

"I don't know," Trent said. "But those things are facts and right now we are short on that particular commodity. We must acquire a few more. When we have enough we will be able to finish the story."

Calista looked at the folders on her desk. "I don't have a file on Nestor Kettering. There was never any need for one. Why would he want to frighten me? He was an out-and-out fortune hunter. He never loved me."

"That does not mean that he is not obsessed with you," Trent said. "Some people cannot tolerate any form of rejection. He is evidently a man who is accustomed to being able to charm women, but he failed with you."

Calista shook her head. "Even if that is true, why would he wait a year to approach me again?"

"I don't know," Trent said. "We need more information."

"I knew something like this would happen sooner or later." Andrew stormed across the room and turned his head to glare at Calista. "Didn't I warn you that rumors about your agency would start to leak out and that they might attract the wrong people?"

"Yes," she said. "You have mentioned that risk on a number of occasions. But given my employment options, I do not think your comments are useful."

"Enough," Trent said. "There is no point arguing about this. We must stick to the matter at hand. What we have is a killer who is not in your files, Calista, but who likely has some connection, however remote, to Nestor Kettering. It cannot be a coincidence that he is back in your life."

Andrew stopped halfway across the room. "That gets us precisely nowhere."

"We also have a fairly accurate description of the killer who, judging by appearance and attire, can move comfortably in respectable society," Calista pointed out.

Andrew swept out a hand. "It could be any one of thousands of men in London."

"Except for two more interesting facts," Trent said. "The first is that he doesn't mind using a knife to commit murder. That is not an especially common hobby among members of the upper classes."

Curiosity flashed in Andrew's eyes. "What, exactly, do you mean, sir?"

"Think about it," Trent said. "Slicing a woman's throat is a very messy way to kill a person. The average well-dressed gentleman is inclined to prefer a tidier approach—a blow to the head, perhaps, or a gun or poison."

Andrew nodded thoughtfully. "A method that would not risk ruining his good clothes."

"But this well-dressed murderer does not seem to mind the blood," Trent said. "Furthermore he seems to know how to kill without getting a lot of the stuff on himself. That is another skill."

"What are you implying?" Calista asked, more uneasy than ever.

"It occurs to me that the man we are hunting might actually revel in killing," Trent said. "That speaks to the depths of his obsession."

"Dear heaven." Calista sat very still. "You believe that he might have done this sort of thing before, don't you?"

"I think it is a very likely possibility. He did not strike me as an apprentice learning his trade. He is a skilled master of his craft."

Calista gripped the arms of her chair. "What sort of madman are we dealing with? And why has he fixed his attention on me?"

"We do have one more bit of information about the man we encountered tonight that might prove useful," Trent said.

Calista and Andrew both looked at him.

"What?" Calista asked.

"I managed to do some damage to his skull with that floral display stand," Trent said. "There was a fair amount of blood. As Calista pointed out earlier, it is likely he will require the services of a doctor."

"How does that help us?" Andrew demanded.

"I'm not sure yet but we shall see." Trent looked at Calista. "Is there anything else you can think of that might help us get to the bottom of this affair?"

"No, I don't think so," she said. "None of this makes any sense."

"It will, eventually," Trent said. He looked at Andrew. "Calista tells me that you conduct research into the backgrounds of those who wish to become her clients. You verify marital status, finances, and so forth."

Andrew shrugged. "It's not hard to determine whether or not they are married. Spotting the out-and-out fortune hunters is a bit trickier, of course, because they can be quite clever. They are, after all, hiding the truth from everyone in Society, not just Calista. They are practiced liars."

Trent raised his brows. "You obviously have a talent for that sort of work."

Andrew tried to appear blasé but he flushed a faint red. Calista knew the compliment pleased him. It occurred to her that he never looked that happy when she thanked him for his investigative work. Evidently Trent's remark, coming as it did from an older male, made more of an impact.

"Let's return to the subject of Nestor Kettering," Trent said. "We know more about him than we do about anyone else who is involved in this thing. We have a name, an address, and the fact that he purchased the memento mori items. That is a great deal of information. We shall focus on him for now."

"Even though he's not the man who attacked us?" Calista said.

Andrew frowned. "Mr. Hastings is right. There must be a connection between Kettering and the man with the knife. It defies logic to think that it is all a bizarre coincidence."

"Yes, it does," Trent said. "I can think of one version of a story that fits the facts that we have obtained. The tale goes like this: After having married his heiress, Kettering is now back in London. He has what he wanted, a wealthy bride, but he cannot forget that you rejected him. After obsessing on that rejection for many months he decides to exact revenge. He buys the memento mori items and arranges to have them sent to you. But when we turn the tables and track down Mrs. Fulton, he panics and hires someone to get rid of her."

"And you as well," Andrew added. "The note about the appointment at Fulton's was sent to you, sir, not Calista."

Calista looked at Trent. "You're suggesting that Nestor hired a professional killer to murder Mrs. Fulton and you?"

"As I said, it's a story that fits the facts that we have at the moment."

"This is not a story, sir. This is my life we are talking about."

"I'm an author, Calista." Trent sounded abruptly weary. "The older I get, the more I am convinced that a truth only makes sense when it is revealed in the form of a story. Without that context it is simply a random event with no meaning. It cannot teach us anything and it cannot be used for any purpose. But a good story—that is another thing altogether. It can set us on a new path. It may be the wrong path, but at least it takes us somewhere."

"Such as?" Andrew asked.

"In this case, the story raises a logical question," Trent said. "Where does a gentleman go to hire another gentleman who is skilled in the art of murder?"

Calista considered that. "An excellent question, but where does one go for the answer?"

"As it happens, I know someone who may be able to point us in the right direction. But first we need a better understanding of the mind of the killer."

"We know one thing about him," Calista said. She shivered. "It is obvious that he is mentally unbalanced."

"I agree," Trent said. "Which means that my brother might be able to give us some guidance. Harry is a doctor who has developed an avid interest in the new science of psychology."

"Yes, your sister mentioned that," Calista said.

"With luck he may be able to provide us with some insights into the character of the man we are hunting."

"What good will it do us to talk to a doctor?" Andrew asked. "We already know we're dealing with a madman who is capable of murder."

"If we gain some understanding of the nature of the man we are pursuing, we may be able to predict his actions," Trent said.

"I would remind both of you that we are making some very big leaps here," Calista said. "We do not even know why this madman murdered Mrs. Fulton tonight."

"I think we can fit her into our story with a bit of speculation," Trent said. "I wouldn't be surprised if Mrs. Fulton attempted to blackmail the customer who purchased the memento mori objects. That explains why she was so vague about her answers when we interviewed her today."

"She attempted to blackmail Nestor Kettering and got murdered for her pains?" Andrew asked. "Yes, that makes sense."

Calista shook her head. "I don't know what to think, Trent. This is all getting so complicated and so very dangerous."

Andrew and Trent exchanged glances. Belatedly she realized that she had used Trent's name for the first time in the conversation, and in a casual manner that signaled the new level of intimacy between them. So be it, she thought. Trent had been right earlier. Considering what they had been through together, they had every right to employ each other's first name.

"We may be able to untangle some of the threads if we acquire more information about Nestor Kettering," Trent said. He looked at Andrew. "You have had some experience discovering the truth about the finances, marital status, and character of the men who apply to Calista's agency. Would you be willing to dig a little deeper into Kettering's background?"

Andrew frowned. "I told you, he's a fortune hunter who married an heiress. What more do you want to know?"

"I won't have the answer to that question until you discover something that we don't already know about him—something that gives us another chapter in our story."

"The servants," Andrew said. Enthusiasm gleamed in his eyes. "They always know what is going on inside a household. I have had some luck in the past with inquiries among the staff who serve in a gentleman's house."

Trent looked amused. "You do, indeed, have the right instincts for this sort of work."

Andrew made a face. "Some would say it's just an excuse to indulge my natural sense of curiosity. But I like to think that my research into the backgrounds of Calista's clients has helped her keep a few cads and fortune hunters off her list."

"That is very true," Calista said.

It occurred to her that Andrew was looking considerably more cheerful, more enthusiastic, than he had been a moment ago. Trent had assigned him a task to fulfill.

"Perhaps we should give this plan some more thought," she said. "Making inquiries of Kettering's household staff might carry some risk."

Andrew scowled. "I would remind you that I am not without experience in this sort of thing."

"The inquiries you make for me are different."

"Damn it, Calista—"

"I believe Andrew will be reasonably safe, at least for now," Trent said. He gave Andrew a sharp look. "Assuming he exercises some common sense and takes precautions to hide his identity."

"Absolutely," Andrew vowed.

"At this point Kettering has no way of knowing that we are focusing our attention on him. He won't be aware that we have the journal."

Andrew grinned and opened the door. "I'll get started first thing in the morning. Meanwhile, if you will excuse me, I will get some sleep."

He disappeared out into the hall.

*My little brother has now become my protector,* Calista thought. *My world is changing.*

23

THE DOCTOR WAS nervous. His fingers shook a little as he set the stitches in the wound. He'd been paid well to come out late at night to attend the patient. The explanation provided was that the gentleman had suffered a fall down the stairs and taken a nasty blow to his head. One could hardly leave a man to bleed until morning, not when the man was willing to pay double the doctor's usual fee. After all, the address was in a respectable neighborhood, not some dangerous, unlit street in the stews.

But one look at the man who answered the door had chilled the doctor's blood. There was something unnerving about the patient, something the doctor could not put his finger on but that made him wish quite devoutly that he had not been available when the summons had come.

The patient was nude above the waist. There was a pile of blood-drenched garments in the corner of the firelit room.

The patient had said little but when he did speak his accents were those of a well-bred gentleman. That should have been reassuring. But the sight of the strange little altar was almost too much for the doctor's nerves. There was a sheathed knife on top. A photograph hung on the wall above it. He wondered if he had been called out to tend a practitioner of the occult.

"I understand you fell down the stairs?" the doctor said. The last thing he wanted to do was converse with the patient but in his anxiety he found himself needing to shatter the frightening silence.

"Yes."

"You were fortunate. I have stopped the bleeding but a blow to the head is always concerning. Were you unconscious for any length of time?"

"No."

"In that case I don't expect that you will have any lasting problems, although you will likely have a headache for a day or so. I will leave you some medicine to ease the pain."

The patient did not respond. He remained stoic as the last few stitches were set.

The doctor finished up quickly, wrapped the patient's head in a clean bandage, and then hastily closed up his satchel. He headed toward the door, intent only on escape.

"That should take care of things," he said over his shoulder.

"One moment."

The doctor froze. The door was at least three, perhaps four strides away. His mouth went dry.

"Yes?" he managed.

"Your payment."

The doctor turned slowly, his heart pounding. "Quite all right. Happy to have been of service."

Without a word the patient held out some banknotes. The doctor stared at them, mesmerized.

"Your payment," the patient said softly.

The doctor took two steps toward the patient, grabbed the banknotes, and fled to the door.

He did not breathe freely until he was safely aboard the hansom and on his way home. He thought about the strange altar, the sheathed blade, and the photograph. He shuddered. He had no idea of the identity of the woman in the picture but he pitied her. She had the misfortune to be the focus of the attention of a very dangerous man.

He just hoped that the woman was still alive. Because whatever had occurred tonight, he was quite certain that the patient had not taken a tumble down the stairs.

24

WHEN THE DOOR closed behind Andrew, Calista gave Trent a long, considering look.

"I am not quite sure how you did it, but you succeeded in calming Andrew's temper," she said. "For that, you have my gratitude. A short time ago I feared that you and he would come to blows. Now the relationship between the two of you appears almost cordial."

"Your brother needs to feel useful, Calista. Every man, rich or poor, needs a profession of some kind."

"I do understand that." She rose from her chair and crossed the room to stand in front of the fire. "Lately it has become clear that he yearns to be more independent. Soon he will want to move out of this house and into his own lodgings. I suspect that the only reason he is still here is because he doesn't feel right about leaving me on my own."

Trent moved to stand beside her. "In spite of the quarreling this evening—or perhaps because of it—it is obvious that the two of you are close."

"We are the last of our line. There is no one else now that Grandmother is gone. She took us in and left us this house and a little money but she never approved of my parents' marriage. To the end of her days she remained furious with my father because he fell in love with Mama and convinced her to run off with him. They were both engaged to other people at the time, you see. It was a great scandal."

"Your grandmother never forgave your father?"

"No. She cut him off without a penny. But Papa and Mama made do with a little money that came from Mama's side of the family and the money that my father made with his engineering consulting."

"I suppose the fact that they did not come around begging for help from your grandmother only made her all the more bitter," Trent said.

"Yes, but that was not the worst of it. You see, Andrew takes after Papa. If you look at a photograph of my father you cannot miss the resemblance. The likeness is unmistakable."

"In other words, every time your grandmother looked at Andrew she saw her son."

"And every time she looked at me, she saw the daughter-in-law she despised." Calista swallowed hard. "She was very cold to Andrew and me. There was a great bitterness eating away inside her. After Andrew and I came to live with her she focused her unhappiness on us. In a way, she blamed us for my father's death."

"It must have been difficult for you and your brother."

"I would have given anything to avoid living with Grandmother. I had an excellent education thanks to my parents and I could have found work as a governess. But I had Andrew to think of. I was sixteen when our parents were killed. Andrew was only nine. No family would have considered hiring a governess who came with a younger brother as baggage."

"So you sank your pride and accepted your grandmother's offer." Trent got a knowing look. "And then you tried to be both mother and father to Andrew."

"I tried to shelter him from Grandmother's moods. Things got very difficult toward the end because she was determined to see me married before she died. She was convinced that I had inherited what she considered my mother's wild temperament. As I got older she became very agitated at the possibility that I would inflict yet another scandal on the family name with a runaway marriage."

"Obviously your grandmother failed to find a match for you."

"She blamed me for that, I can assure you. I was twenty and still unmarried when she died. I have always believed she deliberately took an overdose of her sleeping tonic in part because she was so angry with me."

"She hoped to punish you by making you feel guilty for her death?"

Calista gave a small, short, humorless laugh. "I think it is far more likely that she wanted to punish me by trying to impoverish me and Andrew as well. It was after her death that we discovered there was very little money left, you see. She had been discreetly selling off her jewelry and the silver for several years to keep up appearances. Her favorite saying was, *appearances are everything.*"

"She is not the first person in Society to survive by those words of wisdom."

"Very true. And I must admit I took that advice to heart when I established my business."

Trent surveyed the elegant library. "You didn't have to sell the house."

"No, but we sold off almost everything of value that we could find, including some paintings and what was left of Grandmother's jewelry. Fortunately she had some rather nice pieces left. I used the money to refurnish the rooms on this floor and make certain the gardens presented a good first impression on potential clients. Then I purchased a couple of new gowns and dedicated myself to fashionable spinsterhood."

Trent turned to look at her. "I admire your ingenuity and your spirit, Calista."

She wrinkled her nose. "Very kind of you to say so but we both know that I am operating a business. In short, I am in trade. Grandmother is no doubt rolling over in her grave."

"She would very likely not approve of me, either," Trent said. "I, too, am in trade."

"You are a successful author. I would hardly call that a trade. It's a respectable profession."

"You don't know much about the writing business, do you?"

"No, I'm afraid I don't."

"It is all about deadlines, a fickle reading public, demanding editors, and the necessity to hound one's publisher for the money that one is owed while enduring endless complaints about lackluster sales. Then one gets up in the morning and repeats the process."

Calista laughed, startling both of them.

"To say nothing of the fact that everyone feels compelled to critique your books," she concluded.

"Very true."

She smiled. "But there is nothing else you would rather do, is there?"

"No," Trent said. He sounded both amused and resigned. "I'm afraid I must admit that the writing is nothing short of an addiction, a drug of sorts. I do not think I could stop if I tried."

"Even if you were unable to sell to a publisher?"

He winced. "Please don't say that out loud. I'm not especially superstitious but there is no sense tempting fate."

"I'm a businesswoman, Mr. Hastings. I hold similar views on the subject of fate, believe me."

He turned back to the fire.

"Not everyone understands, you know," he said after a while.

"That writing is a passion for you?"

"Yes," he said. "They consider it a hobby or an eccentricity—a relatively harmless pastime."

"Perhaps one must experience a passion of one's own before one can comprehend another's."

"You have a passion for your work, don't you?" he said.

"There is so much unnecessary loneliness in the world. Marriage is not necessarily the answer, at least not for women. But an enduring friendship is a great gift and a blessing."

"You find satisfaction in helping others obtain that gift."

"Yes, I do."

Perhaps it was the brandy. Perhaps her nerves had truly been shattered by the violent events of the evening. Whatever the cause she was suddenly feeling curiously light-headed, even a little giddy.

"If Grandmother could only see me now," she said. "Drinking brandy with a dashing author of detective novels after a night spent fending off a fiendish killer in a chamber full of coffins."

"It all sounds so much more entertaining when you tell it as a story."

"Yes it does," she said.

She started to giggle. Trent watched her, bemused. She never giggled, she thought, horrified. The giggles were abruptly transformed into laughter. The laughter was unnatural but she could not seem to contain it.

Then she felt the tears on her cheeks.

"Oh, for heaven's sake," she said, choking on the words.

Humiliated, she hurried toward her desk, intending to find a hankie. But Trent was suddenly there, in her path. His arms closed around her and she sobbed into his shirt for what seemed an eternity.

He did not try to console her with words. He simply held her very tightly. She realized with a sense of wonder and dismay that it felt very good to be in his arms. In that moment it was exactly where she wanted to be.

After a time the tears were purged. She raised her head.

"Please forgive the display of emotion," she said. "I am, of course, quite mortified."

He ignored that. "You forgot the kiss."

"What?

"You mentioned the late-night brandy and the fiendish killer and the room full of coffins but you neglected the kiss we shared. Was that because you did not enjoy that part of the story?"

She would never forget the kiss, she thought.

"I believe that was the very best part," she said.

Trent's eyes heated. He caught her gently by the shoulders, pulled her close and kissed her slowly, as though she were a rare wine to be savored. When he finally raised his head she was shivering a little. Not with nerves, she thought. With a glorious, energizing excitement.

"I'm glad," he said. "Because it was certainly my favorite chapter."

It was as if the library was locked away in another dimension, a place inhabited by only the two of them. *Seize this moment,* she told herself. *Store it up in your memories so that you can take it out and warm yourself with it in the future.*

Common sense descended.

She yearned to remain in Trent's arms but she knew it would be folly to think herself safe there. Reluctantly she pushed herself away from his heat and strength. Reluctantly he let her go.

"My nerves seem to be somewhat wobbly tonight," she said.

"As are mine," he said. "I think it's fair to say that we both have cause to feel a bit unsettled."

She managed a smile. "You do not appear to be at all unsettled by events."

"As you have recently observed, appearances are deceiving. But it is time I let you get some sleep." He picked up the journal. "It has been a very interesting evening but also a rather long one."

"I'll have Sykes whistle for a cab."

"Thanks, but that is not necessary. I need the exercise and the night air to clear my brain so that I can think clearly."

"I understand. Events tonight have been nothing if not chaotic."

"It is not the events at J. P. Fulton's that are clouding my brain at this moment. It is you, Miss Langley."

"Me?"

"Yes, you." He crossed the room in long strides, heading toward the door. "I will call on you tomorrow so that we can discuss our plans in detail, but I believe that our first move should be a consultation with my brother, Harry."

"I would very much like to accompany you when you speak with him."

"Certainly."

Sykes was waiting in the hall. "Shall I summon a cab, sir?"

"No thank you, Sykes," Trent said. "I'll walk."

Sykes led the way toward the front door.

Calista followed, stopping at the threshold. She watched Trent go down the front steps.

"Are you sure it's safe for you to walk home tonight?" she asked.

Trent paused to look back at her. "The killer failed and he is wounded. I doubt he can do any more serious damage tonight. As for Kettering, if he is, indeed, behind events this evening, he will need time to concoct a new scheme. It's not easy to find reliable talent when it comes to murder."

"A sobering thought," Calista said.

Trent looked at Sykes. "You will check the locks on all the doors and windows, will you not?"

"Of course, sir," Sykes said.

25

TRENT WENT UP the steps of his town house and took his key out of his pocket. The walk home had, indeed, proved clarifying but not quite the way he had anticipated. He did not gain any new insights into the investigation, but by the time he let himself into his own front hall he was certain of one thing. He wanted Calista.

Furthermore, his desire for her had not lessened now that the violent emotions aroused by the confrontation in the coffin chamber had dissipated. If anything, his need had only grown stronger. Leaving her alone tonight ranked as one of the most difficult things he had ever done.

She was safe, he thought. At least for now. She was not alone in the big house.

But he could not escape the knowledge that she was being hunted. The need to protect her was so powerful he almost turned around.

He let himself into the darkened hall, hoping that Eudora was fast asleep.

She appeared at the top of the stairs, clutching her wrapper at her throat. He suppressed a groan.

"Trent, what happened? I expected you home hours ago. I have been very worried. Are you all right?" She descended a few more steps and got a closer look at him. "Good heavens. Were you involved in a carriage accident?"

"It was a bit more complicated than that, but I am all right."

"Thank goodness. But you must tell me everything. I will not be able to sleep if you don't."

There was no evading the questions, he thought. Eudora had a right to the answers.

"Come into my study and I will explain," he said.

Eudora was both appalled and fascinated by his tale so it was another half hour before he finally succeeded in climbing into bed. He lay there for a long time, arms folded behind his head, and contemplated the shadows.

It would not be easy to find the sort of evidence required to have a wealthy gentleman like Nestor Kettering arrested for murder. If he had, indeed, hired someone else to do the deed, as seemed likely, it might well be impossible to prove it.

As for the nasty gifts that Calista had received; she was right, there was no law against sending memento mori presents to a lady.

Trent contemplated the memories of the one other occasion when he had confronted a similar problem. Sometimes a man's options were limited.

Sleep finally descended, bringing with it the old dream.

*He heard Eudora's screams echoing from the laboratory. Desperate to get to her he tried to run up the stairs but he was ensnared in a dark fog. The staircase twisted away into infinity. He was consumed with the icy fear that he would be too late, just as he had been too late the last time . . .*

. . .

He came awake in a cold sweat. Out of long habit, he sat up on the side of the bed and breathed deeply for a time. The dream fragments slipped back into the shadows but he knew he would not be able to go back to sleep.

After a while he got to his feet and reached for his robe. He had another chapter of *The Affair of the Missing Bride* due soon. He might as well get some work done.

He made his way downstairs, went into his study, sat at his desk, and started to reach for a sheet of paper and a pen.

But Fulton's journal was in the way. He opened it instead. The pages were filled with neatly recorded transactions that went back for three years.

As he had told Andrew, money always left a bright trail.

It was the matter of motive that concerned him the most. Committing murder always involved some risk. Furthermore, a man—even a madman—needed a reason to cross the sharp boundary between civilized behavior and violence. According to Harry, for some warped minds it was simply the dark thrill of the business that drove the killer. Nevertheless, even that constituted a motive of sorts.

Others were driven by greed or passion or a desire for vengeance. He knew a great deal about that last motive. He touched the side of his jaw where the skin was drawn tight and rigid with scars. When he realized what he was doing he lowered his hand.

If Nestor Kettering had employed a hired killer to murder Mrs. Fulton in order to assure her silence, perhaps it was because he had something more damning to conceal than the purchase of a few memento mori items.

26

"YOU SAY NESTOR Kettering purchased the same set of memento mori items, coffin bells, and coffins four times over the course of the past year?" Harry asked.

"According to Mrs. Fulton's records, yes," Trent said. "The pattern never varied. First the tear-catcher, then a ring, then a safety coffin bell. The only thing that changed were the initials inscribed on the items. Eventually a coffin was purchased but each time it was sent to a different funeral director."

"Patterns and repetitions are always of considerable interest in situations such as this," Harry said. "They indicate an obsessive nature."

They were gathered in Harry's comfortably cluttered study. Trent had been prepared for the fact that Calista would accompany him. Last night she had made her intentions clear and she had every right to be there. But at breakfast Eudora had surprised him by insisting on attending the meeting, as well.

She seemed so determined—even enthusiastic—about the prospect of becoming involved in the case that he did not have the heart to refuse her. He was, in fact, not at all certain that he could have kept her away.

He had to admit that it was good to see Eudora excited about something besides her gardening and her novels. It dawned on him that perhaps she felt the same way about him. We have been dragging each other down for years, he thought.

He shook off the flash of insight and watched Harry move around behind the desk.

Harry had inherited their mother's blue eyes and their father's fascination with science, especially chemistry. His interests had led him into the medical profession but he still maintained a well-equipped laboratory. He distilled and concocted his own medicines using plants and herbs from Eudora's greenhouse. He maintained that one could not trust the quality of the products that could be purchased in chemists' shops and apothecaries.

Harry adjusted his reading glasses on his nose and looked at one of the pages of the journal that had been marked.

"It appears that coffin bells are rather expensive," he noted wryly. "Especially when one considers that there is no record of such a device having been successfully employed."

"Is that so?" Calista asked.

She stood a short distance away near a bookshelf lined with heavy volumes on the subjects of anatomy, surgery, and the new, highly controversial science of psychology.

"I'm quite sure that if there ever is an instance of successful use it will be a great sensation in the press." Harry turned to the next page in the journal. "Those in the grave-digging business will tell you that there have been some false alarms, however."

"What do you mean?" Eudora asked.

"The problem is that the natural decomposition process creates swelling and bloat of the tissues and even small twitchy movements of the body, which, in turn, can cause the bell to sound," Harry explained.

Eudora made a face. "Something to think about when one walks past a graveyard."

"According to Mrs. Fulton's records, over the course of the last month Kettering bought a tear-catcher, a jet-and-crystal ring, and the bell inscribed with Calista's initials," Trent said. "But he had not yet purchased the coffin."

"Interesting," Harry said. He sounded as if he were listening to a patient describe his symptoms.

"As I said, the pattern of the purchases has been repeated four times during the past year, including the items given to Calista. In the last three instances, all of the items were delivered to N. Kettering of Number Five Lark Street. But that was not the case with the earliest orders."

Harry's eyes narrowed slightly in understanding. "Those first few items were sent directly to the victim?"

Out of the corner of his eye Trent saw Calista's mouth tighten at the word *victim*.

"So it appears," he said. "Mrs. Fulton's notes indicate that they were sent to Miss Elizabeth Dunsforth in Milton Lane."

"That provides you with a starting point." Harry leaned back in his chair. "It certainly would be illuminating to talk to one of the other people who received the memento mori items and bell."

"But why would the pattern change?" Calista asked. "Why would the first set of memento mori go directly to the *intended recipient* but the rest directly to Kettering's address?"

"I cannot say for certain, of course," Harry said. "But I can speculate that in the case of the first round of gifts Kettering was new at the business. He was still discovering how he wished to torment his victims. As his obsession grew, he may have found it more satisfying to take possession of the memento mori items first so that he could savor them before sending them to the women."

"An unnerving thought," Eudora whispered.

"It is also possible that he simply did not trust Fulton to see that the items were sent to the right person," Harry continued.

"Or he did not want her to know where they were going," Trent said.

"Yes," Harry said. "But I think it's more likely he discovered that he rather enjoyed delivering them himself."

"Trent and I intend to call at Miss Dunsforth's address after we leave here," Calista said. "Is there anything else you can deduce from the pattern of the gifts?"

"I'm afraid not, Miss Langley." Harry took off his glasses and rubbed the bridge of his nose. "The study of human behavior is still a very new science. There is much we do not know—perhaps much we cannot know. But the manner in which this man is tormenting you convinces me that he has fixed on you in what can only be described as a dangerously obsessive manner."

"It is as if he is haunting me."

Harry looked at her, his eyes grim. "If I am correct, it would be more accurate to say that he is hunting you, not haunting you. He is stalking you the way one does a deer in the forest."

"Before one makes the kill," Calista said.

Eudora put a hand on her shoulder. "You are not alone."

Calista gave her a tremulous smile.

"There is one very significant difference," Trent said. "In the case of the deer, the hunter makes every effort to conceal himself from the quarry before he strikes. But in this case Kettering seems to be playing a very cruel game."

Harry looked at him. "I agree. You must stop him before he gets any closer to Miss Langley."

"Do you really believe that he intends to murder her?" Eudora asked.

Harry kept his attention on Trent. "You have disrupted his pattern. There is no way to know how that will affect his mind. If you are correct, Kettering arranged to have Mrs. Fulton murdered last night. We must assume he will be willing to send his killer after another victim."

Calista took a deep breath and let it out slowly. "I do wish you would stop using the word *victim*, Dr. Hastings."

"My apologies, Miss Langley. But I fear the only other word that springs to mind is *prey*. He sees himself as the hunter."

"I suppose that there is little point in going to the police with this information," she said.

Harry's mouth tightened. "Not unless Trent can find a way to identify the man who murdered the proprietor of J. P. Fulton's."

"I will meet with Inspector Wynn at the Yard but I doubt there is much that he can do until Kettering makes his next move," Trent said. "Meanwhile, you must not go out alone, Calista."

She looked at him with shadowed eyes. Her whole world had been turned upside down by the bastard who was stalking her, Trent thought. He had to use considerable willpower to suppress his rage and another emotion, as well. Fear. He could feel the killer circling Calista, closing in on her. The thought of her being alone and unprotected tore at his insides.

"I understand," she said quietly. "But I cannot live with such constraints indefinitely. I have a business to see to. There must be something we can do."

Harry used his glasses to motion toward Fulton's journal. "I agree that your next step is to interview Miss Elizabeth Dunsforth of Milton Lane. She may be able to provide some insights into the mind of Nestor Kettering and perhaps give you some clue as to the identity of his hired killer."

"Assuming she is still alive," Eudora said.

"And assuming that Kettering actually did hire a killer and that the assault last night did not come from an entirely different direction," Trent said. "We are looking at circles within circles."

Harry shook his head. "We are not dealing with a set of random coincidences. There must be some connections."

"I agree," Trent said.

He could only pray that the assumption was true.

Rebecca Hastings appeared in the doorway. She was an attractive young woman with an intelligent gaze. She had very little close family of her own but she had created a warm and loving home for Harry and their infant son. In addition, she had become Harry's assistant when he saw patients in his surgery. Harry often proudly declared that she had a great aptitude for medicine.

"I'm sorry to interrupt," she said, "but a boy just arrived with a message." She looked at Harry. "Mrs. Jenkins's son is feverish. She hopes you will be able to see him today."

Harry got to his feet. "I am on my way." He came out from behind his desk, took his coat down off a hook, and picked up a large black satchel. "Please keep me informed about this situation involving Nestor Kettering. And be careful, Miss Langley. I don't mind telling you, I believe there is cause for grave concern."

He disappeared out into the hall.

Rebecca looked at Trent, Calista, and Eudora. "Will you stay for tea?"

"Afraid that won't be possible," Trent said. He picked up the journal. "Calista and I must be on our way to Milton Lane to see what we can learn from Elizabeth Dunsforth."

"They are going to take me home, first," Eudora explained.

"I see." Rebecca fixed Calista with a thoughtful expression. "Some other time, perhaps, Miss Langley?"

"I would like that very much," Calista said. "Mr. Hastings tells me that you often assist your husband in his medical practice. That sounds quite fascinating."

Rebecca smiled. "Yes, I do find great satisfaction in the work. At one time I dreamed of becoming a doctor but that is virtually impossible for a woman, as I'm sure you're aware."

Eudora made a soft little sound of disgust. "None of the leading medical schools will accept female candidates."

"True, but I have learned a great deal working with my husband," Rebecca said. "I believe he finds me useful."

Trent smiled. "What Harry says is that you are indispensable. Now, you must excuse us."

Rebecca gave Calista and Eudora a polite but rather pointed smile. "The traffic is rather heavy at this time of day. Perhaps Calista and Eudora would like to take the opportunity to refresh themselves before setting out."

Calista and Eudora both looked as if they were about to decline the offer. But the two exchanged an unreadable expression and then Calista smiled at Rebecca.

"Thank you," Calista said.

"Excellent notion," Eudora agreed.

Rebecca appeared satisfied. "Mrs. Bascombe will show you the way."

The stout housekeeper appeared in the hall. With a last, curious glance at Rebecca, Calista and Eudora allowed themselves to be escorted down the hall.

A moment later footsteps echoed faintly on the stairs that led to the landing where the water closet was located.

"Am I missing something here?" Trent asked.

Rebecca ignored that. She lowered her voice and fixed him with a determined look.

"What is going on, Trent? The news of the murder of the owner of the mourning goods shop is a great sensation in the papers today. Neither you nor Miss Langley were mentioned in the piece but I know you were nearly murdered, and I heard Harry say that the situation is dangerous. Surely this is a matter for the police."

"The police are investigating Mrs. Fulton's death. They may, indeed, succeed in arresting the killer, but even if they do, there is still the problem of proving that Nestor Kettering hired him."

"I fear you are all in over your heads."

He was very fond of Rebecca but there were times when he found her irritating. He seemed to be surrounded by women who felt free to speak their minds and make their opinions known. It was his misfortune that he preferred the company of such females, he thought. They were so much more interesting than the other sort.

"If you can come up with a better approach to the problems we are confronting, Rebecca, I trust you will let me know."

"Meanwhile, you intend to continue with your inquiries into this dangerous matter."

"I cannot walk away now."

"No, I suppose not." Rebecca gave him a knowing look. "The question is how did you become involved in the first place?"

"You must blame Eudora for that. She insisted on becoming one of Miss Langley's clients."

"Ah." Rebecca looked pleased. "I must congratulate her. It is past time she emerged from her martyr's cave."

"I could not agree with you more."

"You and I have always been in accord on that subject." Rebecca paused. "Harry and Eudora adore you, Trent. But neither of them can shed their sense of guilt."

"I am aware of that but what the devil can I do? I have told them countless times that what happened in the laboratory was not their fault."

"Words are of no use in a situation like this. You must take action if you want to help your brother and sister find some peace of mind concerning the events of the past. I can only repeat the advice I have already given you on numerous other occasions. Fall in love, marry, and start a family of your own. That alone will set Harry and Eudora free."

"You make it sound so simple."

"It is anything but simple. It is a great challenge and there is always risk involved. But I suspect that you may have begun the process."

"What the devil are you talking about?"

"There is a certain expression in your eyes when you look at Miss Langley."

"Damn it, Rebecca." He stopped because he could not think of any way to end the statement in a coherent fashion.

Footsteps sounded on the stairs. Calista and Eudora were on their way back to the front hall.

"Off you go," Rebecca said. "Have your adventure with Miss Langley. I think it may be exactly what you need. But for heaven's sake, do not get yourself killed in the process. If that were to happen, Harry and Eudora would lose all hope of moving beyond the past. Indeed, Eudora would likely blame herself again because she is the one who introduced you to Miss Langley."

There was nothing he could say to that, Trent thought. It was the truth.

"I will never forgive you if you leave me alone to deal with your brother and sister under such circumstances," Rebecca warned.

"I will keep your threat in mind."

27

CALISTA PERCHED ON the edge of the carriage seat—the only position that would accommodate the small bustle and drapery of her fashionable walking gown. She envied Trent. His masculine attire allowed him to lounge in the corner, one leg outstretched.

He watched the busy street scene with a pensive air.

"You are quite close with your brother and sister," Calista said.

He glanced at her, his mouth twisting in faint amusement. "For my sins, yes."

They should no doubt be discussing what they had learned from Harry, Calista thought, and planning how to approach Miss Elizabeth Dunsforth. But her growing curiosity about Trent and his family got the better of her.

"You do not mean that," she said gently. "I can see that you are quite fond of all of them, including your sister-in-law." She paused, not certain how far she should step into his private life. But given what they had been through together, surely she had some right to a few intimacies. "Correct me if I am mistaken but I have the impression that Eudora and Harry view you almost as a paternal figure."

"Kindly do me a favor and don't remind me. It makes me feel quite old."

"Nonsense. You are in your prime. But you are most certainly a few years older than Harry and Eudora and it is clear they think of you as the head of the family."

"Very likely because after our mother's death and the death of her second husband, that was what I became." His profile hardened. "Belatedly, I might add."

"When did your mother die?"

Trent was silent for a time. She got the impression that he was not going to answer the question and she was beginning to regret asking it when he surprised her.

"My mother was murdered," he said eventually. "By her second husband."

He said it calmly, as though it were merely a statement of fact and not a shattering revelation.

"Dear heaven." For a few seconds she was so shocked she could not find her voice. "Is that what you meant when you said your stepfather was dead? He was hanged for murder?"

"He did not hang." Trent fixed her with an ice-cold look that chilled her to the bone. "I had left home by the time Bristow moved in but I can assure you that he was never a father to Harry and Eudora, not in any way, shape, or form. He was a venomous snake of a man who somehow managed to appear charming long enough to convince my mother to marry him."

"I'm so sorry," Calista whispered. She could not think of anything else to say.

"Bristow told everyone that my mother took her own life—that she deliberately drowned herself in the pond at our country house. But Eudora and Harry and I never believed that, not for a moment. Bristow married her for her money. Six months after the wedding she was dead."

"How old were you?"

"Twenty-two. As I said, I was away at the time, traveling in America. I had been absent from home for nearly a year. I was intent on seeing the world, particularly the Wild West. It all sounded so exciting. So thrilling. Just the sort of adventure a young man craves."

The bitterness in his words told her that he blamed himself for not saving his mother.

"I got home as soon as I could after I received the telegram informing me of my mother's death," he continued. "I found Eudora and Harry on their own with what few members of the staff remained. Several had given notice because they were terrified of Bristow. But when I arrived, he was gone as well."

"Where did he go?"

"He left for London the day after they pulled my mother's body out of the pond. He did not bother to attend the funeral. When I finally got home, Eudora and Harry were still in shock. They were also very frightened. They told me their suspicions. The remaining servants said they, too, were convinced that Mother had been murdered. But there were no witnesses and no proof."

"I assume Bristow got his hands on your mother's inheritance?"

"A great deal of it, yes, although my mother had been careful to reserve a certain amount for each of her children. Bristow was addicted to gambling. He went through the money very quickly. But at least he seemed content to remain in London and leave Harry and Eudora and me alone. The one asset Bristow could not touch was the country house because my grandfather had left it to me."

"So you did not lose your home."

"Theoretically it was safe, but I knew we could not trust Bristow. As long as he was alive, I believed him to be a danger."

"Is that when you started to write your mystery novels?"

Trent frowned. "How did you know?"

"Given your situation it seemed logical that you might have sought an outlet for your—" She stopped before she said the word *passions.* "An outlet for your talents and energies."

"For a time we lived on some money that my grandfather had left to me but I knew it would not last forever. So I started writing. I have always had a certain facility with storytelling and my travels abroad had given me a number of ideas for the character who became Clive Stone."

"But you were trapped in the country, weren't you? There was no other way for you to guard your brother and sister. You dared not leave for fear that Bristow might return."

"You understand me very well, Calista."

"Perhaps that is because I know how it feels to be responsible for the safety and welfare of a younger sibling."

"One does what one must, of course." Trent returned his attention to the window. "A few months after my mother's death I sold the first chapters of a novel featuring Clive Stone to a country newspaper which published them in serialized form. When the story was completed, the chapters were bound together in a book and sold quite well. The *Flying Intelligencer* made me an excellent offer for rights to serialize my next novel. I discovered I had begun a career."

She thought about the plot of the first Clive Stone novel, *Clive Stone and the Affair of the Midnight Appointment.* It had involved a villain who had married a woman for her fortune and then murdered her. In the end, the killer had come to a bad end, as villains always did in Clive Stone novels. In that particular case, the murderous husband had attacked Clive Stone on a bridge. In the ensuing struggle, the killer had fallen to his death and drowned in the raging river.

"You said Bristow died?" she asked.

"Yes." There was a long pause. "Within a few months after my mother's death."

"I see." She sensed she was on dangerous ground. She chose her words with great care. "That must have come as a relief to all of you."

"I will not deny it, although Bristow managed to go through all of the money he had stolen from Mother before he finally departed this earthly plane."

There was an iron-hard finality in Trent's voice that told her that was all of the story that she would get for now.

28

MILTON LANE PROVED to be a neighborhood of prosperous town houses. The cab halted in front of Number Fourteen. Calista and Trent went up the front steps. Trent clanged the door knocker a couple of times.

"We never discussed what we would do if Miss Dunsforth is not here or if she refuses to see us," Calista said.

"If all else fails we shall have to hope that whoever is home is a fan of Clive Stone."

"Has that approach worked for you in the past?"

"I've only employed it when I've made inquiries related to my research. But, yes, it has been my experience that most people are quite generous with their time when it comes to discussing their areas of expertise with an author."

"Is that how Clive Stone learned to pick locks?"

"Among other things."

A housekeeper opened the door.

"We have a very important matter to discuss with Miss Elizabeth

Dunsforth," Calista said. "We are hoping that she will be good enough to see us for a few minutes."

The housekeeper blinked. "I don't understand. There is no Miss Dunsforth at this address."

An icy finger traced a path down Calista's spine. Beside her, Trent went very still.

"This is very odd," he said smoothly. "We are quite certain of the address. Has something happened to Miss Dunsforth?"

"I wouldn't know. I'm new in this post."

"Is the lady of the house at home, by any chance?" Calista asked. "It is very important that we speak with someone who can give us Miss Dunsforth's new address."

The housekeeper hesitated. "I suppose I can see if Mrs. Abington is receiving visitors. It is very early in the day."

Trent took a card out of his pocket. "You may inform her that Mr. Trent Hastings would be grateful for a few minutes of her time. The matter involves some research that I am doing for a new novel featuring Clive Stone."

The housekeeper's eyes widened. "You're the author of the Clive Stone stories? How thrilling. I have read every one of your books at least twice. My employer is kind enough to pass her copies to me after she is finished with them. I cannot tell you how many pleasant evenings I have spent with a Clive Stone novel."

"Thank you, Mrs.—?" Trent broke off on an inquiring note.

The housekeeper blushed. "Mrs. Button, sir."

"Thank you, Mrs. Button. I'm very glad to know that you enjoy my stories. Now, if you wouldn't mind asking your employer if she will be kind enough to see us—"

"Yes, sir, right away, sir."

Mrs. Button closed the door. Calista listened to the rapid patter of muffled footsteps.

"I must say, that worked rather nicely," Calista said.

Trent looked grim. "It usually does."

The door opened less than two minutes later. Mrs. Button beamed at Trent.

"Mrs. Abington is at home and would be delighted to see you, sir."

"Thank you," Trent said.

More or less ignoring Calista, the housekeeper led the way into a well-appointed drawing room. A fashionably dressed woman of some thirty years was seated on a sofa covered in dark red velvet. She flicked a disinterested glance at Calista and favored Trent with a warm smile.

"Mr. Hastings," she said. "This is an unexpected pleasure. Please be seated."

"Thank you," Trent said. "This is Miss Langley."

Mrs. Abington gave Calista a brief, dismissive glance. "Miss Langtree, was it?"

"Langley," Calista said.

"Yes, of course," Mrs. Abington said vaguely. She turned back to Trent and gave him another gracious smile. "I must tell you that I am a great fan of your novels, sir. Indeed, my entire family enjoys them. We read them aloud in the evenings. Do sit down."

Trent held a chair for Calista and then took his seat.

"I'm delighted that my stories provide you some enjoyment," he said.

"Yes, indeed. But I must admit, I am very curious to know what brings you to my door, sir."

"Research, madam."

"Research? I would be thrilled to assist you but I cannot imagine how."

"Miss Langley and I are engaged in a real-life investigation into the disappearance of a Miss Elizabeth Dunsforth."

"I see." Mrs. Abington frowned briefly at Calista and then returned her attention to Trent. "How very odd. Why would you want to do that?"

"We are making notes of the various steps required to locate a missing person," Trent explained. "The process intrigues me. I intend to use it in the plot of my next book."

"I see," Mrs. Abington said again. "I suppose that explains Miss Langtree's presence. She is your secretary."

"Langley," Calista corrected.

No one paid any attention.

"Something along those lines," Trent said.

He was careful not to look at Calista.

"How on earth did you trace Miss Dunsforth to this address?" Mrs. Abington asked.

"We discovered that some memento mori items were sent to her here," Trent said. "A tear-catcher, a jet ring, and a bell designed for a safety coffin."

"Oh, yes, I remember those things. We could not understand why anyone would send them to Miss Dunsforth. She had no family to speak of, you see. A cousin or two, perhaps, but they never visited. And it wasn't as if Miss Dunsforth, herself, was dying, at least not at the time. She appeared quite healthy. We assumed that it was all some unfortunate mistake."

Calista tensed. "Miss Dunsforth did reside at this address at one time?"

"Yes," Mrs. Abington said. "She was employed as a governess. Quite a good one, actually. I was sorry to have to let her go."

"Why did you dismiss her?" Trent asked.

"After the second memento mori gift arrived she went into a decline. Developed a dreadful case of shattered nerves. She was convinced that someone was watching her and following her. In the end she became quite delusional. Naturally, I couldn't have her around the children, not in her unbalanced state of mind. So I sent her back to the agency. I have no idea where she is now."

"Would you mind giving us the name of the agency?" Trent asked.

"Certainly. It was the Grant Agency in Tanner Street."

Calista stopped breathing for a few seconds, nearly overcome by an eerie, light-headed sensation. The old saying whispered through her head: *as if someone walked over my grave.*

"Are you quite certain that Miss Dunsforth was with the Grant Agency, Mrs. Abington?" she asked.

"Of course, I'm certain." Mrs. Abington switched her attention back to Trent. She lowered her voice in a conspiratorial manner. "Just between you and me, Mr. Hastings, I suspect that I would have been forced to let Miss Dunsforth go, even if she had not become delusional."

"Why do you say that?" Trent asked.

"I cannot be certain but I believe that for a few weeks prior to the arrival of the tear-catcher and the other items, Miss Dunsforth was seeing a gentleman."

Calista could scarcely breathe now. She did not dare look at Trent but she sensed the tension in him.

"What makes you say that?" Trent asked.

"Her mood changed for a time," Mrs. Abington said. "She suddenly seemed happier and more carefree, at least at first."

"Given the nature of a governess's position, it would be extremely difficult for one to conduct any sort of illicit liaison," Calista pointed out.

"I consider myself a generous and understanding employer," Mrs. Abington said, an edge on the words. "Miss Dunsforth was allowed one afternoon and evening off each week and three hours on Sunday so that she could attend church. I assumed she used her free time to visit bookstores and museums and perhaps do a bit of shopping. But in the weeks before the memento mori started to arrive she began returning quite late from her evenings off. There was an air of excitement about her. I don't mind telling you that it caused me some alarm."

"Why didn't you let her go then?" Calista asked. "Most employers would have done so. Generally speaking, governesses are not allowed to form romantic liaisons."

"To be perfectly honest, I did not want to go through the process of hiring yet another governess." Mrs. Abington sighed. "I'm afraid my children are rather high spirited. They have already gone through three governesses. In any event, I thought the liaison was over when she returned one afternoon quite depressed."

"Do you know why she was in low spirits?" Calista asked.

"I assume the gentleman had ended the affair, of course. They always do, sooner or later. Men are happy enough to seduce a poor governess, but everyone knows such relationships always end badly."

"How long after that was it before the tear-catcher arrived?" Trent asked.

"Less than a week," Mrs. Abington said. "She was still moody and depressed, but she had not yet begun to lose her nerve. She was quite alarmed by the tear-catcher, however. It had her initials engraved on it, you see. That was the beginning of her decline."

"Do you have any idea of the identity of the man she might have been meeting on her free afternoons and evenings?" Calista asked.

"No. I can only assume he was one of those men who take advantage of women who find themselves facing the world alone." Mrs. Abington smiled at Trent. "Have I been of any help to you in your research, sir?"

"You have been invaluable, Mrs. Abington," Trent said.

Mrs. Abington turned to Calista. "You'll want to make a note of that, Miss Langtree. My full name is Beatrice Abington."

"I will be certain to jot that down," Calista said.

She was impressed when Trent managed to extricate both of them from the household before tea was served. She went briskly up the cab steps. Trent gave the address of the Grant Agency to the driver, climbed inside the carriage, and settled on the seat across from Calista.

"Sorry about the misunderstanding concerning your role in my life," he said.

"Trust me when I tell you that I am quite content to play the part of your secretary. Mrs. Abington could have made another assumption about my position, one that would have been far less respectable."

Trent appeared irritated by that observation but he made no comment. Instead he changed the subject.

"What was it about the name of the Grant Agency that startled you?" he asked.

"You noticed that, did you? I'm sure it's nothing, really. Merely a coincidence."

"What was it?"

"I have had two clients from the Grant Agency within the past year. I was able to introduce each of them to very suitable men. Both women are married now and living in the country. I don't see how there can be any connection to this affair."

"I'm not a fan of coincidences in my stories."

29

THE SECRETARY USHERED them into the office of the agency's proprietor.

"Mr. Hastings, the author, to see you, Mrs. Grant." There was a
distinct pause. "Oh, and his secretary, Miss Langley."

Mrs. Grant ignored Calista. She glowed at Trent. "Please be seated,
sir. I have read all of your novels. They are so exciting." She waved a
dismissing hand at the secretary. "Thank you, Miss Shipley. That will
be all for now."

"Yes, Mrs. Grant."

Miss Shipley was in her early thirties but there was a rigid quality
about her that put Calista in mind of a headmistress at a girls boarding
school. At one time she had no doubt been attractive, even pretty, but
life had crushed whatever happiness might have been allotted to her at
the outset. Still, she made an attempt at fashion. A massive bun—no
doubt a hairpiece—sat atop her head like a crown. It was anchored
with a number of long, ornamental hairpins.

She gave Calista a disapproving look before moving out into the hall. In a few more years she will look like Grandmother, Calista thought.

The door closed firmly behind Miss Shipley.

Mrs. Grant was a few years older than her secretary but very different in appearance and temperament. She was comfortably plump and endowed with the sort of bubbling personality that can rarely be squelched for long.

She beamed at Trent. "Such a pleasure to meet you, Mr. Hastings. I understand you wish to inquire about one of my governesses. How old are the children?"

Calista frowned. "The children?"

"The age matters, you see," Mrs. Grant said briskly. "All of my governesses are extremely well qualified, but I have discovered that some are better when it comes to instructing very young children. Others excel at teaching older children." She turned back to Trent. "What are the ages of your little ones, sir?"

"Actually," Calista said, "we would like to interview Miss Elizabeth Dunsforth. A friend recommended her."

"Miss Dunsforth?" Mrs. Grant was clearly bewildered. "I don't understand."

"Is she no longer associated with this agency?" Trent asked.

"It's not that. Oh, dear, I see you aren't aware of what happened to Miss Dunsforth."

"No," Calista said. She was vaguely aware that she had a death grip on her satchel. "What happened to her?"

"The poor woman had a complete nervous breakdown. It was a terrible thing to watch. She was convinced that a man was following her everywhere, watching her, entering her lodgings when she was not around. Sending her inappropriate gifts. It was all very sad. She was an excellent governess but in the end I no longer felt comfortable sending her out to interview with potential clients. I had to let her go. Sadly, she was dead within the week."

"Murdered?" Trent asked calmly.

"What?" Mrs. Grant looked horrified at the notion. "Good heavens, no. I believe the funeral director mentioned an infection of the throat. I'm not aware of the precise circumstances of her death but I'm certain that if she had been murdered, there would have been a great sensation in the papers. You know how it is when a respectable young woman becomes the victim of a dreadful crime."

"Yes, of course," Calista said. "There is always a great deal of sordid speculation about her personal life in the press and the penny dreadfuls."

"Indeed. I can assure you, Miss Dunsforth's death was a quiet, altogether respectable affair. I attended the funeral. I felt it was the least I could do for her."

"Were there many people at her funeral?" Trent asked.

"Sadly, no. Just me." Mrs. Grant paused. "But she must have had at least one relative who cared about appearances."

"Why do you say that?" Trent asked.

"Because the funeral director told me in confidence that the gentleman who brought in the body and paid for the funeral was a distant cousin. Although he was not present at the gravesite, I must say he sent her off in proper style. There was an expensive, very modern safety coffin, the sort that has a bell attached to a chain so that the deceased can ring for assistance from inside the casket—assuming she suddenly revived."

"Expensive," Calista said.

"Yes, indeed." Mrs. Grant heaved a long sigh. "I must say, it's been a difficult year for my business."

"Why is that?" Calista asked.

Trent glanced at her, surprised by the question. But she was genu-

162

inely interested. Business was business, after all. She was always curious about other enterprises that were owned and operated by women. There was usually something to be learned.

"One always expects to lose a few governesses over time, of course," Mrs. Grant said. "Sadly, the young, attractive ones all too often allow themselves to be seduced, if not by the master of the house or the eldest son, then by some callous gentleman who takes advantage of their naïveté."

In other words, the women were raped and abandoned, Calista thought. Governesses occupied a very lonely position in a household. They did not mingle with the servants. At the same time, they were certainly not members of the family. The in-between status left them very vulnerable.

"What happens to them?" she asked.

Trent gave her a quick, subtle look of warning.

With an effort she managed to control her temper.

"I'm afraid those poor women usually land on the street," Mrs. Grant said. "As I said, a certain degree of turnover is expected. But for the most part, my ladies are very healthy."

"Healthy?" Calista asked, startled.

"I avoid hiring those who don't appear to be robust. There's no market, you see. Parents don't want sickly governesses around their children."

"I understand," Calista said.

"But in the past year I've had two other governesses die on me— both apparently healthy young women."

Calista could scarcely breathe now. "By any chance, did they suffer from bad nerves, too?"

Mrs. Grant frowned. "Now that you mention it, I remember that Miss Forsyth did seem rather anxious shortly before she died. Miss Townsend handed in her notice a few days prior to falling ill. Both appeared somewhat depressed. Why do you ask?"

"Research," Trent said. "For my next book. *The Affair of the Vanishing Governess.*"

"Oh, yes, of course." Mrs. Grant nodded solemnly. "Let me see if my secretary remembers anything in particular about the other two governesses."

She leaned back and pulled a cord that hung down the wall. Somewhere in the other room a bell rang.

The door opened. Miss Shipley loomed. "Yes, Mrs. Grant?"

"Regarding Miss Forsyth and Miss Townsend. Do you happen to remember if either of them suffered from weak nerves?"

"I have no idea, Mrs. Grant. But, then, it's not the sort of thing one discusses with a secretary, is it?"

Not if one hopes to maintain one's post, Calista thought. Elizabeth Dunsforth had made the mistake of letting her employer know about her growing anxiety and it had cost her the position in the Abington household.

"That will be all," Mrs. Grant said. "Thank you."

"Yes, Mrs. Grant."

The door closed again.

"I'm sorry, Mr. Hastings." Mrs. Grant smiled her cheery smile. "I'm afraid I can't be of assistance on that particular subject."

"Do you happen to know the cause of death in the other two cases?" Trent asked.

"I believe they all suffered from an infection of the throat," Mrs. Grant said. "There must be something going around."

Calista could hardly breathe. "Did you attend the other two funerals?"

"Yes, I did." Mrs. Grant sighed. "I felt it was the least I could do. They were all women who found themselves alone in the world. They had been excellent governesses. And so very young."

"Did someone pay for the funerals of Miss Forsyth and Miss Townsend?" Trent asked.

Mrs. Grant brightened. "Yes, indeed, someone did take care of Miss Forsyth and Miss Townsend, and in a very respectable fashion, I might add. Although, if you ask me, it's rather sad that family stepped forward at the end even though they never bothered to help any of those young women when they were alive. All three of them were quite desperate and alone when they applied for posts at my agency."

"Were the funerals conducted by the same funeral director?" Calista asked.

Mrs. Grant reflected briefly and then shook her head. "No. Each one was handled by a different undertaker."

"About the coffins," Trent pressed. "Were they all expensive?"

"Oh, yes, and quite modern. They all had safety bells. Unfortunately, none of the three governesses ever rang her bell."

30

THE DAY HAD turned mild so Trent suggested that they walk back to Cranleigh Square. It would have been a very pleasant stroll under other circumstances, Calista thought. But talk of murder had a way of ruining a very nice day.

"An infection of the throat." Calista shivered in spite of the sun. "Elizabeth Dunsforth's lover murdered her and likely two other Grant Agency governesses as well, and then he had the gall to buy them expensive coffins. He is like a beast of prey. He is literally hunting governesses. It is difficult to believe that there has been no sensation in the press."

"He is now hunting you, as well." Trent's eyes were stone cold.

"So it seems."

"You are not a governess," Trent said.

She glanced at him. "What does that signify?"

"I don't know. Simply another element in our story, one that does not quite fit as of yet. As for the lack of coverage in the press, that is easily explained. The killer probably paid the funeral directors to conceal the cause of death. It's not an uncommon practice. Short of obtaining permission to dig up the bodies, it will be impossible to prove the women were murdered."

She tightened her grip on her satchel. "Nestor Kettering is a madman. And to think he once asked me to marry him. We've got to stop him."

"We need evidence—something, anything—that we can take to the police. Inspector Wynn is a good man. He will act if we can provide some proof that Kettering has employed a professional killer."

"I keep thinking about what Mrs. Abington said concerning Elizabeth Dunsforth's belief that some man was following her. The poor woman was not delusional. Someone was, indeed, watching her."

"What I find interesting is Mrs. Abington's suspicion that Elizabeth Dunsforth may have been involved in an illicit liaison shortly before she developed the case of shattered nerves."

"It is a terrible game to Nestor, isn't it? He seduces lonely, single women, and then he frightens them, and in the end he orders them murdered."

"So it appears," Trent said.

A young boy was playing with a kite in the park. His governess sat on a nearby bench, keeping an eye on the child as she perused a book. Calista watched the scrap of bright red paper float high above the trees. The child giggled. The governess looked up and laughed with him.

Calista wanted to warn the woman that she might be in danger but she knew that if she tried to speak of madmen and murder the governess would believe her to be crazed and quite possibly a danger to her young charge.

"What are you thinking?" Trent asked.

"About how oddly vulnerable governesses are. They are frequently alone with the children they are paid to teach and watch over. They are isolated from other adults. It would be so easy for a man to approach that young governess over there on the bench, for example."

"Governesses hold a peculiar position in a household, neither upstairs nor downstairs. You are right. In many ways they are isolated and alone."

"And no doubt lonely," Calista said. "There must be something we can do."

"Wynn cannot act yet but there are others with a deep knowledge of the criminal underworld," Trent said. "One in particular might be persuaded to assist us."

"Who?"

Trent's mouth twitched slightly at the corner. "A criminal, of course. Who else? I told you that in the course of conducting research for my novels I have made some interesting acquaintances."

"Eudora did mention that not all of your associates were the sort one could invite for tea."

"I'm afraid Jonathan Pell falls into that category."

She did not know whether to be intrigued or appalled. In the end she concluded that she was simply very curious.

"How many criminals do you number among your acquaintances?" she asked.

"Only a select few, I promise. As it happens, Pell would not care to be considered a common criminal. He is, in his own way, a high-ranking member of his particular social class."

"Ah, he is a crime lord." This was becoming more interesting by the moment. "How in the world did you meet one?"

"Jonathan Pell is a fan of my novels."

She smiled. "Of course. I would enjoy meeting Mr. Pell."

"You, Miss Langley, will not go anywhere near Jonathan Pell."

"But—"

"I will be seeking a favor from him. That means I must go into his world. It is not a world you can enter."

"I would remind you that last night I was with you when we were very nearly murdered. I believe one could say I have more than a passing acquaintance with the criminal world."

"The man who attacked us last night was most certainly a murderous villain, but as to the world he inhabits—that is still an open question."

"How much more dangerous could Mr. Pell be?"

"It's not the danger that concerns me. It's what a visit to one of Pell's establishments would do to your reputation. His business caters to men from all walks of life, including those who inhabit the so-called respectable world. Someone might recognize you or question your reasons for paying a visit to him. That would prove disastrous. Mr. Pell does not even allow his own wife and children to enter his establishments."

"I see." She considered that for a moment. "What sort of businesses does he operate?"

"Pell started out as an orphan on the streets. He rarely discusses that portion of his career. He now owns a number of music halls, taverns, and gambling hells."

"I fear those are the sorts of establishments that Andrew has been frequenting of late."

"You worry about your brother," Trent said. "I worry about your reputation. I trust you will understand my concerns."

She decided to let the argument rest. Trent was right. She was walking a fine line with her business as it was and now she was caught up in a potentially devastating murder scandal. She could not take the risk of entering the underworld lair of a crime lord. It probably did not speak well of her that she regretted not being allowed to do so. Grandmother would have been shocked.

"What, exactly, do you intend to learn from Mr. Pell?" she asked.

"I am hoping that he can tell me something about the villain who tried to kill us last night."

"Do you think he will know one killer in a world that has a number of them?"

"Reliable murderers who work for hire, as we suspect this one is doing, are not as common on the ground as one would think," Trent said. "If the man who attacked us comes from the underworld, I believe Pell will know of him. And if he survived the blow to the head, he will no doubt be wearing a bandage these days. He will stand out in the crowd of professional criminals."

"I see."

"How do you feel about houseguests?" Trent asked.

"Houseguests?" she repeated, surprised by the sudden change of topic.

"My sister and myself. Do you mind if we descend on you until this problem with Nestor Kettering has been dealt with?"

"You don't want me to be alone, do you?"

"Not for a moment."

31

H E AWOKE ON the dark wings of a nightmare and a raging headache.

He wondered again if he should have killed the doctor. But he had been warned not to bring undue attention to himself. Getting rid of a body was always a problem that took planning and considerable energy. He was in no condition to undertake such a task. The wound to his head had weakened him. He needed time to recover.

He got up from the pallet and dressed in the cold bedroom. The pain in his head made him clumsy. He looked at the small bottle sitting on the floor beside the pallet. He did not want to cloud his mind with the drug the doctor had given him.

The voices murmured in his head, assuring him that it was safe to take the medicine.

He hesitated a moment longer and then, reluctantly, he opened the bottle and swallowed some of the contents.

After a time the pain receded somewhat. When he was certain he would not lose his balance, he made his way slowly downstairs. He forced himself to eat a little cheese and some bread and then he made a pot of strong tea.

When he finished the small meal he went into the unfurnished parlor and sat cross-legged in front of the altar. He lit the white candle and contemplated his failure. The injury to his head would heal but the wound to his honor was deep.

He gazed at the photograph that hung on the wall above the altar. The voices in his head whispered to him, reminding him that he had a quest to fulfill.

"I will not fail again," he vowed.

He spoke to the voices but he did not take his attention off the woman in the photograph.

He was a knight. His oath was his bond.

He would cleanse himself of the taint of failure and the dishonor that it had brought down upon him. And then he would fulfill his quest.

"'Til death do us part," he said to the woman in the photograph.

32

"YOU ARE GOING to pay a visit to a crime lord tonight?" Andrew paused his fork halfway to his mouth. He was clearly fascinated. "Why? Bloody hell, how did you meet him in the first place?"

Calista winced. "Really, Andrew. Language. We have guests."

Although she routinely hosted the salons and teas she used to facilitate introductions among her clients, dinner guests were a novelty at Cranleigh Hall. In spite of events, she was discovering that she was enjoying the experience. Probably because Trent was seated at the other end of the table, she thought.

Trent and Eudora had arrived with their luggage a few hours ago. Mrs. Sykes had been elated at the prospect of houseguests. She and Mr. Sykes had spent the afternoon opening up two bedrooms and preparing them for visitors. Mr. Sykes had made a show of serving dinner in grand style.

Andrew flushed and looked across the dining table at Eudora, who calmly buttered a roll, evidently unconcerned with his language.

"My apologies, Miss Hastings," he muttered.

"Think nothing of it." Eudora gave him an airy smile. "I have two brothers. I assure you I am not the least bit delicate when it comes to language."

She took a healthy bite of her roll.

Relieved, Andrew turned back to Trent. "Well, sir?"

"It's a complicated story," Trent said. "Suffice it to say that Pell is a fan of my Clive Stone novels and from time to time he has assisted me in my research."

"What questions will you put to Mr. Pell?"

"I am hoping that he will be able to identify the man who attacked your sister and me last night."

"I should accompany you," Andrew declared. "You will no doubt be entering a dangerous neighborhood. Don't you think that it would be a good idea to take a companion with you? I purchased a gun last week."

Calista put her fork down so quickly it clanged on the dish. "You did *what*? You never told me that you bought a gun."

"Didn't want to worry you any more than you already are," Andrew mumbled.

Calista started to argue but Trent silenced her with a look. Then he turned to Andrew.

"I would appreciate your company," Trent said. "Mr. Pell will be in his office tonight. Although his men will be patrolling the nearby streets to secure the safety of his clientele, it is only common sense to take a few precautions."

"Excellent," Andrew said. "I will bring my gun. I have not had much chance to practice with it, but I expect that most villains would run from the sight of a revolver."

"You will not be allowed to take it into Mr. Pell's office," Trent said. "But it might not be a bad idea to have it with us on the journey."

Calista found herself torn. Her instinct was to forbid Andrew to take such a risk. At the same time, she knew she no longer possessed that sort of authority over him. He was a man now. He made his own decisions. And he appeared positively thrilled at the prospect of the adventure into the criminal underworld. *Just as I would be if I could accompany Trent.*

Trent would be with him, she reminded herself. Trent would protect him. But she was also worried about Trent. On the other hand, logic dictated that the two men would be safer together.

She caught Eudora's eye and in that moment she knew that both of them were concerned. It occurred to her that Eudora would also feel at least somewhat better about the plan if Trent had a companion at his side.

Trent ate some of his potatoes and fixed his attention on Andrew. "I am curious about what your research on Nestor Kettering has produced."

"Not much more than what we already knew, I'm afraid," Andrew said. "After Kettering left London he went heiress-hunting in the countryside. Managed to get himself invited to a number of shooting parties, country house weekends, that sort of thing. In the course of one of those forays he met a young lady, Anna Wilkins, who by all accounts is quite lovely and quite rich. Her father was dying and eager to see her wed and settled before he left this world."

"The wedding occurred a year ago?" Trent asked.

"Eleven months ago, to be precise. The couple moved to London where, evidently, Kettering immediately set about enjoying his wife's money." Andrew stabbed a chunk of roast beef with his fork. "As I said, most of that I already knew. But I did learn a couple of interesting facts when I chatted up one of the maids. Turns out the father's will left Anna in control of her inheritance."

"For which she can thank the new property laws," Eudora said.

"Yes, indeed, but there is another intriguing aspect of the father's will," Andrew continued. "The maid I spoke with is involved in a romantic relationship with the coachman. He overheard a conversation between Kettering and another gentleman. Kettering was complaining about his circumstances. It seems that Anna's father might have had a few concerns about his daughter's new husband."

"Why is that?" Calista asked.

"According to the maid, the father's will stipulates that if Anna dies, the money goes to distant relatives in Canada, regardless of the cause of death. The same holds true if she is committed to an asylum for any reason."

"The two most popular methods for removing people who stand in the way of a fortune," Eudora observed.

Trent was intrigued. "You're right, the father must have had some serious concerns about his daughter's safety. He tried to protect her by making certain Kettering would not profit if he harmed his wife or locked her up in a private asylum."

"If we are right about Nestor," Calista said, "that will is probably the only thing keeping Anna alive."

"I wonder if she knows that she is living with a madman," Eudora wondered.

"Probably not," Andrew said. "The staff certainly seems unaware of Kettering's propensity for murdering governesses. I doubt they would remain in his employ if they knew the truth. According to the maid, Anna Kettering is a very lonely woman. Her husband is rarely at home. She takes solace in séances. Attends a sitting at least once a week, sometimes more often."

Calista put down her butter knife. "I wonder who she is trying to contact on the Other Side?"

"Does it matter?" Eudora said. "Séances are nonsense. The mediums who claim to be able to summon the spirits of the departed are all frauds."

33

TRENT AND A very excited Andrew left in a hansom an hour later. Eudora joined Calista at the front door to see the men off. When the cab disappeared into the fog, Mr. Sykes closed the door.

"Why don't you wait in the library?" he suggested gently. "I'll have Mrs. Sykes bring in some tea."

"Thank you," Calista said. "It's going to be a long night."

"The important thing," Sykes said, "is that none of you will be alone tonight."

"Quite right, Mr. Sykes," Eudora said.

Calista led the way into the library. A cheerful fire burned on the hearth. Mrs. Sykes carried a tea tray into the room and poured two cups.

"Don't worry about the gentlemen," she said. "I'm sure they will be fine. Mr. Stone appears to be very competent."

Calista smiled. "You mean Mr. Hastings, don't you, Mrs. Sykes?"

"Oh, right," Mrs. Sykes said. "Very easy to confuse the two, isn't it? Mr. Hastings appears to have a great deal in common with his creation."

She departed, closing the door.

Calista looked at Eudora. "I feel perfectly dreadful about having dragged you and your brother into this mess. But I must admit I am very grateful to both of you."

Eudora smiled. "On the contrary, I think it is I who should be grateful."

"For putting your brother in harm's way? I very nearly got him murdered, Eudora."

"I'm aware of that." Eudora's expression grew serious. "And I will admit that aspect of the situation is unnerving. But it is so good to see Trent exhibiting some degree of interest and enthusiasm for something other than his writing."

"What about you?" Calista asked. "I have the impression that you feel a certain degree of enthusiasm for Edward Tazewell."

Eudora turned pink. "Is it that obvious?"

"You went so far as to stand up to your brother when he expressed his disapproval of my agency. You made it clear that you intended to continue attending my salons. I'm assuming that Mr. Tazewell was one of the reasons you were so adamant about remaining a client of my business."

"Trent meant well. He was only trying to protect me."

"I know."

"Over the years there have been other men who have displayed a certain interest in me. At least three were simply after money. It is no secret that Trent has used the income from his writing to rebuild the family finances. He has been very successful with his investments in properties and he has been careful to share the income with Harry and me."

"I see."

Eudora wrinkled her nose. "I've had another sort of admirer, as well. You would be surprised by the number of people—male and female—who have befriended me in hopes of persuading me to convince Trent to read their manuscripts and recommend them to his publisher."

"Oh, my." Calista laughed and sipped some tea. "I can understand why you are wary of suitors."

"I'm afraid I've had some unpleasant experiences," Eudora said. "But Mr. Tazewell is different. He does not need my money—he has a nice income of his own."

"I would never have introduced him to you if I thought he might be a fortune hunter."

Eudora smiled. "In addition, he has no interest in writing a book. He prefers to invent things. Did you know that he holds at least four patents for various types of machines designed to do complex mathematical calculations?"

"No, I wasn't aware of that."

"He also is convinced that oil will be the fuel of the future. We are running low on coal, you see."

"I'm afraid I haven't given the subject much thought. What is it, exactly, about Mr. Tazewell that intrigues you?"

Eudora considered the question for a moment. "I have asked myself that question many times since meeting him. The truth is, I cannot say for certain. He is not what most people would consider a charming conversationalist. When he does get interested in a topic, it is difficult to stop him from exploring it in excruciating detail."

"The engineer in him, I expect."

"He is not at ease in frivolous social situations. That is why your salons appeal to him. They are always of an educational or instructional nature. In that sense, he reminds me a little of Trent and Harry. For better or worse, they are all serious men, perhaps to a fault."

"They are certainly not shallow."

"Indeed not." Enthusiasm warmed Eudora's voice. "When it comes to serious matters, Mr. Tazewell's interests are quite wide ranging. He is keen on investigating the latest advances in engineering and science. And he is very modern in his views on the subject of women's rights. He is a widower with two young daughters, you know."

"I know," Calista said, amused.

Eudora flushed. "Yes, of course. As it happens, he is very concerned that his little girls be given the same education that would be given to boys. I applaud that notion, most likely because I had a rather unusual education, myself—at least it was unusual for a girl."

"Is that so?"

"Our parents held very modern views on such matters. After Papa died my mother continued to teach us. My education came to a halt when she married that terrible man, Bristow. Everything changed after he came to live with us. And then Mama . . . died."

Eudora broke off and got to her feet. She moved to stand in front of the fireplace and stood watching the flames in silence.

Calista rose and crossed the room to stand beside her.

"Trent told me that he was away from home, traveling in America, when your mother died," she said. "He also told me that you and Harry and the servants were convinced that Bristow murdered her."

"Trent told you that?" Eudora looked up, startled. "That is very . . . interesting. Trent almost never talks about what happened to Mama. I have never known him to confide in anyone outside the family."

"I think he has concluded that there are certain similarities between the situation in which I find myself and the circumstances of your mother's death."

Eudora gripped the mantel with one hand. "One thing certainly seems to be true—in both cases there is no evidence to take to the police, at least none that would provide cause for an arrest."

"I'm so sorry, Eudora."

"That bastard Bristow used to beat Mama, you know."

Calista could not think of anything to say. She put her hand on Eudora's shoulder.

"Harry tried to interfere but Bristow simply turned on him and beat him, as well. After that Mama tried to conceal the bruises from us. Trent never knew about the beatings because Mama never told him in her letters. I think she understood that he might do something violent—something that might get him arrested or even killed—if he knew what was happening at home."

Calista considered what she knew of Trent's personality. "Your mother had every reason to worry."

Eudora did not take her attention off the fire. "It's so very easy for a man to hurt his wife or even kill her and get away with it. One can only wonder how many times it happens. But we hardly ever read about it in the press."

A deep sense of knowing unfolded inside Calista. "Is that the real reason why you have never married?" she asked quietly. "You fear being trapped in a marriage like your mother's?"

"Her marriage to Bristow lasted less than six months but it was quite frightening. My mother insisted that I lock myself in my bedroom every night when he was in the house. Mercifully, he spent most of his time in London, going through Mama's money."

"Dreadful, dreadful man."

"Marriage is a terrible risk for a woman, isn't it?"

"Yes."

Eudora managed a rueful smile. "Yet, even knowing the risks, sometimes the thought of having a family of one's own—a good man and children to love—can be quite . . . compelling."

"I think that, deep down, most decent people wish to love and be loved in return," Calista said.

"So we sometimes take the risk."

"Eudora, it is not my place to say this, but I'm quite certain that your brothers would take steps to protect you if you were to find yourself in a terrible marriage."

"Don't you think I know that?" Eudora turned away from the fireplace and picked up her cup and saucer. She tried to take a sip of tea but her fingers were trembling, so she hastily set the cup back on the saucer. "Trent risked his life to save me on one occasion. And as for Harry, he would do the same if he believed I was in danger."

"But you fear marriage all the same?"

"It is not marriage I fear, Calista. As you say, I have two brothers to protect me. But I cannot abandon Trent. I told you, he lost his true love because of me. I will not be free of that burden until he finds another love."

"I don't understand how you can possibly blame yourself for what happened," Calista said.

"The scars," Eudora said. "Bristow threatened to throw acid in my face, you see."

"Dear heaven."

"There was a terrible scene in Harry's laboratory. In the end, Trent was the one who was struck with the acid. Afterward Althea could not bring herself to look upon his face."

"What of Bristow?" Calista asked.

"He fled that day. He went back to London. After Trent had begun to heal he followed Bristow. Harry and I were terrified that Trent would kill Bristow and then hang for murder. But in the end, Bristow died of a fever."

"I am very glad he is no longer in your life."

"No one shed any tears for him, I can tell you that much."

"You do realize that Trent does not want you to be burdened with guilt because of what happened, don't you?"

"I understand," Eudora said. "But that does not change how I feel."

There was nothing more to be said on that subject, Calista thought.

Guilt was a terrible taskmaster. She looked at the clock. It was going to be a very long night.

After a moment she turned to look at the file drawers that stood against one wall.

"The other day you mentioned that it might be helpful to have some sort of system that would make it easier to match people with similar interests," she said.

Eudora gave a small start, as if yanking herself out of her gloom-filled thoughts. She looked at the files. "Yes, a way to cross-reference interests and, perhaps, certain characteristics of your clients' personalities. I think you would find such a system quite useful. I have a similar system set up to keep track of the plants I grow in my greenhouse. I use it for any number of purposes."

"It appears we are fated to spend a very long evening together, worrying. I suggest we put the time to good use. I would be very grateful if you, in your position as my new assistant, would give me some practical instructions on how to go about setting up a proper filing system such as you have described. In the process we might be able to discover something in the client files that connects to Nestor Kettering."

Eudora assumed a professional demeanor. "I would be happy to take a look at your present system and see what modifications might be made."

34

"Hastings, always a pleasure." Jonathan Pell came up out of his chair and rounded his desk to greet his visitors. "I am quite enjoying your latest in the *Flying Intelligencer*, by the way. Very clever twist tossing in the mysterious female character, Wilhelmina Preston. Expect she'll prove to be the villainess, right?"

Andrew followed Trent past the two hulking guards who bracketed the doorway like a pair of large statues, and came to a halt in the crime lord's office.

"You know I never discuss my plots, Jon," Trent said. "But I'm pleased that you are enjoying *The Missing Bride*. Thank you for seeing us on such short notice tonight."

"Anytime, anytime. You are always welcome, you know that." Jonathan gave Andrew a considering look. "I trust you will introduce me to your new associate."

"Of course," Trent said. "Mr. Andrew Langley. Andrew, Mr. Jonathan Pell."

"Sir." Andrew inclined his head in a small, polite acknowledgment of the introduction.

He was uncertain of the rules of social etiquette expected in such an unusual situation. But judging by Trent's manner it appeared that the code of conduct that one would apply in a gentlemen's club or a drawing room seemed to hold in a crime lord's office.

"Have a seat, both of you." Jonathan waved Trent and Andrew to the two chairs that stood in front of his desk.

Andrew took his seat and looked around, trying to conceal his curiosity. If it had not been for the guards at the door and the muted sounds of drunken voices raised in song in the adjoining dance hall, the room could have been the private study of a wealthy, respectable gentleman.

Like his office, Jonathan Pell did not fit the newspapers' popular image of a crime lord. Pell was a tall, slender man who appeared to be in his early forties. His sharply etched features were framed by fashionably styled whiskers. He wore an expensive-looking suit and a crisp white shirt and tie, all in the latest style. A faint echo of the streets in his accent was the only hint of Jonathan Pell's origins.

But it was the wall of bookshelves that struck Andrew as the most surprising element in the room. The Clive Stone series occupied half a shelf, but there was also a wide variety of novels sitting on the neighboring shelves. He spotted Stevenson's *The Strange Case of Dr. Jekyll and Mr. Hyde*, Wilkie Collins's *The Moonstone*, and Jules Verne's *Around the World in Eighty Days* and *Twenty Thousand Leagues Under the Sea*. The latter two titles were in the original French, another surprise.

In addition to the fiction, there was an assortment of journals devoted to science and invention. Darwin's *On the Origin of Species* had been given special pride of place.

It struck Andrew that perhaps Pell considered himself to be a human example and living proof of Darwin's theories—a man born to the hard life of the streets who had been strong enough to survive and gone on to build an empire.

It was clear that Trent and Pell treated each other as equals. There was an uncommon accord between the two men. Although they came from very different worlds, Trent had somehow earned Pell's respect, and the feeling was mutual. Andrew wondered what had happened to form such a bond. He doubted that it had anything to do with Trent's detective novels.

There was something vaguely familiar about both Pell and the office. It took Andrew a moment to realize that he had been introduced to both in the character of one of Clive Stone's underworld connections—Bartholomew Drake, a crime lord who played chess with Stone and offered insights into the criminal underworld.

"I have just opened a new bottle of brandy," Jonathan said. He picked up an elegant cut-crystal decanter. "Will you join me?"

"Brandy sounds like an excellent idea," Trent said. "The fog is oppressive and damp tonight."

"So I'm told." Pell splashed brandy into three snifters. "I make it a point to stay indoors as much as possible on nights like this. My doctor tells me the fog is not good for my lungs."

Trent looked at the gold cigarette case on the desk. "My doctor informs me that cigarettes are also bad for the lungs."

Jonathan's brows rose. "I assume you refer to your brother. I've heard that theory, but my doctor insists that is scientific nonsense. Then again, my doctor is quite fond of his pipe so it is possible that he is not interested in medical theories that conflict with his own pleasures."

Trent took the snifter of brandy and nodded appreciatively. "We all have our blind spots, do we not?"

"Indeed." Jonathan sat down behind the desk and lounged back in his chair. "Now, then, to what do I owe the honor of this visit?"

"Mr. Langley and I came here to ask for your professional advice."

Jonathan looked amused. "The two of you propose to open a music hall or a gaming house?"

"Rest assured we have no intention of setting ourselves up as your competition," Trent said.

"I am relieved to hear that." Jonathan sat forward and clasped his hands on the desktop. "Because my competitors have a way of going out of business."

"I am aware of that," Trent said. "Let me explain our problem. Someone has been threatening a lady who happens to be a friend of mine."

"My sister," Andrew said quickly.

Whatever Jonathan had been expecting to hear, apparently that was not it. He frowned.

"I will admit I am more than a little surprised," he said.

"This same individual came close to murdering her last night," Trent continued. "Although I suspect that I was the intended target. I believe that it was just bad luck that Mr. Langley's sister was with me at the time. Regardless, I would very much like to learn the name and address of the man who attacked us."

Jonathan leaned back in his chair and considered briefly. "Was this some footpad who tried to rob you?"

"No," Trent said. "A trap was set. Miss Langley and I walked straight into it. The man I am looking for was dressed as a gentleman but he used a knife in a manner that strongly suggested he has employed such weapon on prior occasions. We believe that he has murdered at least four people, all women. You may have read about one of the victims in today's newspapers—Mrs. Fulton, the proprietor of J. P. Fulton's Coffins and Mourning Goods."

Jonathan narrowed his eyes ever so slightly. "The woman's throat was slit."

"I know. Miss Langley and I discovered the body."

"The press made a great sensation of the story—body found in a blood-soaked coffin and so on. Are you telling me that most of the facts are correct?"

"Astonishingly, yes. Whoever murdered Fulton also attacked Miss Langley and me but we were able to fend him off."

"I'm impressed." Pell inclined his head in appreciation and glanced at Trent's walking stick. "But, then, I know that you are very skilled with that particular device."

"My walking stick proved useless," Trent said. "The range was too short. However, I was able to wound the bastard with an iron stand of the sort used to display floral wreaths. I believe I did considerable damage. He very likely needed stitches. At the very least, he will be wearing a bandage on his head today."

Pell took another sip of brandy while he contemplated the information. Andrew began to wonder if perhaps Trent had made a mistake by seeking help from such a dangerous man.

But to his surprise, Pell lowered the snifter and smiled a faint, amused smile.

"Where in blazes did you come up with the iron stand?" he asked.

"We were in a chamber full of coffins and other funeral paraphernalia. It was handy."

Pell shook his head. "You never cease to astonish me, Hastings. One can only wonder how many other novelists go to such lengths to conduct research."

"You told me that one of the reasons you enjoyed my books was because of the effort I made to get the details right," Trent said.

"So I did. Very well, then. You came here to see if I can point you toward the killer."

"Can I assume that he was not working for you last night?"

Pell's eyes went cold. "He was most certainly not in my employ."

"I am, of course, happy to hear that. Not that I actually thought you would hire such unreliable staff."

A fleeting gleam of icy amusement came and went in Jonathan's eyes. "You know me very well, my friend."

"I am wondering, though, if the killer might have been working for one of your competitors."

"As I said, my competitors rarely thrive for long. I do have some business colleagues, however. One or two of them have been known to accept contracts that involve the removal of a certain individual. There is always the odd businessman from the so-called respectable world who will pay well to see a competitor suffer an untimely accident. And then there are the wives who are anxious to be free of difficult husbands, and husbands hoping to be free of difficult wives. That sort of trade is always available to those who are willing to take certain risks. But I have never gone into that line. I prefer less hazardous financial endeavors."

"And Clive Stone admires your choice in that regard," Trent said. "But about this man who tried to murder me and quite possibly Miss Langley last night—"

"I will make inquiries," Pell said. "It is the very least I can do to repay you for all the hours of reading pleasure that you have provided me."

"Thank you," Trent said. "I will be grateful for any useful information."

"Of course." Pell put his snifter down. "Now, then, as I told you, on the whole, I am enjoying *The Affair of the Missing Bride*. But I did feel that the first chapter was a bit slow. Not your usual quick-off-the-mark start to the case. The murder did not take place until chapter two. I believe the problem is the woman in the story."

"Miss Wilhelmina Preston," Trent said.

"Exactly. You don't want to spend too much time suggesting that Clive Stone might be developing a romantic liaison with her. Slows things down, you know."

189

35

THE SITTERS AT the séance heard the ethereal chimes first, faint and distant. The sound shivered in the darkened room.

"Listen closely," the medium intoned. "The music is faint because it is coming from the Other Side. It is one of the few ways the spirits can communicate with us."

Hope infused with desperation made Anna Kettering's heart race. There had been so many failed séances. She had been attending sittings with various mediums for months, only to be disappointed time and again.

"Whatever you do, don't let go of each other's hands," the medium continued. "If any one of you breaks the circle of energy the connection will be shattered."

Anna tightened her grip on the hands of the sitters who were positioned on either side of her chair. No one moved. They hardly dared to breathe. Most had closed their eyes against the glary light of the lantern that sat in the center of the table. But Anna kept her eyes open. If the one she hoped to contact appeared, she wanted to be able to see him.

It was nearing midnight, the hour when the veil between the normal world and the Other Side was at its weakest. Florence Tapp had come highly recommended as a medium who could open a pathway to the Other Side.

"I sense a presence trying to reach through the veil," Florence said. "I think, yes, I'm quite sure it is a man."

There were several anxious, enthusiastic murmurs around the table.

"Yes, it is definitely a man," Florence said. "Is anyone in this room attempting to reach a dear son or perhaps a brother or uncle who has gone before?"

"Yes," said the woman sitting on Anna's right. "That may be my older brother, George. He died without telling anyone where he kept his will. George? Is that you?"

"No," Florence said, firmly. "It isn't George. I believe this is an older man."

There was another round of affirmative murmurs.

The table began to levitate. It rose a few inches off the floor.

"The table," one of the sitters exclaimed in a hoarse whisper. "It's moving. There really is a spirit in the room."

The chimes grew louder, echoing eerily in the darkened space.

The rapping started.

The murmurs around the table grew more excited. Anna held her breath.

"Definitely an older man," Florence said. "I think he wishes to speak to his wife."

There was no response from the sitters.

"No, not his wife," Florence said quickly. "His daughter, perhaps."

"Papa?" Anna whispered. She hardly dared to breathe. "Papa, is that you? Please, you must help me."

36

ANDREW GOT HIS gun back from one of the large bodyguards and followed Trent out of Pell's office. They made their way through the crowded, smoky music hall. The tables were filled with well-dressed, upper-class young men drinking shoulder-to-shoulder with members of the working classes.

On stage a singer dressed in a low-cut red gown sang a bawdy ballad laced with sexual innuendo. The audience joined in at the chorus. One had to look twice to realize that the chanteuse was a man dressed as a woman.

Outside on the street the fog had grown thicker. Trent pulled up the collar of his greatcoat. Andrew did the same. They walked toward the line of waiting cabs.

"Do you get that sort of thing a lot?" Andrew asked.

Trent selected the first hansom and stepped up into the cab. "What sort of thing?"

Andrew bounded up into the vehicle and sat down on the narrow bench seat. "Readers like Mr. Pell who feel obliged to tell you how to write your books."

"Everyone's a critic," Trent said.

"It must be rather annoying."

"One grows accustomed to it." Trent thought for a moment. "Perhaps it would be more accurate to say one learns to endure it without resorting to outright violence except on rare occasions. On another subject, it occurs to me that it might be interesting to see what Kettering does at night. Do you know the address of his club?"

"Beacon Lane. Why?"

Trent used his walking stick to rap on the trapdoor in the roof of the hansom cab. The driver opened the door and looked down.

"Aye, sir?"

"We've changed our mind," Trent said. "We wish to go to Beacon Lane."

"Aye, sir."

The trapdoor closed and the cab rolled forward into the fog.

Andrew contemplated his observations in Jonathan Pell's office.

"I noticed that you did not tell Mr. Pell to take his critique and go to the devil," Andrew said.

"I'm not an idiot. The man is a crime lord, Andrew. He employs very large men who carry guns and knives. He's entitled to his opinions."

"Good point. Do you think he will be able to help us?"

"If the man who attacked Calista and me last night happens to work for any of Pell's associates, we will have a name by morning."

"And if he isn't employed by any of Pell's associates?"

"Trust me, Pell will want to identify him almost as badly as we do. His associates will be equally determined to find the villain."

"Why?"

"The most successful lords of the criminal underworld are, at heart, excellent businessmen," Trent said. "And as is the case with business-men at every level of society, they are always eager to stamp out free-lance competition."

"I understand." Andrew watched the passing carriages materialize out of the fog only to disappear back into the mist. "As Clive Stone says, the criminal world is a dark mirror of the respectable world."

"There are certainly predators in both spheres. What was your impression of Pell?"

Andrew thought for a moment. "He is a very dangerous man."

"Do you say that because of his guards?"

"They certainly make an impression. But I would consider Mr. Pell dangerous with or without the guards."

"Why?"

"To be honest, he puts me in mind of you, sir."

Trent gave him a sharp look but he did not seem to know how to respond to the remark.

"On the surface he appears to be a wealthy, respectable gentle-man," Andrew continued. "But if you look deeper there is something hard and determined underneath."

"He had to be hard and determined to survive and prosper in his world."

"Do you mind if I ask how you became acquainted with him?"

"I once had occasion to seek his advice and assistance," Trent said. "He agreed to help me. We made a bargain."

Andrew was fascinated. "You did a deal with the devil?"

"There are devils in the world and they exist at every level of soci-ety. I do not consider Pell one of them."

"Did you take the risk of approaching him because you wanted insights and details about the criminal world for your novels?"

"No," Trent said. "At the time I was looking for a man who had disappeared into the streets of London. When I began to make inquiries I was told that Pell might be able to assist me. I was also warned that if I sought Pell's help I must be prepared to someday repay the favor."

"Did you find the man you were looking for?"

"With Pell's assistance, yes, I did."

"Did Pell ever call in the favor that you owed him?"

"Let's just say that Pell considers that the scales are even."

In the shadows it was impossible to be certain, but Andrew got the impression that Trent was amused.

"What could a man from our world do for a crime lord?" Andrew asked.

He did not expect an answer but he was surprised.

"Mr. Pell makes a great deal of money," Trent said. "He happens to have two young daughters and a baby son. His fondest wish is that his three children will not follow in his footsteps."

"Ah," Andrew said. "He wants them to move in respectable circles."

"Of course. He does not want them to be tainted by the scandal of being known as the offspring of a crime lord."

"I understand. But how can you assist him in reaching his goal? You're an author."

"Pell has been pursuing a clever plan for the past several years. The first step was to convert the sources of his income into legal investments such as the music hall. That move has been accomplished."

"Music halls are legal but not entirely respectable."

"True, but that was only the initial step. Eventually he plans to retire altogether, disappear, and reinvent himself as a member of the very respectable country gentry. If all goes according to his scheme, he will soon quietly vanish from the criminal underworld and from London. He and his family will make their home in some picturesque countryside village."

Andrew chuckled. "He intends to hide in plain sight in respectable

Society where no one will ever think to look for him. It is quite brilliant. But how are you involved in his scheme?"

"As it happens, I'm rather good when it comes to making speculative investments in properties."

"Bloody hell." Andrew grinned. "You invest his money for him."

"I have the connections in the respectable world that are required to gain access to potentially profitable investments. It is the bargain I made with Pell back at the start of our association. It has worked well for both of us."

"Perhaps, but you are not simply repaying a favor. I could tell that the two of you are friends."

"Pell is an intelligent, well-read man who hungers for conversation with others who share his many and varied interests. Such companions are scarce in his world."

"I saw his bookshelves," Andrew said. "Not the sort of titles that one expects to find in a crime lord's study."

"He is a self-taught man as well as a self-made man. I settled my account with Pell, and now he and I meet on occasion to share a bottle of brandy and talk about the latest books and politics and other matters."

Andrew mulled that over for a moment. "Why did Pell agree to help you find that man when you first sought him out?"

"I have asked myself that same question on several occasions. I cannot be certain, but in hindsight, I think the answer is that he had some sympathy for me."

"*Sympathy?* Mr. Pell?"

"I realize most people would not expect that particular emotion from him," Trent said. "But he understood my reasons for wanting to find the man I was hunting."

"Will you owe him another favor after tonight?"

"Not in the way you mean. We are friends now. Friends do each other favors without keeping a close accounting."

"Trust is a rare jewel," Andrew said.

"In any world," Trent agreed.

"Who was this man you were searching for?" Andrew asked after a moment.

"His name was Bristow."

"Do you mind if I ask why you were so determined to find him?"

"He murdered my mother."

Andrew went very still. "Is he—?"

"Dead? Yes."

The next logical question whispered through Andrew's head. *Did you kill him?* But he could not bring himself to ask it. Some secrets were meant to be kept.

37

Beacon Lane was shrouded in a wispy fog. Several hansoms were lined up on one side of the street, waiting for business. The horses dozed. The drivers took nips of gin to ward off the damp. It was a familiar scene outside a gentlemen's club, Andrew thought.

A pair of gas lamps burned at the entrance to the club. A sprinkling of mostly inebriated gentlemen—their laughter too loud, their gaits unsteady—went up the steps and disappeared through the doorway into a warmly lit front hall.

"We don't even know if Kettering is inside," Andrew pointed out.

"That should be easy enough to discover."

"How?"

Trent's mouth kicked up a little at one corner. "Sometimes the simple approach works best. I'll try asking."

He waited until the door opened again. A well-dressed man came down the steps and started across the street. He was not so drunk that he staggered but Andrew could tell from his weaving stride that he'd imbibed a fair amount.

Trent got down and steered a course across the street. He managed to neatly intercept the intoxicated man, making it look like an accident. Andrew could not hear what was said but it appeared that Trent was apologizing. He then engaged the other man in brief conversation, clapped him on the shoulder as though they were old pals, and started toward the front steps of the club.

The man who had been intercepted climbed into a hansom. The cab clattered off into the fog.

Trent stopped at the foot of the steps and returned to the hansom.

"Kettering is inside," he said, stepping up into the cab.

"So we wait?"

"We wait."

They did not have to sit and wait for long. Some twenty minutes later two men emerged from the club. When they passed through the light from the streetlamps, Andrew got a look at their faces.

"The one on the right is Kettering," he said. "I don't know the other man."

"Neither do I, but that is hardly surprising. As Eudora insists on reminding me, I don't get out much."

Kettering and his companion climbed into a hansom and set off into the night.

"Now we follow them," Trent said.

Andrew felt his blood quicken. He leaned forward slightly, very conscious of the weight of the revolver in his pocket.

"Be careful," Trent advised. "It's addictive."

Andrew glanced at him. "What is?"

"This business of uncovering secrets."

"Huh. Hadn't thought of it as a business."

Trent gave him an unreadable look but he did not speak.

The hansom carrying Kettering and the second man left the crowded streets behind and entered a fashionable neighborhood of elegant town houses. It stopped in front of one of the residences. Both men got out and went up the front steps.

Kettering's acquaintance opened the door. The pair disappeared into a dimly lit front hall.

"This is not Kettering's address," Andrew said. "It must be his companion's residence."

"Do you know the name of his associate?" Trent asked.

"No. I never had a reason to investigate his acquaintances."

"We need to learn the name of this one."

"How do you propose to do that?" Andrew asked, genuinely curious.

"The cab is waiting, probably for Kettering. Perhaps the driver can answer a few questions. I'll see what he can tell us."

"I'll come with you."

Trent got out of the hansom and Andrew followed him. They started toward the waiting cab.

Somewhere in the fog a whip cracked with the force of lightning. A startled horse whinnied in alarm and lunged forward, breaking into a frantic gallop. Its hooves thundered on the pavement. Andrew heard the clatter of carriage wheels.

In the next instant a dark vehicle loomed in the softly glowing fog. It slammed forward at a reckless speed.

Andrew had just enough time to realize that the runaway carriage was barreling toward them before Trent gave him a powerful shove.

"Move," Trent shouted.

Jolted out of his state of frozen disbelief, Andrew bolted toward the side of the street. He stumbled against the bottom step of a town house and grabbed the railing to steady himself. Trent made it to the opposite railing.

They both swung around just as the carriage, swaying wildly, rumbled furiously down the street before vanishing into the fog.

Andrew listened to the vehicle racing away into the night. A strange, dazed sensation gripped him. He could hear Trent speaking to him in harsh, urgent tones but it took him a moment to process the meaning of the words.

"Did you get a look at the driver?" Trent said.

"What?" Andrew pulled himself together with an effort, trying to remember what he had seen. "No. I just saw the carriage bearing down on us."

"We know one thing. That wasn't Kettering or his friend, either. They're both inside the town house."

Andrew tried to catch his breath. "The man who attacked you and Calista?"

"Possibly. If so, it's clear that I did not do nearly enough damage with the floral display stand."

38

"THIS SITUATION CANNOT be allowed to continue," Calista said. "It is clear that you have become a target for this violent criminal, Trent. Andrew is also at risk now. We must find a way to stop this madman before he murders one or both of you."

"Uh-huh." Trent drank some of the brandy that Sykes had poured for all of them.

They were gathered in the library. Calista prowled the room like a caged cat. Eudora sat, tense and grim-faced, on a dainty, satin-covered chair. Andrew was sprawled in one of the leather-padded reading chairs in the languid pose that only a young male could achieve.

The careless posture reminded Trent quite forcibly of the fact that he was no longer nineteen. The vigorous events of the night, combined with the excitement of the previous evening, had left him with some sore muscles and a few bruises. He wondered if he was getting old.

Calista stopped and glared at him. "Are you listening, sir?"

"To every word," he said. "We are making some progress in our investigation, Calista."

"You call this progress?" She spread her hands in a wide arc. "You and Andrew could have been killed tonight. At the very least you both would have been severely injured if that vicious man had succeeded in running you down."

"There's no need to carry on like this, Calista," Andrew said. "Try to remember that Mr. Hastings and I were not hurt."

Trent winced and braced himself for the reaction he knew that Andrew's admonishment would bring down on his head.

Calista whirled to confront Andrew.

"Do not tell me to calm down. You were nearly killed tonight. Because of me."

"No," Eudora said. Her tone was calm and quite firm. "It's not because of you, Calista."

They all turned to look at her.

"Trent and Mr. Langley were endangered by some madman who has fixed on you, Calista," she continued. "It is not your fault. It was never your fault."

Calista's mouth tightened but she seemed subdued by Eudora's tone. She resumed her pacing.

"We must come up with a plan to stop him," she said in seething tones.

"We are working on a plan." Trent turned the glass between his palms, watching the firelight dance in the brandy. "The question I keep asking myself is, how does the hired killer fit into this business?"

"It's obvious that Nestor Kettering employed him," Calista said.

"She's right," Eudora said. "It's the only explanation that makes sense."

"Yet Mr. Pell knew nothing of this paid killer who dresses like a wealthy gentleman." Trent set aside his glass and leaned forward, elbows braced on his thighs, fingers loosely clasped between his knees. "Where did Nestor Kettering find him? It is not as if one can go into a shop and purchase the services of a villain who will commit murder for pay."

Calista paused, frowning. "What are you thinking?"

"I'm thinking that this killer comes from the respectable world, not Pell's world," Trent said. "But that still leaves us with questions."

Andrew paused his glass halfway to his mouth and looked at Trent. "We need more information about Kettering, don't we?"

"Yes," Trent said. "I propose that you follow him tomorrow as he goes about his daily affairs. But you must be careful not to let him see you."

Andrew grinned. "Don't worry, he will never notice me. I'm rather good at following gentlemen around, if I do say so. I've done it for Calista's business for years."

Calista stopped pacing again. "I'm not so sure that's a sound plan."

"We don't have a lot of alternatives," Andrew said, going for a placating tone. "I give you my word I will be very careful not to let him see me."

Calista started to protest again.

"Trent is right," Eudora said in the same determined tone of voice. "We need to find the link between Kettering and his hired killer."

"The associate, perhaps?" Andrew suggested. "The one who left the club with him tonight? Maybe I should look into his background."

"We definitely need to identify him," Trent said. "That shouldn't be hard now that we have an address."

"Hmm," Calista said.

Trent looked at her. "What?"

"Nestor Kettering lied to me. I think it is safe to assume that he lied to Mrs. Fulton about his reasons for ordering so many memento mori gifts. He no doubt has a long history of lying to women."

"We are dealing with a practiced liar," Trent said. "No surprise. Where does that take us?"

"I don't know." Calista made a small fist with one hand. "But it strikes me that by now Mrs. Kettering must have some idea of the character of the man she married."

Trent shook his head. "Forget it. There is no point speaking to Anna Kettering. She may not have any great fondness for her husband, but it is highly unlikely that she would do or say anything that would even hint at scandal, let alone murder. She will not give you any evidence that might lead to her husband's arrest."

"Nor could she be made to testify against him," Eudora pointed out. "Always assuming she actually is aware of his illegal activities."

Calista's eyes narrowed. "But if she suspects what her husband is doing, she must be terrified."

"That doesn't mean she would have any incentive to talk," Trent said. "She is in the same situation as you are. There's no point going to the police. Doing so would probably get her killed."

Calista managed a shaky smile. "I doubt if she is in quite the same situation as I am."

"Why do you say that?" Eudora asked.

"From what Andrew could discover, she is alone in the world. She doesn't have the sort of friends and family that I have." Calista paused. "I am quite fortunate in that regard."

She seemed surprised to discover that was the case, Trent thought.

"No," Eudora said. "You and Andrew are not alone."

"I don't know how to thank both of you," Calista began.

Andrew stirred in his chair, sat forward, and fixed his attention on Trent. "On top of everything else, you saved my life tonight, sir."

Trent groaned. "It's the least I could do, considering that I'm the one who suggested we follow Kettering. But enough. No more thanks."

Eudora looked troubled. "Calista is right about one thing. We need a bit more of a plan."

"I agree," Trent said. "But it will have to wait. It has been a very long night. We all need sleep."

"You are correct, sir." Andrew bounded up out of the chair. "I've got to rise early so that I can get to Kettering's address before he leaves his house for the day."

Eudora rose and looked at Calista. "The men have a point. We all need sleep."

"What we need," Calista insisted, "is a useful plan."

"We will all be able to think more clearly if we get some rest," Eudora said.

39

"I'M LOSING PATIENCE, Kettering." Dolan Birch poured more brandy into the glass. "Have you made any progress?"

Kettering stared at the brandy. He had not wanted to accept the invitation to share a late-night drink but he had not dared to refuse. Nevertheless, Birch was the last person he wished to spend time with tonight. With the exception of his frigid little whore of a bride, of course.

He wrapped one hand around the glass.

"I just need time, Birch."

"I thought we had an agreement, Kettering."

"We do," Nestor said. He gulped some of the brandy. "Give me a few more days."

"I have held up my end. The arrangements have been made with my associate in Seacliff. The plan will go forward just as soon as you fulfill your side of the bargain."

"There have been some . . . complications."

"What sort of complications?"

"The silly bitch is involved with the writer Trent Hastings. The bastard and his sister are living in Cranleigh Hall at the moment."

"Yes, I know."

Nestor stiffened. "How?"

"Hastings and Miss Langley showed up at the offices of the Grant Agency. They were asking questions about Dunsforth and the others."

"Bloody hell."

"Indeed. Now I must take steps to make certain that they don't find a way to link me to the agency. I do not appreciate being put into this position, Kettering. Among other things it will mean a loss of income. I am not happy about that."

"What are you going to do?"

"That is my problem. I will deal with the matter. But in the meantime, I must insist that you fulfill your part of the bargain."

"I will, I swear it."

"Soon, Kettering."

"Yes. Soon."

40

"THE NAME OF Kettering's associate is Dolan Birch." Andrew sprawled in a reading chair and flipped through the pages of a little notebook while simultaneously stuffing his mouth with the small tea sandwiches that Mrs. Sykes had provided. "A few years ago Birch married a much older woman, a widow, who conveniently died in her sleep soon after the wedding."

"Leaving Birch with a nice inheritance, I assume?" Trent said.

They had gathered in the library to listen to Andrew's report. Trent had one shoulder propped against the end of a bookcase. Eudora was seated in one of the reading chairs.

Calista had stationed herself behind the desk. She was as riveted by Andrew's report as the others but she was also acutely conscious of Andrew's air of excitement. He's enjoying this, she thought. Danger and secrets are like a tonic to his spirits.

There was a focused determination about him that was new and unsettling. She was no longer taking care of her little brother. He was helping to take care of her. She did not know whether to be relieved or terrified.

"Birch did inherit a sizeable fortune," Andrew said. "But by all accounts he has managed to go through a great deal of it. However, he seems to have found another source of income."

"What is it?" Eudora asked.

Andrew popped another sandwich into his mouth. "I haven't been able to ascertain that. Meanwhile, regarding Kettering, as of now his day appears to be quite ordinary. He paid a call on his tailor this morning, attended a boxing match in the afternoon, had tea at his club, and then went home to dress for the evening. I just came home to get something to eat before I return to watch his club."

"A typical day for a gentleman," Calista said. "But I suppose that is only to be expected. Even a murderer must at least appear to live a routine life if he wishes to remain undetected."

"A man like Kettering will keep his most interesting appointments after dark," Trent said.

Eudora's mouth tightened. "Yes, of course."

"Don't worry, I'll be back in front of his club in short order to see what he does tonight," Andrew said. "It won't be hard to keep up with him because the traffic will slow his cab."

"You will be careful, Andrew," Calista pleaded. "Please promise me that much."

He grinned. "Don't worry about me. I've paid the driver of a hansom to remain readily available for me as long as I require his services. Costs a bit, naturally, but in a hansom it's a simple matter to follow Kettering."

Trent looked at him. "In the process of keeping an eye on Kettering today, did you happen to see his wife?"

"Mrs. Kettering? She did not leave the house while I was watching it but there is nothing strange about that. Can't say whether she went out shopping or visiting while I was trailing around after Kettering, of course." Andrew glanced at the clock and got to his feet. "I'd better be on my way. No telling when he'll leave this evening. I have the impression that he spends as little time as possible at home. That is not a happy marriage."

He collected one last sandwich and went quickly toward the door.

"One moment," Trent called after him.

Andrew paused. "Yes, sir?"

"You have your revolver?"

"Of course."

"Good. Keep the gun within reach at all times. We know that Kettering and his hired killer are dangerous men. We must assume that the same is true of Dolan Birch."

"Rest assured, I will be cautious. Don't wait up for me. Gentlemen like Kettering often stay out until nearly dawn. I will give you a full report at breakfast."

Andrew vanished out into the hall. Calista heard him speaking to Mrs. Sykes, thanking her for a packet of sandwiches, and then the front door closed behind him.

She looked at Trent and Eudora. "Well, one of us, at least, appears to be enjoying this venture."

"One's definition of entertainment is different at the age of nineteen," Trent said.

"Yes, I suppose that is true," Calista agreed. "But it is a bit unnerving to see Andrew *thriving* like this. Now I understand why he gets some pleasure from the process of verifying the information my clients provide me."

"I would tell you not to worry about him but in truth I'm concerned about the safety of both of you," Eudora said.

Trent watched Calista with grim eyes. "We need to find a way to end this matter and quickly."

A brisk knock sounded. Mr. Sykes opened the door. He looked at Trent.

"A message for you, sir."

Sykes held out a small silver tray. Calista and Eudora watched Trent pick up the envelope. He carried it to the desk and used a letter opener to slit the seal.

"It's from Jonathan Pell," he said.

He read it aloud.

> *The blade man you are hunting is from your world, not mine. He is not in the employ of any of my colleagues. Rumors about him began circulating nearly a year ago. He is believed to be quite mad.*
>
> *No address as of yet but will continue to make inquiries. I am pleased to say that I have learned something about the detective business from Clive Stone. It is a most interesting profession.*

"How on earth did Nestor Kettering manage to hire a madman who enjoys murdering women?" Eudora said.

"Perhaps he had some assistance from his associate, Dolan Birch," Trent said.

"If that is true, then they are both guilty of hunting women who are alone in the world," Calista said, oddly numb. "What kind of person could do such a thing?"

Eudora rose, crossed the room, and put her hand on Calista's shoulder.

"Together we will solve this puzzle," Eudora said gently.

Calista managed a shaky smile. "Thank you."

Trent went to the desk, found a piece of paper, and selected a pen.

"What are you going to do?" Calista asked.

"Send a note to Pell telling him about Dolan Birch. Pell is always very keen to learn everything he can about his competition. Trust me, he will want to make inquiries about Birch. I will make it clear to Pell that we would appreciate knowing whatever he discovers and that we, in turn, will convey to him any other useful information that we learn."

41

S HORTLY BEFORE FOUR o'clock in the morning Calista heard a hansom in the street. Relief shot through her. Andrew was home.

She leaped out of bed, grabbed her wrapper, and hurried out into
the hall. A door opened at the far end of the corridor. Trent appeared,
tying the sash of his dressing gown. Another door opened and Eudora
joined them.

They all gathered at the top of the stairs and looked down at
Andrew.

"Sorry," Andrew said. "Didn't mean to wake you."

"Any news?" Trent asked.

"Afraid not." Andrew shoved his fingers through his hair. "Kettering went to the theater, had supper with friends, and spent much
of the rest of the evening playing cards at his club. When he left the
club he met briefly with Dolan Birch. Unfortunately, I could not
get close enough to hear what was said but I got the impression they

were quarreling. I think Birch was demanding something from Kettering."

"Where is Kettering now?" Trent asked.

"I followed him back to his residence on Lark Street a short time ago. All quite routine. Now if you don't mind, I'm going to get some sleep."

42

THEY DID NEED sleep, Calista thought. But for her, at least, that was going to be hard to come by.

She tossed and turned for a few minutes before she gave up the attempt altogether and got out of bed.

The only solid evidence they had to work with consisted of Mrs. Fulton's sales journal, Andrew's notes, and her own client files.

All of those things were downstairs in the library.

She pulled on a wrapper and let herself out into the night-darkened hallway. The big house seemed especially gloomy at night. It was as if her grandmother's ghost hovered in the atmosphere, complaining endlessly about ill health, slatternly servants, and ungrateful offspring who brought scandal and shame on the family name.

But tonight she and Andrew and the Sykeses were not alone in the big house. For the first time in all the years they had lived here, there were houseguests. More than houseguests, she told herself as she started down the stairs—Trent and Eudora surely qualified as loyal friends.

It was good to have friends.

She reached the bottom of the stairs and went toward the library. There was a thin bar of light under the door. For a few seconds she froze, pulse skittering wildly. It struck her that she might be about to surprise an intruder. Someone had managed to enter the house in a clandestine fashion on one other occasion. Perhaps he had come back.

Common sense descended in the next moment. The flaring light under the door told her that the fire was still going strong in the hearth.

No intruder would bother to light a fire.

Nevertheless, her nerves flickered and sparked a little when she put out the candle and opened the door.

Trent lounged in one of the large armchairs. He was still in his dressing gown. His legs were stretched out toward the hearth. Mrs. Fulton's journal was open on his lap.

He looked up when the door opened. Setting the journal aside, he got to his feet.

"Couldn't sleep?" he asked.

"No," she said. "It would appear that you couldn't, either."

"I've been thinking about what you said earlier. You were right. I have made inquiries and I am hopeful that Mr. Pell will be able to provide us with a lead. But this situation has become extremely dangerous. We need to act now—not wait for answers to fall into our lap."

"I agree." She walked forward a few steps and stopped. "I came down here tonight to take another look at my client files. The question I keep asking myself is, why did Nestor Kettering come back into my life recently? He showed no interest at all in me for most of the past year."

"Perhaps because he was occupied with hunting governesses."

She tightened her grip on the lapels of her wrapper. "Yes."

"I have a theory," Trent said deliberately.

"About Nestor?"

"Yes. It occurred to me that if he is, indeed, the one who seduces and then murders the governesses, he may wish to expand his hunting territory beyond the Grant Agency. After all, over time someone would be bound to notice so many young, healthy women succumbing to infections of the throat. Your introductions business offers many of the same advantages as the Grant Agency. You have a roster of single women who seek companionship and love."

"But to get access to those files, he must first convince me to let him back into my life, is that what you are saying?"

Trent's expression was grim. "Something along those lines, yes."

"I suppose that explains why he sent the flowers and then showed up in my office a few days ago. But if that was the plan, why did he attempt to frighten me with the memento mori gifts at the same time? It doesn't make sense."

Trent went to stand, looking down into the fire. "Damned if I can see the whole story at this point but it's all connected somehow. I'm sure of it. We must find a way to link him to the murder of Mrs. Fulton or one of the governesses. We need evidence."

"But how can we obtain it? We don't have anything except our suspicions."

Trent watched the flames. "I've been thinking about that. If there is any evidence to be found it will no doubt be in Kettering's house."

"That is the reason I suggested that we talk to Anna Kettering."

Trent shook his head. "I told you, the odds are she won't help us. Worse yet, she might warn her husband."

"Then what on earth can we do?"

"A small act of burglary might solve our problem."

Raw panic crackled through her.

"No," she said. "It's too dangerous."

"Perhaps not—if I plan well."

"No, you must not even consider such a scheme," she said. She hurried across the room, the skirts of her wrapper flaring out around her legs. "I will not allow you to break into the Kettering house. You might be arrested, or worse. If that hired killer is guarding the place you could be killed."

Trent looked up from the flames. The ice-cold determination in his eyes alarmed her as no words could have done.

"Trent, please," she whispered. "You have taken so many risks already. I could not bear it if you are imprisoned or murdered because of me."

Gently he captured her chin on the edge of his hand. His thumb traced her lower lip.

"It's my choice," he said. "Always remember that."

"Trent—"

He silenced her by the simple act of covering her mouth with his own. In that moment she knew that the deep hunger that had swept through her the first time he had kissed her had been no spark of fleeting passion brought on by nerves and the dark thrill of danger. The same sensation was heating her now, more intense than ever. She was on fire with a bright, sparkling, disorienting energy.

In Trent's arms she was learning the true power of passion. It was a precious gift, one she had given up all hope of ever receiving. And even as she surrendered to the fever, she knew it was also a very dangerous gift because it so easily could be lost.

But tonight it was hers to savor.

The kiss went from tender and seductive to dark and desperate in the space of a heartbeat.

Trent groaned, framed her face between his hands, and wrenched his mouth away from hers. He looked down at her with hot eyes.

"I want you," he said, his voice rough around the edges. "No, I *need* you. Tell me you want me, too. I must hear the words."

"Yes." She gripped his shoulders to steady herself. "Yes, I want you, Trent Hastings."

He released her. Without a word he walked across the room and very deliberately locked the door. When he returned to her she smiled and opened her arms.

He uttered a deep, low growl, a sound that could have been interpreted as either desperation or soaring triumph. Perhaps it was both. He undid the sash of her wrapper. When the garment fell away his fingers closed gently over her breast. She could feel the heat in him through the thin fabric of her nightgown.

He deepened the kiss. The intense intimacy left her shivering in a hot whirlpool of sensation. When he finally tore his mouth away from hers to kiss the side of her throat she could scarcely catch her breath.

The world spun around her. She thought she was falling, but in the next instant she realized that he had picked her up and was carrying her across the room. A strange panic assailed her. It was unnerving to be hoisted off the floor in such a fashion.

She clenched the front of his shirt. The old fear that had troubled her dreams for years—the fear of knowing that she and Andrew were alone in the world and that she was the only one who could protect Andrew—somehow blended with the physical reality of being lifted off her feet.

But in the next moment she felt the strength in his arms and knew that he would never let her fall.

He carried her to the desk and seated her there, her legs dangling over the edge. One by one Trent undid the front buttons of the nightgown. He made a place for himself between her knees and kissed her again.

Her fingers shook a little as she undid the front of Trent's dressing gown. She eased her palms inside the garment—and caught her breath when she felt the rough, etched skin that covered his left shoulder.

He was nude above the waist. Below that, he was garbed in a pair of loose-fitting trousers of the sort men wore as nightclothes. She could see the clear outline of his rigid erection pressing against the fabric. The sight made her go very still.

He raised his mouth from hers. Shadows moved in his eyes.

"I should have warned you," he said, his voice raw with some edgy emotion and the control that he was exerting to mask it.

"About what?" she asked.

"The scars are not limited to my face."

Very deliberately she rested one hand on the ridged skin of his shoulder.

"It is not the look and feel of your scars that shocks me," she said. "It is the knowledge that you must have endured a great deal of pain at the time you acquired them. Eudora told me Bristow hurled acid at you—acid that was intended to destroy her face."

Trent took a deep breath and exhaled slowly, as though a great weight had been lifted from his shoulders.

"It was a long time ago," he said. "The only thing that matters to me tonight is whether or not you are so repulsed by the sight of my scars that you cannot allow me to make love to you."

"There is nothing about you that I find repulsive. Quite the opposite. You are the most attractive man I have ever met." She risked what she hoped was a sultry smile. "And I assure you, I have met a number of gentlemen in my business."

He ignored her weak attempt at humor. Instead he watched her with a seriousness that tore at her emotions.

"Have you loved any of those other gentlemen?" he asked.

"No."

"I'm glad."

He kissed her and she was once again lost to passion.

She barely noticed when he drew the hem of her nightgown up above her knees. But the feel of his warm hand on the inside of her thigh sent a shock through her. She went still, her breath tight. Everything inside her was tight, as well. A tension unlike anything she had ever known seethed deep within her.

He moved his mouth to her throat. "You are so soft. I could spend the rest of the night just touching you."

"I think I would enjoy that very much." There was a shivery note in her voice now. "I like the feel of your hands on me."

He groaned again and his touch became ever more intimate. She knew a sudden wave of embarrassment when she realized that she was growing damp. Trent's hand was wet and slick now—because of her. She stirred uneasily, at the mercy of a great confusion of the senses. She wanted more, needed more, but she was not sure exactly what it was that she craved.

He did something with his hand and she drew a sharp breath. She gripped his bare shoulders, desperate now. What was happening to her?

"Trent. *Trent.*"

"Come for me," he said.

"I don't understand." She was breathless.

"There is nothing to understand. Just abandon yourself to pleasure. I want to know that I can give this to you."

He probed deeper, slipping his fingers inside her. She almost shrieked aloud. She would have done so had she been able to catch her breath. Instinctively she tightened herself around him, searching for an escape from the impossible tension.

It was as if he were drawing a bowstring tighter and tighter until it threatened to snap.

When the release came she was overwhelmed by the cascading waves of sensation. Lost in the wonder of the moment she was only dimly aware that he had opened his nightclothes and freed himself.

He gripped her legs and wrapped them around his waist.

"Hold me," he said.

It was a command and a plea.

She obeyed because there was nothing she wanted to do more than hold him. She wanted the moment to last forever. She tightened her legs around him and gripped his shoulders with all of her might.

He thrust deeply, heavily into her. A sharp, lancing pain shocked her nerves, jolting her back to reality.

Trent froze. "Calista."

"It's all right," she managed. She gripped him very tightly between her thighs. "It's all right."

Trent hesitated and then, when she did not release him, he began to move within her. Slowly, deeply, deliberately at first. And then with more force.

She was still struggling to adjust to the feeling of being so tightly stretched when Trent stiffened. The muscles of his shoulders were like steel bands beneath her hands.

With an effort of will he pulled free of her body, grabbed a handkerchief out of his pocket, and sheathed himself in the large square of linen.

With a barely muffled groan, he gave himself up to his release.

When it was over he clutched the damp handkerchief in one hand and braced himself with his other hand planted on the desk beside her thigh. He loomed over her.

"Calista," he said.

She dared not move. She could not move.

His eyes burned with the heat of spent passion.

"Calista," he said again. "You should have told me."

"It was my decision," she said. "Never forget that."

He drew a deep breath. "May I say that I am very glad you chose tonight to make the decision?"

She smiled. "You may."

He gave her a perfunctory little kiss on the forehead, made his way to the nearest armchair, and collapsed into it.

Now that the passion and drama had subsided she was overcome with a sense of awkwardness. She had no idea how a woman of the world was supposed to act in such circumstances. Grandmother had offered no advice for such delicate situations. Then again, Grandmother would have been horrified by such a situation.

She jumped down from the desk. But her knees proved unsteady. She swept out a hand to catch her balance and accidentally knocked a pile of client folders onto the floor. Her neatly detailed notes were scattered across the carpet. She ignored them to pull her wrapper securely around herself and tie the sash.

Trent watched her intently, as if he could not take his eyes off her. She took a deep breath and seized what she could of her composure.

"You're certain you are all right?" Trent asked.

She did not know what she had been expecting him to say but that particular question was not it. She was shocked to realize that, deep down, she rather hoped he would make a passionate declaration of undying love. She reminded herself that they were barely acquainted with each other. Which only made the entire affair all the more scandalous.

Nevertheless, she thought, he certainly could have said something mildly romantic, or merely polite. At the very least he might have indicated that he had enjoyed himself. He was a writer, after all. He was supposed to have a certain fluency with words.

On the other hand, he was not at his best when he wrote about Clive's feelings toward the mysterious Wilhelmina Preston.

"Of course I'm all right," she said. "Why wouldn't I be all right?"

She crouched on the carpet and began to gather up the papers and folders.

"Calista?"

He pushed himself up out of the chair and went down on one knee beside her. He started to help collect the folders.

"Don't," she said, more sharply than she had intended.

He looked at her, brows slightly elevated. "I was only trying to help."

"I know." Now she was angry at herself for the unwarranted flash of anger. "But it will be faster if I do it. I can identify my own notes more quickly."

"As you wish."

He sat back on his heels and watched her gather up the papers.

"Calista," he said again. "I'm sorry. It never occurred to me that this might be your first experience of this sort of thing. I swear, I never meant to hurt you."

She gave him what she hoped was a bright little smile. "No need to apologize, sir. But I will admit I am very curious about something and I would be glad of an explanation."

"What?"

She stopped collecting papers and sat sideways on the rug, her legs curled beside her. "Will you tell me more about how you came by those scars? Eudora told me only a little. I realize it is none of my affair but given that you know so many of my secrets—"

"You feel you have a right to some of mine." He nodded and got to his feet. "You are correct." He crossed the room, picked up the brandy bottle, and splashed some into a glass. "In and of itself, it's no great secret, but we do not talk about it outside the family."

"I understand. Forgive me for prying."

He swallowed some brandy and looked at her. "Sometimes I think the real problem is that we don't talk about it inside the family, either. You know how it is with family secrets."

43

H<small>E DECIDED TO</small> tell her the truth, or at least the part of it she had asked for. He owed her that much, he thought. And as it was the only thing she seemed to want from him tonight, he would give it to her.

In that moment he knew that he would give her anything she asked of him.

An eerie sense of recognition—of *knowing*—slammed through him, stealing his breath. This was not how sexual desire felt. Desire hit a man hard and fast and then dissipated rapidly because there was nothing to anchor it. This was something more, something that went deep; something that felt timeless. Inescapable.

This was the kind of powerful emotion that could alter the course of a man's life—or seal his doom.

The sight of Calista curled up on the carpet, disheveled and bewildered by what had just happened between them, unlocked a gate somewhere inside him. A new path was revealing itself, one he had long ago assumed he would never discover.

Simultaneously, the realization that she might be regretting their passionate encounter filled him with a dread unlike anything he had ever experienced.

He let the heat of the brandy warm him while he searched for a way into the story.

"I told you that my mother's second husband, Bristow, did not remain at the country house for her funeral," he said. "He went straight to London and there he remained for several months. But eventually he returned to the village where Eudora, Harry, and I lived."

"Why did he come back?"

"He managed to gamble away almost all of my mother's inheritance. He found himself in debt to a very dangerous man."

"The crime lord, Mr. Pell?"

"No. One of Pell's competitors. The day Bristow showed up at the house I was not there. I had walked into town to browse in the local bookshop. When I got home the housekeeper was in a panic. Bristow had forced his way into the house. He was upstairs in my brother's laboratory, shouting at Eudora."

"She told me that he had a terrible temper," Calista said.

"Bristow was screaming at her, insisting that she pack a bag and accompany him back to London. I told the housekeeper to fetch Tom, the gardener. Then I went up the stairs to the laboratory. Bristow was in a rage. It became clear that he had promised Eudora to a crime lord named Jenner."

Calista's mouth dropped open in shock. "What?"

"Jenner owned one of the gambling hells in which Bristow had lost a great deal of money."

"Your stepfather intended to use Eudora to pay his debts?"

"Jenner was one of those men with a taste for innocent young girls. There was no shortage of them in London, of course, but most of his prey came from the slums. The thought of acquiring a respectable, gently bred young lady as his mistress evidently appealed to him."

"Poor Eudora. She must have been terrified."

"When he was finished with her, Jenner would have put her to work as a prostitute in one of the brothels he operated. On that day in Harry's laboratory Eudora did not fully comprehend the fate Bristow intended for her but she knew more than enough about him to be terrified. When I walked into the laboratory I saw that he had backed her up against a wall. He had a flask of acid that he had picked up from Harry's workbench."

"Dear heaven."

"Bristow was threatening to hurl the acid straight into Eudora's face if she continued to defy him. Harry was also in the room. He was pleading with Bristow."

Horrified, Calista climbed to her feet, a couple of folders in one hand. "What did you do?"

"When he saw me in the doorway, Bristow ordered me to leave. He threatened to throw the acid at Eudora if I took so much as a single step closer to him."

"He used her as a hostage?"

"That was his plan but he was starting to panic. The three of us faced him from three different sides of the room. He could not watch all of us at once and it was me he feared the most."

"Yes, of course. You were the oldest."

"I told him that I would give him a family ring that had been handed down to me by my grandfather. I explained that it was worth a great deal of money—more than enough to pay off his gambling debts. Bristow didn't believe me, not at first, so I described it in great detail—a single large ruby set all around with diamonds and sapphires."

"It must have been worth a fortune," Calista said.

"Bristow was suspicious, of course. He said my mother had never mentioned such a valuable ring. I explained that was because it was my inheritance. She had always feared that if he got his hands on it he would sell it. I told him that the ring was hidden in a secret drawer in my grandfather's cabinet of curiosities."

"Where was the cabinet?"

"It sat in a corner of the laboratory. Bristow told me to get the ring and show it to him. I went to the cabinet, opened one of the drawers, and took out a small box."

"What happened?" Calista asked, riveted by the tale.

"Bristow became very excited at the sight of the box. He demanded that I put it on one of the workbenches. I went to stand at the open window instead. I threatened to toss the ring out into the same pond in which he had drowned my mother unless he released Eudora."

"He believed you?"

"By then he was desperate to get his hands on that ring. I also pointed out that it would be very difficult to drag Eudora to London holding that flask of acid. I agreed to let him have the ring in exchange for Eudora. He was desperate so he took the bargain. I set the box on a workbench. He was still holding the flask in one hand so he was forced to release Eudora in order to pick up the box. The instant she was free I told her to run. She fled out into the hall. Bristow was enraged. But his rage was directed at me because I had tricked him."

"That was when he hurled the acid at you?"

"By then he had opened the box and realized it was empty."

Calista's eyes widened. "It was all a bluff?"

"I told him a story, Calista. People will follow you anywhere if you tell them a tale they desperately want to believe. It's astonishing, really, how gullible even the most skeptical person can be if he or she wants to believe."

"There never was a ring?"

"If I'd owned such a ring I would have sold it and invested the profits immediately after my mother's funeral because Bristow had devastated the family finances. No, there was no ring."

"That was quite brilliant thinking on your part, Trent."

"I make my living writing fiction, remember? I have always been rather good at inventing stories."

"But in that instance you paid a great price."

"I did the only thing I could think of under the circumstances."

"Yes, of course," Calista said. "You had to protect Eudora."

She understood, he thought. Of course, she did.

"I managed to turn partially aside and cover my eyes with my arm," he continued. He looked down at the scars on the back of his hand. "The day was very warm. I had removed my jacket, opened the collar of my shirt, and rolled up my sleeves in the course of the long walk home. Not that the fabric was much protection. The acid burned through my shirt in places."

"What happened next?"

"Tom, the gardener, arrived on the scene. He was armed with a stout shovel. With the flask empty, Bristow was unarmed. He fled toward the door, screaming at the gardener to get out of the way. I told Tom to let the bastard go."

"You could not allow Tom to be arrested for assault."

Again, she understood, he thought.

"Harry doused me with the buckets of water he kept handy in case he accidentally set a fire with one of his experiments. It was all very chaotic for a time. When events calmed down, Bristow was gone. I learned later that he caught the train to London that same day."

"Eudora told me that Bristow died soon after that day. A fever, she said."

This was the tricky part of the story, he thought. He drank a little more brandy to give himself a moment to think. He had told the tale in its entirety to only one other person—Jonathan Pell. Until now only he and Pell knew the real ending.

"I realized that when he'd had time to recover from events at the country house, Bristow would not rest until he found a way to get rid of me. Eudora was his only hope of escaping Jenner. I also knew that he probably did not have a lot of time. Jenner was not a patient man."

"You went looking for Bristow, didn't you?"

"Just as soon as my wounds had partially healed. But Bristow had gone to ground in London. It was not me he feared, but the man to whom he owed money."

"What did you do?"

"I went into the hells and started asking questions. Jonathan Pell was an up-and-coming crime lord at the time. At first I think he was merely intrigued, perhaps even amused, by my determination. He told me that if he helped me, there would be a price to pay. There is always a price, he said."

"You agreed to pay it."

"Yes."

"Pell helped you find Bristow?"

"He did, yes. But fate had already taken a hand. When I finally tracked him down, Bristow was alone and dying of a fever. He was delirious but he recognized me. He pleaded with me to pay for a doctor. Harry told me years later that it was unlikely a doctor could have saved him."

"But that is not your point, is it?" Calista asked gently.

"There were things I could have done. I could have purchased some laudanum or another drug to ease his suffering. I could have paid for a nurse to tend him. But I walked away and left him there, Calista. Three days later they pulled him out of the river. Evidently in his delirium he had managed to drag himself to the end of a dock. He either jumped or fell in. We'll never know and I don't particularly care."

"I am very glad that you were not forced to kill him," Calista said. "I realize that you would have done it to protect your family and I understand. But I am glad you do not have to carry that particular burden."

The atmosphere was very still in the library. He was afraid to shatter it but he had to ask the question.

"Do you?" he asked. "Understand, I mean? I did cross a line, Calista. I left Bristow to die. Had he not been dying, I would have killed him."

She moved a few steps closer to him.

"I can see that the knowledge of what you did and what you know you would have done haunts you," she said. "I am sorry that you were obliged to confront that aspect of your nature. I realize that knowing such a truth about yourself must be a hard thing to live with but you have mourned the death of your lost innocence long enough. It is past time for you to get on with living your life."

He stared at her, stricken by the insight. "Do you think that is what I've been doing all this time? Grieving for the truth I discovered about myself?"

"That certainly appears to be the case," she said. She bent down to scoop up a few more folders and pages of notes. "I suggest you give yourself more credit, sir. You are a man of honor who was willing to sacrifice himself for those who depended on him. I respect that. You should respect that about yourself, as well."

"Calista, about tonight. And your own innocence."

"I assure you I have not been innocent for a very long time." She straightened and put the folders on the desk. "No woman who must make her own way in the world can retain her illusions. And that is what innocence is at its core, is it not? Illusions."

"It seems we are both rather jaded."

She gave him a wry smile. "We are, indeed. Nor are we alone. I certainly am not. Every governess and every paid companion I have ever met is just as realistic, I assure you." She stopped and looked down at the folders in her hand. "The governesses. Yes, of course."

"What are we talking about now?"

"The murdered governesses from the Grant Agency." She put the folders on the desk and started shuffling through the pile. "The three women Mrs. Grant said were buried in modern safety coffins."

"What are you looking for?"

"None of the women was a client of my agency. But as I mentioned, I did have two Grant Agency governesses as clients. Both were successfully matched. I seem to recall that one of them told me that she had referred another woman at the agency to me. But that woman never came for an interview."

"Why is that important?"

"I don't know. But it is troubling me. I have a vague recollection of making a note of the name."

She sat down behind her desk and opened the folders. He angled himself across one corner of the desk and watched her page carefully through the notes.

"Yes." She paused at a page, reading quickly. "Here it is. Virginia Shipley."

She said it as if he ought to recognize the name.

"I don't—" He stopped. "The secretary at the Grant Agency?"

"Wasn't that her name? Shipley?"

"Yes, I think so, but what does that signify?" he asked.

"It occurs to me that Nestor Kettering selected his prey with some care. The three women who died all had a few things in common."

"They were all young, alone in the world, and worked for the Grant Agency. What of it?"

"Think about it, Trent. How did Nestor go about selecting his prey? On his own, he would not have had any way to know which women were young and alone and attractive. Yet he managed to find three such ladies at the Grant Agency. It was only after they were dead that he started sending flowers to me."

Understanding dawned.

"You think he had access to the Grant Agency files, don't you?" he said. "Someone allowed him to select his prey."

"Who would have better access to those files than the secretary?"

44

"I'M AFRAID MISS Shipley did not come in to the office today." Mrs. Grant tapped one finger impatiently on her desk. "She did not even bother to send a note explaining her absence. I can only assume she fell ill during the night. She has always seemed quite healthy but one never knows, does one?"

"No," Calista said. "It is very important that we talk to her. Would you mind giving us her address?"

"Why?" Mrs. Grant looked at Trent with obvious misgivings. "Are you going to put Miss Shipley into your new novel instead of me?"

"I wouldn't think of it," Trent said. "But it is imperative that I speak to her to confirm one or two small facts. I would be grateful if you would be so kind as to give me her address."

"What facts do you wish to confirm? Perhaps I can help you."

"Very well," Trent said. "Among other things we wish to know if Miss Shipley is acquainted with a man named Nestor Kettering."

"I've never heard of him. I have no clients named Kettering. Why would Miss Shipley know him, and why is that information important to you?"

Calista decided it was time to take command of the situation.

"Let me put it this way, Mrs. Grant," she said. "There is every reason to believe that Nestor Kettering is a very dangerous man. We think he may be responsible for the death of several women. If that is the case, Miss Shipley may be in grave danger."

Mrs. Grant stared at her. "You're serious." She turned back to Trent. "This is not part of your plot research, is it, sir?"

"Unfortunately, our concerns for Miss Shipley are genuine," he said.

Mrs. Grant did not appear enthusiastic about cooperating but it was clear that she was shaken.

"I'll give you the address," she said. "Miss Shipley recently moved to a very nice neighborhood. Said something about having received a bequest from a distant relative. I've been afraid she would give notice one of these days. I got the impression that she no longer needs the income from her post here at my agency. Fortune has evidently smiled upon her."

45

TWENTY MINUTES LATER Trent stood in the center of a small but nicely furnished little parlor. Calista stood across from him. Together they looked down at the body of Virginia Shipley. The expensive silk necktie that had been used to strangle her trailed away from her bruised throat.

"Fortune did not smile upon her," Trent said. "Someone murdered her."

"Nestor Kettering," Calista said. "It must have been him."

"Perhaps, but she did not die like the others. That raises some questions."

"He didn't consider her prey the way he did the others, so he did not follow his usual pattern," Calista said. "He murdered her so that she would not talk to us."

"Which means she knew something that could lead us to him."

"The same reason Mrs. Fulton, the proprietor of the mourning goods shop, was killed."

"Perhaps." Trent went out into the hall. "Let's have a look around before I send for the police. We may find something that will link Miss Shipley to her killer."

"I'll search her bedroom," Calista said. "It will be easier for a woman to spot something unusual in another woman's bedroom."

"I'll deal with the ground-floor rooms," Trent said.

He went down the hall toward the small dining room and kitchen. Calista hoisted her skirts and hurried up the narrow staircase.

She stopped at the first bedroom doorway and looked into the room. There was a small writing table near the window. The wardrobe stood open, as if Shipley had been interrupted in the midst of getting ready for bed. The towering hairpiece she had been wearing at the Grant Agency and the long, sturdy pins required to anchor it were neatly arranged on a dressing table.

There was a very large, expensive mirror on the table. The brush and comb set were backed with silver. A small jewelry box occupied a prominent position.

Miss Shipley was doing quite well on a secretary's salary, Calista thought.

It occurred to her that many women would keep the things they valued most in their jewelry boxes. She went toward the dressing table.

She was reaching out to lift the lid of the jewelry box when a man appeared in the mirror. There was a gun in his hand.

Instinctively she started to turn, her mouth open to scream a warning to Trent but the newcomer was upon her so swiftly she could not get the words out.

He slapped a large palm across her lips and hauled her back against his chest. His eyes met hers in the mirror and she knew that he would murder her without a qualm.

"Not one word," the man said. "I've already killed one inconvenient woman today. I don't mind silencing another."

46

S HE HEARD TRENT's footsteps on the staircase.

"Calista?" he called.

She struggled in the stranger's grip, trying to make enough noise to warn Trent, but her captor jerked her away from the dressing table and turned so that both of them faced the bedroom doorway.

Trent appeared, his walking stick gripped casually in his hand.

"One more move and I'll shoot you first and then kill the woman," the gunman said.

"I understand," Trent said.

The gunman took his hand away from Calista's mouth in order to get his arm more securely around her. He pinned her to his chest.

"You must be Hastings," he said. "I assume this irritating female is Miss Langley. I knew Shipley was going to be a problem sooner or later, but I had hoped to deal with her before she became a liability."

"You were too late, Birch," Trent said.

Calista's heart was pounding but she felt the jolt of alarm that went through the gunman's body.

"How do you know my name?" Birch demanded.

"Well, as you clearly are not Kettering, I went with the next logical choice. Incidentally, a number of people are aware that Miss Langley and I came here today to interview Miss Shipley."

"I was afraid of that. The two of you have ruined a very profitable business. It was so easy to sell the names of the young governesses to wealthy, jaded men who enjoy seducing innocent, well-bred women without having to bother with the nuisance of dealing with irate fathers and brothers."

"You sold those young women?" Trent asked.

"I provided names, addresses, and descriptions for a fee. It was up to the client to seduce the merchandise. But you'd be amazed how many wealthy, jaded men enjoy the chase, so long as they know they can walk away when the game is finished. And it really is so easy with governesses. The nature of their work means that they spend a great deal of time alone with their charges. They take the children to parks and other sorts of outings and they generally stick to their routines like clockwork. There really is no great trick to starting up a flirtation with one if you know where to meet her."

"And you knew their schedules because Miss Shipley kept you informed," Calista said.

"Shipley kept track of the merchandise and their routines, yes. The women considered her a friend and confidante."

"What happened to the women you sold to your clients?" Trent said.

"Who knows? I imagine most of them wound up on the streets. A few of the smart ones, like Shipley, no doubt managed to conceal their time as whores and find new posts as governesses. It wasn't my concern. All I guaranteed my clients was that the merchandise was young, attractive, well-bred, and alone in the world. The rest was up to them."

"Were you the one who murdered the three governesses?" Trent asked almost casually—as if the answer was only of passing interest.

"Why would I want to do that? I made a great deal of money off those silly women. They were all so willing to believe that a wealthy, respectable gentleman wanted to marry them."

"It was a story they wanted to hear," Trent said. "When did you make your business arrangement with Miss Shipley?"

"Shipley and I met when she was a governess. She was quite pretty in those days. But the looks didn't last. I lost interest in her. Eventually she went to work as the secretary at the Grant Agency, and then, a few years ago, she approached me with her business plan. I think she actually believed that if she made herself valuable to me—if she became my business partner—I would find her attractive once again."

"If you didn't murder the governesses, who did?" Trent asked.

"Kettering, obviously. I began to wonder about him after the second one succumbed to a mysterious illness. When the third governess went into the ground I concluded that Kettering was a problem. I was about to inform him that I would no longer provide him with names from the Grant Agency list. It was simply too risky. But at about that time he pleaded with me to help him get rid of his wife. I saw an opportunity because I had recently learned of Miss Langley's very interesting business."

"Miss Shipley told you about my introductions agency, didn't she?" Calista said.

"Yes. I was amused at first. You and I are in the same business, Miss Langley."

"No, we are not, you bastard."

"I had already begun to speculate about the possibilities of taking over your introductions agency but I could not see a clear way to achieve my objective."

"Until you realized that one of your clients, Kettering, might be in a position to get his hands on my files, is that it?" Calista asked.

"I had been acquainted with Kettering long enough to learn that he had once seduced you, Miss Langley."

"He did not seduce me."

"Call it what you will. Kettering mentioned in passing that he had come very close to marrying you, only to discover that you were not an heiress, after all. He seemed to think he'd had a very narrow escape."

"He was not the only one," Calista said.

"My point is that I was aware of your past relationship with Kettering but I had not understood the exact nature of your business or realized the potential until Shipley outlined the possibilities for me. A list of single women, many with respectable incomes. So much more valuable than penniless governesses."

"You thought you could use Nestor to get access to my roster of female clients," Calista said. "You assumed that I would allow him back into my life."

"In my experience, lonely women are usually eager to give a man a second chance," Birch said.

"So you made a bargain with Kettering," Trent said. "You told him that if he could gain access to Miss Langley's list of clients, you would help him make his wife disappear."

"That is a very shrewd deduction, Hastings," Birch said. "Only to be expected from a novelist who specializes in detective fiction, I suppose. Yes, that was the plan, but things have obviously gone awry."

"So you are trying to snip off loose ends," Trent said. "You had to get rid of Miss Shipley first because she could connect you to the three dead governesses and the brothel business you are operating. I imagine Kettering is next on your list?"

"He was until you and Miss Langley showed up here at Shipley's house. Now you have the honor. You really are a damned nuisance, Hastings. I should have gotten rid of you first."

Calista felt Birch's body tense in preparation for the shot. Her arms were at her sides. She opened her right hand, revealing the long, sturdy hairpin with its two steel prongs that she had concealed within the folds of her skirts.

Trent met her eyes and she knew he understood what she intended.

She could not hesitate a second longer. Birch was going to shoot Trent. She set her teeth together and raised her arm as high as possible. She stabbed the hairpin backward, hoping to drive the steel into Birch's eye and, at the very least, distract him long enough to give Trent a chance to act.

She felt the twin prongs hit flesh and thought she might be sick to her stomach.

Birch shrieked in agony and rage. Instinctively he shoved her aside with such force she fell to the floor. She heard the gun roar but Trent did not go down. She knew that in his panic, Birch had missed his target.

Trent leaped forward, the walking stick raised for a blow.

Birch staggered back, howling with fury. Calista saw that the hairpin had lodged in his jaw, not his eye. As she watched, he yanked it out. Blood spurted.

And then Trent was upon him, swinging the stick in a savage arc that caught Birch on the arm. Calista heard bone crack. The revolver thudded heavily to the floor.

Birch screamed again and fled toward the door.

Trent went after him. Both men disappeared into the hall. There was another panicky scream. Birch, Calista thought. Not Trent.

The scream was followed by a terrible cascade of heavy thuds on the staircase.

Calista scrambled to her feet, hoisted her skirts, and ran out into the hall.

"Trent," she shouted.

He was standing at the top of the stairs, unharmed.

She ran to him and stopped beside him.

"Are you all right?" he asked.

"Yes," she said. "You?"

"Yes," he said.

Together they looked down at Birch, who lay sprawled at the foot of the staircase. He did not move. It seemed to Calista that his head was at an odd angle.

Trent went slowly down the stairs. When he got to the bottom he put two fingers on Birch's throat. After a moment he looked up and shook his head.

Calista was quite certain she would be sick then. She sank down on the top step and hugged herself.

"I killed him," she whispered.

"No," Trent said. He said it very firmly. "The hairpin did no lethal damage. He stumbled on the stairs and broke his neck."

She nodded and took some deep breaths.

"Come. I will put you in a cab and then summon a constable," Trent said.

"Wait, there is something I must do first." She forced herself to her feet. "I never got a chance to search Shipley's desk."

The little notebook was tucked into the back of one of the drawers.

47

"SOMEDAY," TRENT SAID, "I would very much like to do something normal when we go out together—a stroll through the park, perhaps, or we might go to the theater if we want a bit of excitement."

"Either would certainly be a novelty," Calista said.

They were back in the library at Cranleigh Hall. Calista was behind the desk, paging through the notebook she had discovered in Shipley's bedroom. Trent was at the window. Eudora was sitting in front of the fire, sipping a cup of the strong tea that Mrs. Sykes had produced. Andrew was making inroads into another plate of sandwiches.

Calista's nerves were stretched to the breaking point and she doubted that she would sleep much that night, but at least she no longer felt physically ill. Focusing on Shipley's notebook was proving a useful distraction.

"Elizabeth Dunsforth, Jessica Forsyth, and Pamela Townsend—those are the names of the three dead governesses," she said. "But there are several other names in this book, as well. There is a sum beside each name. Twenty-five pounds and so on."

Eudora shuddered. "Those are the amounts Dolan Birch paid her for the names and addresses of the women he, in turn, sold to his clients."

"To think Birch had the gall to call himself a gentleman," Andrew said. "Jonathan Pell is a paragon of virtue compared to him."

Trent looked at Calista. "Anything else of interest in that diary?"

"Not unless you count my name," Calista said. "It appears that Miss Shipley sold me to Dolan Birch for a thousand pounds."

Trent's jaw hardened. "You were potentially the most valuable one of all. When she sold your name, she was selling your whole agency and, with it, another list of spinsters who could be seduced and carelessly abandoned by Birch's wealthy clients."

"Or in the case of your wealthy spinster clients, seduced and married for their fortunes," Eudora added.

Calista closed the journal. "Obviously one of my clients from the Grant Agency confided in the wrong person."

"She no doubt thought she was doing Miss Shipley a favor by recommending your agency to her," Eudora said.

"Instead, Shipley sold the information to a man she hoped would come to love her if only she could make herself valuable to him." Calista shook her head. "It is all so sad."

"At least we have one more chapter in the story." Trent crossed the room and selected a sandwich from the tray Mrs. Sykes had provided. "We discovered the connection between Kettering and Birch, the Grant Agency and you, Calista."

Calista closed the notebook and absently tapped one finger against the cover. "The thing I don't understand is why Nestor Kettering murdered those three women. Evidently he seduced them, but why kill them?"

"It is obvious that he is a madman," Eudora said. "As Harry suggested, he is in the grip of some bizarre obsession."

Andrew frowned. "Perhaps he killed the women in an attempt to permanently conceal the evidence of his affairs from his wife."

"I doubt if he cares about his wife's feelings," Calista said.

Trent eyed the uneaten portion of his sandwich. "That might not be true. Perhaps he does care a great deal about her feelings."

"That's hard to believe," Calista said.

Trent looked at Andrew. "You said that Anna Kettering's father attempted to protect her by stipulating in his will that if anything happens to her the money goes to distant relatives."

"That's what the maid told me," Andrew said.

"What if the will went a step beyond that?" Trent continued. "If Mrs. Kettering actually controls her own inheritance, she could decide to leave her husband."

"And take the money with her," Calista finished very quietly.

"A man like Kettering might see that as reason enough to commit murder," Andrew said.

48

"YOU WERE RIGHT," Jonathan Pell said. "I did have some interest in Dolan Birch—at least I did until I learned of his rather convenient fall down a flight of stairs yesterday."

He smiled benignly at Trent.

"What did you discover?" Trent asked.

Calista's first impression of Pell was that he did not look like a crime lord. He was a distinguished-looking man, well-dressed, with excellent manners and a respectable demeanor. If he had sought out her introduction services she would not have hesitated to consider him as a possible client.

It also occurred to her that if she had seen him standing with Trent in a crowded room and not been aware of the truth about each man she would have assumed that Trent was the crime lord. It wasn't just the scars, she thought. There was no doubt in her mind that, under the right circumstances, both men could be equally dangerous.

The three of them were sitting in a closed carriage parked at the edge of a deserted graveyard. Pell had arrived in an anonymous cab.

The coachman, however, did not look quite so anonymous. He wore the heavy, many-caped overcoat and slouchy, low-crowned hat common to the men in his profession, but he had the thick shoulders and big, powerful hands of a boxer.

A heavy fog afforded additional privacy for the appointment. The mist was so thick that Calista could make out only a few of the closest headstones. There was a distinct chill in the atmosphere and not all of it was inspired by the weather.

How had her calm, orderly, lonely life taken such a bizarre turn? she wondered.

She certainly was not lonely these days. The feeling that she was watching her own life from the perspective of a spectator had evaporated entirely. It was as if she had awakened from a long sleep. She had experienced a chaotic mix of powerful emotions in the past few days—fear, anger, a fierce determination to survive, and a breathless passion.

And something else as well, she thought.

She looked at Trent, who was deep into a serious conversation with Jonathan Pell. *I'm falling in love. So this is how it feels.*

The realization stole her breath.

"What news do you have for us?" Trent said to Jonathan.

"I let it be known in certain quarters that I was interested in any information relating to Dolan Birch," Pell said. "As it happens, there have been rumors about him circulating for some time now. I had not paid any attention because Birch's business did not infringe on any of my own enterprises."

"What do you know of him?" Trent asked.

"It appears that Birch was, in fact, a crime lord of sorts who provided a variety of services to a rather exclusive clientele—wealthy gentlemen who moved in Society."

Calista pulled herself together and focused on the conversation.

"We are aware that he was selling the names and addresses of young governesses to his clients," Calista said.

Pell's mouth tightened, his disgust obvious. "Quite true. That was not his only business, however. He offered other services to those who could afford him. I suspect he may have managed to make a few inconvenient wives and assorted relatives who were standing in the way of inheritances disappear."

"Birch told us that he had agreed to get rid of Kettering's wife," Trent said. "But he died before he could tell us how he intended to do that."

"I believe I know the answer," Pell said. "I discovered that a few days ago Birch bought a ticket on the morning train to Seacliff, a small village on the coast. He returned on the evening train that same day. Yesterday I sent one of my men to Seacliff to make a few inquiries."

"What made you do that?" Calista asked.

Trent glanced at her. "It's safe to say that Dolan Birch was not the sort of man who would take a short day-trip to a small village unless he had pressing business there."

"Precisely," Pell said. "Men in his position usually book passage to New York or Rome when they want a change of scene. Yet he chose a day-trip to a rather boring little village on the coast."

Calista leaned forward, gloved hands tightly clasped, anticipation sparking. She knew that Trent was also paying very close attention.

"What did you discover?" Calista asked.

"My man spent most of the day in a local pub. He learned that there was a very odd business operating out of an old mansion some distance outside the village. On the face of it, the owner of the house is running a seaside hotel and spa for a very exclusive clientele that demands absolute privacy. The guests arrive in closed carriages."

"I don't understand," Calista said. "Why does that matter?"

"It matters," Pell said, "because according to my employee, there are rumors in the village that the hotel guests tend to remain for extended stays. When they do leave, it is always in another closed carriage. There is a high wall around the grounds and the gate is locked and guarded at all times."

"Are you telling us that the owner of this spa may be operating a private asylum?" Trent asked.

"I believe that to be the case," Pell said. "But my agent returned with another rumor, as well. Evidently the owner of the establishment will make a guest disappear altogether," Pell said. "For a price."

"Even if it's true," Calista said, "what good would that do Kettering? If we are correct, he will lose the fortune if he tries to have his wife committed, just as he would if she dies."

"The critical word here is *disappear*," Pell said.

Trent looked thoughtful. "I understand what you are saying. The question is, what would happen if Anna Kettering is said to be enjoying an extended stay in a health spa? Perhaps, after some time had passed, it could be made to look as though she had left the spa on a sea voyage."

"Months or even years might pass before anyone questioned her absence from London," Pell said.

"Assuming anyone ever did notice," Calista said. "Anna Kettering has no close family, only some distant relatives in Canada. They would never be able to prove that something terrible had happened to her."

"Even then, how could anyone prove that she was imprisoned or dead?" Trent said. "All that would be required to put the fortune in Kettering's hand would be a few forged papers."

"Which would be easy enough to produce provided Anna was not around to deny the legality of the papers," Pell added.

"The scheme would hinge on making certain that the body was never found, but that wouldn't be difficult," Trent concluded. "There are a number of ways to make one disappear. It's really quite ingenious when you think about it."

Calista looked at him, startled.

A flicker of amusement came and went in Pell's cool gaze.

"As I have noted on more than one occasion, it's just as well you didn't pursue a career in my world, Hastings," he said. "I believe you would have proven to be serious competition."

49

"YOU INTEND TO go inside the Kettering house," Calista said quietly.

Trent walked across the library to the windows and looked out at the expansive gardens.

"I cannot delay it any longer," he said. "I can think of no other way to search for evidence that will link Kettering to the deaths of those women."

"I must remind you that there is one other thing we can try before you take such a risk. I have no idea if it will work—I admit the odds are against it—but we have little to lose."

Trent turned to look at her. "You want to confront Mrs. Kettering with our concerns."

"At the very least, we must warn her about her husband."

Trent shook his head. "I told you, she will not talk, and even if she did, no wife can testify against her husband. It would be worth her life to assist us. If she does know what is going on, she will understand that. She's trapped, Calista."

"She must at least suspect what her husband is doing," Calista said. "But she thinks she has nowhere to turn. Don't you see? That is why she is seeking help from the mediums who conduct séances. She must be desperate. We must at least offer to help her. It is the least we can do."

50

A NNA KETTERING WENT shopping in the morning.
"How can she live her life in such a normal fashion?" Calista
asked. "She is married to a killer, for heaven's sake."

"As I keep reminding you, she may be unaware of her husband's
habits," Trent said.

"She knows," Calista said.

They were in a carriage outside a dressmaker's shop, waiting for
Mrs. Kettering to appear. Andrew had sent a note earlier advising them
that Kettering had left the house and was headed toward his club. By
the time Calista and Trent arrived at Kettering's address their quarry
was just getting into a carriage to go on the shopping expedition.

"This may prove to be a stroke of good luck," Trent said. "It might
be easier to convince her to talk to us on a busy street where she will
feel somewhat anonymous."

"Yes, I see what you mean."

The door of the dressmaker shop opened. Mrs. Kettering appeared,
followed by a young clerk who carried two large packages.

"It's now or never," Calista said.

Trent got out and handed her down the carriage steps. He took her arm and escorted her across the busy street.

"Mrs. Kettering," Calista said, striving for a polite but firm tone. "How nice to see you. Would you care to join Mr. Hastings and me for a cup of tea? There is a very nice little tea shop around the corner."

Anna turned quickly, eyes widening. Shock and alarm shivered through her slim, delicate frame. She was very much on edge, Calista decided.

"Have we met?" Anna glanced uneasily at Trent before returning her attention to Calista. "I'm afraid I don't recall—"

Calista came to a halt directly in front of her. She lowered her voice.

"My name is Miss Langley. Calista Langley. This is Mr. Trent Hastings." She paused when she realized that Anna was about to bolt. "The author," she added.

For once Trent's name had no visible impact.

"I don't understand," Anna said. "I'm quite sure I have never met either of you."

"Mrs. Kettering, it is absolutely imperative that I speak with you about your husband," Calista said. "I am quite concerned that you might be in danger. If that is the case we may be able to help you."

"How dare you?" Anna took a step back. There was panic in her eyes. "I have no idea what this is about. Leave me alone, both of you." She turned to the coachman. "Take me back to Lark Street immediately."

"Aye, ma'am."

The coachman handed her up into the carriage. The door slammed shut.

Calista watched the vehicle disappear into the traffic. "She is quite terrified. I'm certain of it."

"So much for your plan," Trent said. "It appears we are left with mine. If Anna Kettering keeps to her routine she will attend a séance tomorrow night and the servants will have the evening off. Kettering will no doubt spend most of the night playing cards at his club. I will visit Lark Street while they are all away and see what I can find."

51

ANNA WATCHED THE street from her bedroom window. The night seemed endless. It was nearly dawn when Nestor finally came home. He got out of a hansom and fumbled for his key. He was drunk, as usual.

She turned away from the window and stood in the darkened room, listening to his heavy tread on the stairs. The spectral light under the door flickered briefly when he went past. A moment later she heard him enter his own bedroom at the far end of the corridor.

They had not shared a connecting room since their honeymoon. In those days she had loved him with glorious abandon. She had been slow to awaken to the knowledge that he despised her.

She gripped the lapels of her gown and told herself that she had to confront him. She had to know the truth.

She lit a candle, opened the door, and went down the long, shadowed corridor to the door of Nestor's bedroom. She could hear him moving about inside, undressing. She nerved herself to rap twice.

There was an abrupt silence inside the room. Then Nestor opened the door.

"What the devil do you want?" he asked. The words were thick with drink.

"Calista Langley stopped me on the street today."

Stunned, Nestor just stared at her for a few seconds. "What are you talking about?"

"She was not alone. Mr. Hastings, the author, was with her."

"What did Langley and Hastings want from you?" Nestor raged softly.

"I'm not sure," Anna said. She retreated a step. "Miss Langley said she wanted to talk to me. Naturally, I refused to speak to her. We have never been introduced, after all. I got into the carriage and came straight back here."

"Bloody hell."

"Nestor, please, what is going on? What have you done?"

"Go back to bed, you bloody stupid woman. Don't you understand? I cannot abide the sight of you. Marrying you was the biggest mistake I have ever made in my life."

Nestor slammed the door shut.

She stood very still in the hallway for a moment longer and then slowly made her way back to her room.

She could no longer escape the truth. She had known for months that it was only the terms of her father's will that kept Nestor from finding a way to get rid of her. But now she knew she could no longer continue to rely on that flimsy protection. She had seen the look in Nestor's eyes tonight. Murderous. He was no doubt telling himself that he had found one heiress; he could find another.

She had to escape.

52

"Congratulations," Eudora said. "You have produced another successful salon. The lecture on photography was quite
informative and now your clients are enjoying themselves and Mrs.
Sykes's excellent tea."

Calista surveyed the crowded room, pleased with the atmosphere.
There was, indeed, a cheerful level of lively conversation going on
among the guests. The photography lecture had provided a topic that
everyone could now discuss with enthusiasm while they munched
small cakes and drank lemonade and tea.

"It is very gratifying when the salons go well," she said. "But it is
not always the case. Next time I would like to try matching people
more scientifically using your system of cross-referencing my clients'
areas of interest. Perhaps we should also attempt to categorize people
by temperament."

"Don't you think that it might be difficult to construct a useful set
of categories for temperament? One can certainly define your clients

in broad terms, such as shy or outgoing and so forth, but I'm not sure it would tell you much about the sort of person who would be a good match for each individual."

"You are right. I am frequently amazed by the matches that come about during the course of the salons. The most successful are not always predictable." Calista watched a very serious-looking gentleman in his early thirties approach. She smiled. "However, I am happy to say that I am not the least bit surprised that you and Mr. Tazewell enjoy each other's company."

Eudora brightened at the sight of Edward Tazewell forging a path through the crowd, a glass of lemonade clutched in one big hand.

"Mr. Tazewell," Calista said smoothly. "I'm delighted you were able to attend the salon today. I hope you enjoyed the lecture."

"Fascinating," he said, but he was looking at Eudora. "I brought you a glass of lemonade, Miss Hastings."

"Thank you, sir." Eudora took the glass from him. "Very thoughtful of you."

"The talk made me curious about the possibility of using photography to record action as it happens," he said. "Currently the process is quite cumbersome. One must take a series of still pictures and imprint them on a rotating glass plate. Just think of the applications for a camera that records live action."

"I can imagine several uses for such a camera," Eudora said. "Especially in the area of entertainment. Why, one could film a play as it takes place on the stage and then watch it again and again."

"What a brilliant idea," Edward said. "Would you care to walk out into the gardens with me so that we can discuss it in detail?"

"I would be delighted," Eudora said.

Edward took her arm. "You are always brimming with creative ideas, Miss Hastings. You inspire me."

Eudora smiled but she paused to give Calista a questioning look. "Will you excuse us? If you need me, I can stay here to help you with your guests."

"Run along, I'll be fine on my own." Calista smiled. "This isn't the first salon that I have hosted, if you will recall. Enjoy the gardens."

Eudora smiled and winked. "I'm sure we will."

Calista watched the pair depart through the open French doors. A good match, she thought. Now, if only Eudora could convince herself that Trent would do quite well without her to manage his household— assuming that he did not get himself arrested or murdered that night when he carried out his plan to search the Kettering residence.

At the moment he was closeted with Andrew in a small sitting room at the back of the house. The two were drawing up a strategy for the venture. Thus far she had heard only the barest outlines of the plan. There had been a low-voiced discussion to the effect that Andrew would keep watch outside the house on the street and blow a cab whistle twice if he saw anyone returning while Trent was inside.

Mrs. Sykes appeared out of the crowd, a concerned expression on her face.

"Excuse me, ma'am, Mrs. Kettering has just arrived."

"*What?* Is she alone?"

"Yes. There's a carriage waiting out in front with some luggage strapped on top but no one else inside. She says she has very important information for you. Seems quite nervous. She asked to speak with you immediately and in private."

"Where is she?"

"I put her in your study."

"I will see her immediately. My guests seem to be doing well enough on their own. Please notify Mr. Hastings that Mrs. Kettering is here. He and Andrew are in the sitting room."

"Yes, miss."

Calista slipped out into the hall and hurried toward the study. The door was closed. She opened it and saw Anna Kettering at the window, gazing out into the gardens. She was dressed for travel in a dark carriage gown and a veiled hat.

She turned quickly at the sound of the door being opened; too quickly. The motion reminded Calista of a startled deer.

"Miss Langley." There was an audible tremor in Anna's soft voice.

"Yes."

"I am so sorry to interrupt you." Anna pushed her veil up onto the brim of her hat, revealing her tense, tightly drawn features. "I had no idea that you were entertaining."

"It's quite all right, Mrs. Kettering." Calista took a couple of steps into the room but she left the door open. She had no doubt Trent would arrive in short order. "Please be seated."

"No, thank you. I cannot stay. I am on my way out of London. I am taking a terrible risk stopping here for a few minutes."

"What is wrong?"

"Yesterday, when you spoke to me on the street, you put me in a dreadful panic. You see, I have been living a nightmare for months, but I kept trying to convince myself that it was my imagination conjuring up all the dark fantasies. When you said you were worried that I might be in danger, I knew I could no longer ignore the reality."

"What do you think is the reality?" Calista asked.

Anna took a sharp breath and briefly closed her eyes. When she opened them again her gaze was shadowed with fear.

"I am afraid to say this aloud, but the truth is, I believe Nestor is quite . . . insane."

There was a slight movement in the doorway. Trent walked into the room. He never took his eyes off Anna, who gave another nervous start when she saw him. He closed the door very softly.

"Mrs. Kettering," he said.

Anna flicked an anxious glance at Calista.

"It's all right," Calista said. "Mr. Hastings is my friend."

"I see," Anna said. "I am glad you have a man to protect you. I don't think the others were so fortunate."

"Who were the others?" Calista asked.

"Miss Dunsforth, Miss Forsyth, and Miss Townsend." Anna's lower lip trembled. "I know their names, and I also know what they looked like because of the photographs."

"What photographs?" Trent asked.

"There is always a portrait," Anna whispered. Tears leaked from her eyes. "In the locked room where Nestor keeps his *collection*. I don't know what else to call it. Every two or three months the photograph disappears and a new one takes its place."

"Mrs. Kettering—" Calista began.

"I told myself they were his mistresses," Anna said. "I cried myself to sleep for weeks after I discovered the first picture. Foolish woman that I am, I had believed that he truly loved me when he married me."

"When did you first start to think that the women might not be your husband's lovers?" Calista asked.

"I'm quite certain they were his lovers, at least for a time. But I have come to believe that something dreadful may have happened to each of them. I could not allow myself to acknowledge the truth. It was too terrible. Yesterday, however, when you confronted me, I knew I could not deceive myself any longer. You see, I recognized you."

"What do you mean?"

"It is your photograph that now hangs on the wall in that terrible chamber, Miss Langley. In the picture you are much younger—a girl of sixteen or seventeen, perhaps. But I know it was you because it is your name on the funeral announcement."

Calista took a deep breath. "I see."

"What, exactly, do you believe is going on, Mrs. Kettering?" Trent asked.

"I'm not certain." Anna turned away to look out into the garden. "But in addition to the photographs there is always a funeral announcement."

The tremor shivering through her words was starting to affect her entire body. Her gloved hands were visibly shaking.

"What is this collection you mentioned?" Trent prodded.

"There are always a few memento mori items at the start." Anna looked down at her hands and then, as if surprised to see that they were trembling, she tightened them into small fists. "The sort of things that one purchases for an elegant funeral. Tear-catchers. Jet-and-crystal rings. And a bell that is attached to a chain. Each is engraved with initials. One by one over a period of several weeks, the items disappear. Eventually, so does the portrait. The date of death appears on the funeral announcement. A few weeks later, there is another picture on the wall and a new collection of memento mori."

"How do you know all this, Mrs. Kettering?" Calista asked.

"Because I defied my husband and entered the locked chamber on the fourth floor of our house. Nestor ordered me to never go inside. He does not even allow the maid to clean it. He claims it is his dark room and that the chemicals inside are dangerous. But I know where he keeps the key and from time to time when he is gone and the servants are not around I . . . I let myself into the room."

"What exactly have you concluded, Mrs. Kettering?" Calista asked.

Anna closed her eyes briefly, composing herself. When she looked at Calista again her gaze was stark.

"I told you, I believe my husband is mad," she said. "I suspect that he has murdered the women whose portraits appear in that locked chamber. When you confronted me yesterday I realized I had to get away, but I could not leave until I had warned you. It seemed the least

I could do. I cannot go to the police. Even if they believed me I have no evidence to give them."

"What about the things in that locked chamber?" Calista asked. "They constitute evidence."

Anna shook her head. "I'm afraid that if the police confront Nestor he will tell them that he pursues a somewhat eccentric hobby. And they would believe him."

"Where will you go?" Trent asked.

Anna looked at him. "I left a note telling Nestor I am traveling to the country for a much-needed rest. But as soon as I am safely away from London I will make some excuse and tell my driver to stop at the first railway station. I will buy a ticket for someplace far, far away. No one will know where I've gone. It is my only hope. If my husband discovers that I am aware of his . . . activities or that I came here today to warn you, I fear for my life. I am now certain that there is only one reason I am still alive, as it is."

"What do you mean?" Calista asked.

"I think my father had some concerns about Nestor, although I'm sure he didn't realize exactly what sort of man I was marrying. But before he died, Papa wanted to be certain that I was married and well protected. He was very careful about the terms of my inheritance in his will. If anything happens to me the money goes to distant relatives in Canada. Lately I have begun to believe that is the only thing keeping me alive."

"You are going into hiding?" Trent asked.

"Yes. I cannot think of anything else to do."

"You are very brave, Mrs. Kettering," Calista said.

"On the contrary. I would not call my decision to vanish an act of bravery. In truth, I am quite frightened. But I am even more terrified of spending another night in that house—not now when I can no longer deny the truth."

"Where is your husband today?" Trent asked.

"I don't know. He left after breakfast as is his custom and he has not returned. Perhaps he is at his club. He may not think to question my whereabouts for some time. He can barely stand the sight of me."

Calista took an impulsive step forward. "Do you need help, Mrs. Kettering?"

"Thank you, but there is nothing you can do for me, Miss Langley. I must disappear. I will leave now. The coachman will be wondering what is keeping me. I told him that I wanted to say good-bye to a friend."

She went toward the door. Trent hesitated and then reluctantly moved aside. He opened the door for Anna and looked at Calista.

"I will see Mrs. Kettering to her carriage," he said.

Calista nodded. "Yes, of course."

Trent returned a short time later, his hard face etched in grim lines. He walked into the room and closed the door.

"Did you learn anything more?" Calista asked. "That is why you escorted her out to her carriage, isn't it?"

"Yes, but it proved fruitless. She is a frightened woman on the run."

"What will we do now?" Calista asked.

"Our plans have not changed but they have been somewhat simplified by Mrs. Kettering's absence. Now Andrew need only watch for her husband and the servants to return to their residence while I am having a look around inside. With luck, Kettering will stick to his usual schedule and remain out of the house until nearly dawn."

"You heard what Anna Kettering said, there is no proof to be found in that house."

"Mrs. Kettering may not have recognized hard evidence when she saw it. The police might view things differently."

"That poor woman. Her nerves have been shattered by this situation. Imagine what it must have been like living night and day with a husband you were beginning to believe might be a murderer."

53

T HE DARKNESS INSIDE the large town house was oppressive but it was not absolute. The lamps had been turned down low but they gave off just enough light to enable Trent to make out objects in his path.

He stood very still for a moment in the hall outside the kitchen. It was the servants' afternoon and evening off. There had been no sign of Nestor Kettering. Even though his wife was gone, Kettering was evidently sticking with his customary nightly routine. With luck he would not return before dawn.

There was a heavy sensation of emptiness about the house. Satisfied that he had the premises to himself, he went slowly down the hall. His ultimate goal was the locked chamber that Anna Kettering had described, but he did not want to overlook anything that might constitute evidence.

He took a little time with the desk in the study. The correspondence and business records appeared unremarkable—the sort that accumulated in any wealthy homeowner's desk drawer. He flipped through the leather-bound journal of household accounts. There were always secrets to be found in a person's financial records but it took time and study to ferret them out.

He put the journal back into the drawer and made his way upstairs to the bedroom floor. Only two rooms showed signs of occupancy.

Anna's room featured several empty drawers and a nearly empty wardrobe. It was obvious that she had taken as many things with her as possible when she packed her bags.

Nestor's bedroom was at the end of the hall. Trent searched the wardrobe and the bureau and found nothing that looked like evidence.

He stepped into the dressing room intending to take only a quick look around. But he paused when he saw a wide, dark stain on the carpet.

Blood. A great deal of it. But there was no body.

He left the bedroom and made his way up the stairs to the fourth floor at the top of the house and began to search the rooms. In other circumstances they would have been assigned to the servants but most were empty. The household staff had their lodgings belowstairs.

The door at the end of the hall was locked.

He took out the lock pick and got the door open. A dark, disturbing miasma wafted through the opening, lifting the hair on the back of his neck. Death had a distinctive odor.

He moved cautiously into the gloom-filled chamber; found the lamp, and turned it up.

Nestor Kettering's body was on the floor. That answered a few questions, Trent thought. Kettering had been shot in the temple. The gun had been placed on the carpet near his right hand.

A funeral announcement hung on the wall. The name of the deceased was written on one of the lines: Calista Langley. The date of death had not yet been added.

There was also a photograph, just as Anna had said. Someone had taken a pair of shears to the Langley family portrait, excising out everyone except Calista.

Trent took a careful look around the room and then made his way quickly back downstairs. He went back into the study and helped himself to the financial journal. Nestor Kettering would not need it in the future.

54

"D O YOU THINK she killed him?" Calista asked.

"One can scarcely blame her," Eudora said.

The four of them—Andrew, Trent, Eudora, and herself—were once again in the library.

"I think there is a very good possibility that Anna Kettering is responsible for her husband's death," Trent said. "The question is who assisted her."

"What do you mean?" Calista asked.

"Kettering was not shot in that chamber," Trent said. "I'm sure of that much. There would have been considerably more blood. It looks like he was killed in his dressing room and then hauled upstairs to the chamber. Anna is a small woman. She might have been able to drag the body along a hallway but she could not have carried it up a flight of stairs."

"You're right," Andrew said. "She must have had help. Perhaps one of the servants was persuaded to assist her. The staff was no doubt aware that she was terrified of her husband."

"There may be a lover involved in this affair," Eudora suggested quietly. "Anna Kettering has evidently been a frightened, lonely woman for some time now. It's not inconceivable that she has become involved in a romantic liaison."

They all looked at her.

"Yes," Calista said. She thought about her impressions of Anna Kettering. "We know she was in fear of her husband. So she took the only way out that she could imagine. She or her lover shot Nestor and tried to make it look like suicide. And then, afraid that she might be accused of the murder, she fled London."

"It's possible," Trent said. He gripped the edge of the mantel and studied the fire. "There is some logic to that story. Regardless, I'm almost certain that the police will view the situation as a suicide. Even if they suspect otherwise, I doubt very much that there will be a serious investigation."

"I suppose," Eudora said, "that it doesn't really matter how Kettering died. The important thing is that he is dead."

Trent gave her a hard look. "It matters. We need all the answers."

She took a breath, clearly startled by the urgency in his tone. "Yes, of course."

"You are right, sir," Andrew said. "We still need to identify the man with the knife."

"This isn't going to be finished until we discover where he fits into this tale," Trent said.

"We have all agreed that the madman with the knife can easily pass as a gentleman," Calista said slowly. "And according to Jonathan Pell, he is not employed by any of the London crime lords."

Eudora looked at her. "What are you thinking?"

Calista looked at the journal that Trent had brought out of the Kettering house. "It occurs to me that if the man with the knife was working for Kettering it is likely that Kettering was paying him on a regular basis—and paying him quite well, judging by the good clothes he wears. Perhaps there will be some record of the payments in that journal."

Andrew smiled. "As Clive Stone likes to say, money is like murder—it always leaves a stain."

Trent walked to stand behind the desk. "Clive Stone will also tell you that there is little that can shed more light on the state of affairs in a household as the family's financial accounts."

"I'm sure that is true," Eudora agreed. "But that journal can wait until morning."

"The rest of you can go to bed," Trent said. He opened the journal to a midpoint. "I want to take a quick look first."

No one got up to leave. They sat quietly, sipping tea. Consequently, they were all in the room when, a short time later, Trent looked up from the journal.

"Bloody hell," he said. "Of course. Should have thought about this angle sooner."

Andrew watched him expectantly. "What angle?"

"The mediums," Trent said. "The latest one is Florence Tapp. It appears that Anna went to see her quite recently. There is a payment for a séance session."

"I told you that Anna Kettering was attending séances on a regular basis," Andrew said. "Why are you interested in Florence Tapp?"

"Mediums are all frauds and charlatans," Calista pointed out.

"Precisely," Trent said. "Which is why the most successful mediums are very, very skilled at studying their clients. Who would know more about Anna Kettering and her problems than the woman who claims to be able to summon the spirits of the dead?"

55

"Mrs. Kettering was attempting to contact her father, who passed on to the Other Side about a year ago." Florence Tapp glanced at the envelope containing the money that Trent had just given to her. "Evidently she was quite close to him. I believe her mother died in childbirth."

Calista found herself oddly intrigued by Florence Tapp. The medium had received them in the shadowy parlor of her small but comfortable house. The heavy drapes were pulled against the afternoon sunlight.

The furnishings were large, substantial pieces that seemed much too big for the space, Calista thought. They were no doubt designed to conceal an assistant or two who could provide mysterious rappings and chimes and moans at appropriate moments during a séance. A table draped in black fabric was set off to the side. An unlit lantern stood in the center.

Florence was an attractive woman in her late twenties with a heavy blond mane that cascaded down her back. She was dressed in an exotic gown fashioned of colorful, flowing material and a turban-style

274

cap. A brilliantly patterned scarf was draped around her throat. Large earrings dangled from her ears, complementing the multitude of bracelets stacked on her wrists. Rings glittered on nearly every finger.

Society would have been quick to condemn most women who dared to dress in such a flamboyant style and who went about with unbound hair, but it made an exception for mediums. It was generally understood that those who possessed the psychical sensitivity required to summon spirits were expected to strike an eccentric note, not only when it came to matters of fashion, but in their private lives as well.

It was not unknown for practitioners skilled at summoning spirits to give private sessions to gentlemen clients who paid extra for the exclusive séances. In past years there had been considerable speculation in the press as to precisely what sort of spirits were aroused during those intimate sessions, but no amount of innuendo could quench the public's enthusiasm for séances. The result was that they continued to be a thriving business, and many of the most successful practitioners were women. Holding séances was one of the few respectable career paths open to females.

"Do you know why Mrs. Kettering is attempting to contact her father?" Trent asked.

"I couldn't say, not for certain." Florence waved sparkling fingers in a vague gesture. "But in my practice I have seen a number of clients who are quite desperate to speak with loved ones. They usually fall into one of three categories. There are those who seek the whereabouts of a missing will or some other valuable object that has disappeared. Those attempting to assuage their grief due to the loss of someone dear to them. And those who want advice on love or financial matters."

"Which category does Mrs. Kettering fit?" Calista asked.

"That's the odd thing," Florence said. "I'm not sure why she was so anxious to speak with her father. At first I assumed it was grief that motivated her. I was able to summon her father's spirit, who communicated to her that he was at peace on the Other Side, but that did not satisfy her."

"How did he communicate that information?" Trent asked.

"In the usual manner," Florence said. "The table floated in midair for a time. There was some rapping inside a closet, which I was able to interpret. And then, of course, there were chimes."

"Chimes?" Calista repeated.

"Music is one of the few methods the spirits can use to communicate through the veil."

"I see," Calista said.

"You said Mrs. Kettering was not satisfied," Trent prodded.

"At first she seemed enormously relieved that contact had been made," Florence said. "But then she immediately started to ask him for help. However the veil that separates this world from the next is quite fragile. It was disturbed by outside forces that evening before Mrs. Kettering's father could respond. I'm afraid contact was lost."

"Did Mrs. Kettering return for a second séance?" Calista asked.

"I suggested a private session," Florence said. "We made an appointment for tomorrow night. May I ask why you are so interested in Mrs. Kettering?"

"Mr. Hastings is doing research for a new novel that involves a medium who solves mysteries," Calista said.

Trent glanced at her, brows slightly elevated. She thought he appeared impressed. She was rather impressed with her clever response herself.

"A fascinating premise." Florence looked at Trent. "Dare I ask if Miss Wilhelmina Preston is secretly a medium with strong paranormal powers?"

"I never reveal plotlines," Trent said.

"I see." Florence gave him a smile that was every bit as brilliant as her jewelry. "You must admit that would certainly make for an exciting plot twist."

"Yes, it would," Trent said. He surveyed the parlor with a speculative expression. "If I do decide to make Wilhelmina Preston a medium I shall endeavor to get the details correct. Make a note, Miss Langley. Levitating tables, spirit rappings, and chimes. Have you got all that?"

Calista shot him a withering look, which he appeared not to notice.

"Yes, Mr. Hastings," she said in steely tones. "I believe I have all the details we will need."

"You mustn't forget the manifestations," Florence added.

Calista looked at her. "Manifestations?"

"That is my signature, you might say, the reason why I attract so many clients. I can summon a manifestation of my spirit guide, an ancient Egyptian princess."

"Do you think you will be able to cause the spirit of Anna Kettering's dead father to materialize?" Calista asked.

"Perhaps," Florence said. "Although I doubt that he will look like he did in life. The spirit world changes the physical body, you see."

"I'm not at all surprised to hear that," Calista said.

She dropped her notebook and pencil into her satchel and closed the bag with a sharp snap.

Florence eyed Trent. "I'm happy to be of assistance to you, sir, but perhaps you could learn more if you scheduled a private séance. I would be delighted to conduct one for you."

"Sorry," Calista said crisply. She jumped up and hoisted her satchel. "Mr. Hastings is too busy for a private séance. Deadlines, you know."

She caught a flicker of amusement in Trent's eyes but he did not say anything; just got to his feet in an unhurried manner.

"I see." Florence was disappointed but she appeared resigned. "Very well. I must admit I am curious about your interest in Mrs. Kettering."

"Characterization," Trent said. "She sounds like a typical séance client. I will need one or two of those in my story and I wanted to get the details correct."

"Oh, I wouldn't say that Mrs. Kettering was typical," Florence said. "Not at all."

Trent went quite still.

"What makes you think that Mrs. Kettering isn't a typical client?" he asked.

"I told you that my customers usually fall into one of three categories," Florence explained. "But I think Mrs. Kettering may be in a fourth. I don't know why she is so anxious to speak with her father, but I can tell you that she is desperate to make contact. In fact, I would say that Anna Kettering is a very frightened woman. I suspect she believes that her dear papa can save her."

"From what?" Calista asked, very careful now.

"I have no idea," Florence said. "But I know a woman who is panic-stricken when I see one. It was obvious she was afraid to be alone. Someone escorted her to the séance and waited outside for her."

Calista froze, hardly daring to move. Trent was also very still.

"Mrs. Kettering was accompanied by someone when she attended the séance?" he said.

He spoke in a remarkably casual manner, Calista thought, as though the answer would provide just another detail for characterization purposes.

"I'm quite certain there was someone else in the carriage," Florence said. "A man. He did not come inside, however, so I never got a look at him."

"But you're certain it was a man inside the carriage?" Calista said.

"Oh, yes," Florence said. "He got out and opened the door for her. Dressed quite well, I must say. Excellent manners. A gentleman."

56

"EUDORA WAS RIGHT," Calista said. "Anna Kettering has a lover, someone who is trying to protect her."

Trent considered that for a moment, adding the new information to the plot outline he was building.

"That would explain a few things," he said, "such as how she managed to move her husband's body into that chamber in the mansion."

Calista exhaled softly. She sounded exasperated. "But aside from that interesting fact, we did not learn much from the medium."

Trent lounged in the corner of the carriage seat and considered his impressions of Florence Tapp. "We did pick up one additional piece of information. As of today, Anna Kettering has not canceled her appointment for a séance tomorrow night."

"She was in a panic when we saw her. It's likely that she forgot about the appointment in her haste to leave London."

"Perhaps."

"What are you thinking?" Calista asked.

"London is a very large place. It would be quite possible for a woman of some means and the assistance of a close friend or a lover to lose herself in the city—at least long enough to keep that appointment tomorrow night."

"Do you think that Anna Kettering really believes the medium can put her in contact with her father's spirit?" Calista asked.

"Judging by Miss Tapp's description, I'd say yes. Anna was willing to book a private séance. That indicates something more than casual curiosity. In addition, Tapp said that Anna is quite frightened. Yes, I think that Anna Kettering wants very much to believe the story the medium is telling."

"What does that signify? Florence Tapp invited you to book a private séance, too."

"Research," Trent said.

"Hah."

"I perceive that you are somewhat skeptical of the séance business."

"It's all rubbish and you know it."

"Nevertheless, Florence Tapp seems to be doing rather well at her trade."

Calista waved that off with one gloved hand. "Tricks and illusions."

"What of it? When you think about it, a successful séance is a form of storytelling. One creates a small, intimate theater in which the members of the audience take active roles in the play. For that to happen, the medium must be very good at inducing people to set aside their doubts and common sense. She must coax them to believe. If they fail to do so, the script falls apart."

"It's a wonder any séance practitioner can keep an audience coming back."

"You are overlooking a very important aspect of the business," Trent said. "A medium has one crucial factor working for her when she conducts a séance—the members of the audience *want* to believe that the performance is real."

"Yes, I suppose that is true. What do you think Florence Tapp plans to reveal to Anna Kettering tomorrow night, assuming that Anna keeps the appointment?"

"I suspect that Tapp has scheduled a private appointment with Mrs. Kettering for the purpose of obtaining a better understanding of the client. I'm sure that after that séance—if the client shows up for it— Tapp will know considerably more about Anna Kettering than she does now. I think we should pay another visit to the medium the morning after she meets with Anna."

Calista drummed her fingers on the cushion. "I doubt that Mrs. Kettering will risk revealing that she's married to a killer. But even if she did, where would that leave us?"

Trent watched the street through the window. The day was bright and sunny, a radical change from Florence Tapp's gloom-filled parlor. In spite of the dark mystery twisting around them, at that particular moment he was intensely aware of the simple pleasure of being alone with Calista. He was in no rush to return to her household. Eudora and Andrew would both be waiting with questions. Mr. and Mrs. Sykes would be bustling around inquiring if anyone wanted tea.

In short, there would be no privacy at Cranleigh Hall.

"We have some nice, shiny answers but we need more," he said. "Nestor Kettering is dead. His widow has deliberately disappeared. Now we must identify the hired killer."

"This cannot go on indefinitely," Calista said. She clasped her hands very tightly together. "We are playing a dangerous game with a madman who has become an expert at the same game."

"It's not the same game for him, not this time."

"Why do you say that?"

"He is accustomed to being the hunter," Trent said. "But this time someone is hunting him."

She watched him with her brilliant eyes. "I do not know how to thank you, Trent."

"It's all in the name of research, remember?"

She gave him a wry smile, which was probably all that his weak attempt at humor warranted.

He wondered—not for the first time—what would happen to his relationship with Calista when the killer was no longer a threat. He told himself not to think too far ahead.

"Is there any pressing need for you to return to Cranleigh Hall?" he asked.

"I have no appointments, if that's what you mean. And no particular task. Eudora is probably deep into my files now, creating cross-references and so forth."

"My sister is very good at organizing things."

"It's a talent," Calista said.

There was considerable admiration in her tone.

"I'm sure you're right," Trent said. "But she has employed her gift to a fare-thee-well in my household and I confess there are times when it is difficult to appreciate her abilities. For some time now I have hoped that she would find some other way to satisfy her passion for organization and management."

"You mean you wished that she would marry and turn her attention to running her own household."

"Well, yes, to be quite truthful. I love my sister but I find it oddly exhausting to have every detail of my life so precisely organized."

This time Calista's smile was genuine. "Are you trying to tell me that your life lacks a bit of spontaneity? You surprise me, sir. You are a writer, after all. One would think that you would experience all the surprises a man could wish for in your work."

"I find my writing deeply gratifying. As I told you, it is a drug of sorts. If I go for long periods of time without it I become irritable and restless. But that is only one aspect of my life."

"I do understand," Calista said quickly. "I was merely teasing you a little. I realize that you are concerned for your sister's happiness. As it happens, she is also worried about you."

"If I could only make her see that I am content with my circumstances." Except that he wasn't, he thought. Not now that he had met Calista. That realization was accompanied by a jolt of inspiration. "Among other things, Eudora has organized a truly astonishing conservatory. It is quite beautiful at the moment. Would you care to see it? My address is not at all out of the way and there is nothing like a stroll through an indoor garden to clear one's thoughts."

Calista hesitated, and for a heart-stopping moment he was afraid she would decline the invitation. It was only then that he realized how desperately he wanted to see her in his house, even if it was only for a matter of a few minutes. He was certain that she would look very good under his roof—right at home, in fact.

And then she smiled again and there was a lovely flush on her cheeks. He started to breathe again.

"Yes," she said. "I would enjoy that very much."

57

"YOU WERE RIGHT," Calista said. She stopped halfway down an aisle formed by rows of palms and turned slowly to take in the interior of the conservatory. "Eudora has done wonders in here."

The iron-and-glass room was a meticulously arranged world furnished in a thousand shades of opulent, verdant green. But all Trent wanted to look at was Calista. She riveted his senses. There was a kind of magic about her, he thought. He did not want to look away.

Until the shattering moment a few days ago when he walked into her office and encountered her for the first time, he would have said that he was too old and too set in his ways to experience such a passionate reaction to a woman. The kind of risk she made him want to take was best taken in fiction where no lasting harm would result to either the writer or the reader.

He forced himself to concentrate.

"I can assure you the whole damn place is organized," he said. "Medicinal plants and herbs to your left. Decorative flowers and shrubs to your right. Creepers and vines on the trellises at the rear. Palms and other exotics to mark the aisles."

She smiled. "I see."

"You will note the markers on each plant. All cross-referenced, of course. And then there is the stillroom. It is a wonder of scientific apparatus. My brother helped her furnish it with the latest equipment."

Calista laughed. "You mock your sister, but you will admit that she has great talents."

"Yes, she does. But I fear she is wasting them on me."

Calista walked slowly toward him. "I believe that Mr. Edward Tazewell appreciates her abilities."

"So Eudora tells me. Evidently he considers her brilliant and she admires his engineering mind. She also thinks that he is a devoted and loving father."

"Yes."

"What do you really know about him, Calista?"

"There are limits to how much anyone can know about another person," she said. "But Andrew investigated Tazewell, just as he does all of my clients. Tazewell is a widower who studied engineering and mathematics. His two young daughters adore him, which I take as an indication of his good character as a parent. Like you, sir, he invests in properties and has been quite successful."

"Is that so? Properties?"

"Perhaps you would like to discuss that business with him."

"Huh."

"But Tazewell's real passion is for invention. He holds a number of patents for various sorts of calculating machines."

Trent grunted. "None of which have been successfully manufactured and sold."

"Eudora is convinced that he is a man ahead of his time."

"That is rarely a good position in which to find oneself."

Calista smiled. "Eudora and Edward Tazewell will not starve, if that is what you fear. I know you wish to protect your sister forever but that is not possible. I'm afraid that happiness always comes with risk."

The vibrant atmosphere of the conservatory whispered around him, hot with the raw energy of life. And in the center of the intoxicating whirlpool stood Calista.

"I am discovering that truth with you," he said.

She walked closer to stand in front of him, rose on tiptoe, and brushed her lips across his. "And I, with you."

When she stepped back, her eyes were luminous with feminine invitation.

He caught one of her hands in his. Without a word—he had no words now—he drew her back along the palm-studded aisle, through the arched entrance of the conservatory, and down a hallway.

At the foot of the stairs he stopped and turned to face her.

"The servants?" she whispered.

"I gave them the time off while Eudora and I stayed with you at Cranleigh Square."

She was in his arms before he could ask her if she would go upstairs with him. The answer he wanted was in her kiss. She put her arms around his neck and the gathering storm broke.

He half carried her up the staircase. It was a struggle because he was trying to peel off the layers of clothing that separated him from her warm, silken body. He got the bodice undone by the time they were a third of the way. The entire gown was lost at the halfway point. The petticoats and small bustle followed in short order. He thanked whatever providence was shining down on him at that moment that there was no corset with which to contend.

Calista was not idle. She managed to get him out of his coat early on and flung his tie across the bannister. And then she fumbled with the buttons of his shirt.

When they reached the top of the stairs she was in her chemise and stockings, her shoes having been left behind on one of the steps. His shirt was undone and he, nearly so. A glorious excitement set fire to his blood.

He grabbed her hand and ran down the hall with her. They were both laughing by the time he got to the doorway of his bedroom.

He scooped her up into his arms, carried her to the big four-poster bed, and fell on top of her.

"Like falling into heaven," he said against her throat.

"What?"

"Never mind."

He kissed his way down her soft, sleek body, thrilling to the feel of her beneath him. Her scent was a drug to his senses.

When he had rid himself of his low boots and the last of his clothes he sank himself deep into her welcoming heat.

She wrapped her stocking-clad legs around his waist and held him tight and close; held him as though she would never let go.

Her release shivered through her a short time later. The irresistible currents swept him away and for a moment he thought himself lost. Then he realized that he was anything but lost. He was exactly where he wanted to be; where he needed to be—in Calista's arms.

58

SOMETIME LATER HE became vaguely aware that Calista was no
longer tucked against him. He opened his eyes to the fading afternoon sunlight and found her standing beside the bed.

"I was just about to wake you," she said.

"I wasn't asleep. Just resting."

"The hour grows late." She tied the tapes of her petticoats with quick,
efficient movements. "People will wonder what has happened to us."

"Damn." He groaned and sat up on the side of the bed.

Evidently the passion that had so thoroughly relaxed him had produced the opposite effect on Calista. She appeared astonishingly ener-
getic as she went about the business of getting dressed.

"I rescued our clothes from the stairs," she said.

She tossed his trousers at him. He grabbed them out of the air and
removed his watch from one of the pockets. He groaned again when
he saw the time.

"You're right," he said. "I suppose we must return to Cranleigh Hall
before everyone becomes alarmed."

Not the words he wanted to speak at that particular moment, he thought. But nothing more suitable came to mind. He watched Calista adjust her stockings.

The sight of her elegant leg almost did him in again. But he summoned his willpower and got into his trousers. He picked up his shirt and smiled.

"What is amusing you, sir?" she asked with some suspicion.

"The thought of you collecting our clothes from the stairs."

"Thank heavens there was no one around to witness the scene. Really, it looked quite . . . quite scandalous."

"How odd. It did not feel scandalous."

She narrowed her eyes. "You *are* laughing at me."

"Not at all." He crossed the room, caught hold of her chin, and kissed her lightly. "I was just amused by the thought of our clothes scattered along the staircase. It would certainly have made an impression on the other members of our families."

Calista gave him a repressive glare. "You're right. But that being said, I am very grateful that we are alone."

"So am I." He smiled again. "I was correct about one thing, you know."

"What was that?"

"I knew you would look very good in my house. You look even better in my bed."

He found his tie draped over the newel-post at the bottom of the stairs. He slung it around his collar and knotted the strip of silk while Calista retrieved a missing glove from the bottom step.

When he chanced to catch sight of himself in the mirror above the console in the front hall he noticed that he was grinning.

"Trent?"

He met her eyes in the mirror. She looked unexpectedly serious.

"Mmm?" he said.

"Eudora thinks that the reason you lost your first love—a young woman named Althea—was because of the acid scars. Your sister is convinced that your heart was broken and that is why you have never married."

He turned around and put his hands very firmly on Calista's shoulders. "I love my sister but she has a flair for the melodramatic. Yes, I was very fond of Althea—but not so fond of her that I did not leave England and set out to see the world. And yes, perhaps I would have married her eventually had matters developed in a different way—and if she had been willing to wait, which I very much doubt. But it was not my scars that put an end to our association."

"What, then?"

"When word got out that my inheritance had vanished her parents whisked Althea off to London. She was launched into Society and was very soon engaged to a wealthy young man. As far as I know, they are happy. More to the point, so am I."

At least for now, he thought.

59

E UDORA TOOK A dainty bite of mashed potatoes and gave Trent and Calista a knowing look.

"While the two of you were out interviewing the medium and apparently enjoying some healthy exercise in the excellent weather," she said, "I went through the portion of Kettering's household journal that covers the past six months."

Calista concentrated on forking up a bite of salmon. "How very efficient of you."

"It wasn't like I had anything better to do," Eudora said. She smiled. "You will be pleased to know that the expenditures for the items he purchased from Mrs. Fulton's mourning goods shop are all there, but aside from those, most of the other entries are quite ordinary—the sort of expenses one would expect given Kettering's financial status. Bills to various tailors, and so forth."

Trent ate some of his salmon while he contemplated that information. He discovered he had worked up an appetite that afternoon in his bedroom. In spite of the dangerous situation in which they were all embroiled, he was savoring everything on his plate. Something to do with Calista being seated at the opposite end of the table, he decided. He could easily become accustomed to the sight of her there. He met her eyes and smiled.

She blushed and concentrated on her potatoes.

Andrew was the only one at the table who seemed oblivious to Eudora's innuendos concerning the afternoon's activities. He was busy cleaning his plate with enthusiasm.

Trent focused on Eudora's comments.

"I suppose it would have been too easy to find payments to a hired killer listed amid the bills to his tailor and the fishmonger," he said. "What about expenses that were entered as miscellaneous?"

"Nothing like that," Eudora said. "I can report, however, that although he was decidedly stingy with his servants, Kettering appears to have been rather generous to his wife. Her quarterly allowance is quite handsome."

Calista paused her fork halfway to her mouth, and frowned. "Well, it was her money, after all."

Andrew looked thoughtful. "That small fact needn't have stopped him if he had been inclined to be less than generous. We know that her father's will protected Mrs. Kettering to some extent but that does not mean that she actually controlled the money on a day-to-day basis."

"True," Trent said.

"No, indeed," Eudora said. "My mother's second husband succeeded in going through her inheritance in a matter of a few short months."

Calista gave that some thought. "So, what does Kettering's unexpected generosity to his wife tell us?"

"That he wanted to keep her quiet?" Andrew suggested.

"I agree," Trent said. "For whatever reason—perhaps simply to maintain peace in the household—he was willing to give Anna Kettering a sizeable allowance."

Calista tapped her fork absently against her plate. "Perhaps he had other reasons. It occurs to me that a large quarterly allowance could mask a wide variety of expenses."

"Yes, it could." Eudora put her fork down so quickly it clanged on the delicate china. "What if Kettering used the allowance money to cover the expenses of the hired killer?"

"Huh." Trent pondered that.

Andrew was equally thoughtful. "But why bother to conceal such expenses?"

"Because they could constitute evidence in a court of law," Trent said. "If the hired killer is ever captured and he names his employer to the police, a record of a series of payments from Kettering would be damning."

"So he concealed the killer's fees as his wife's quarterly allowance?" Eudora said. "That is an interesting theory."

"At this point it is only a theory," Trent said.

He watched Eudora help herself to some more vegetables. It was not just his appetite that had increased of late, he realized. She was eating more heartily than usual, too. It was as if both of them had been hibernating for some time and had finally emerged from their dark cave.

It was good to be among friends, he thought. Good for the body and the soul.

"There was only one other expense that caught my eye," Eudora said. "Kettering purchased a house in Frampton Street—Number Six. Evidently it was an investment. But there is no record of any rent having been paid by a tenant and no indication that it was sold."

Trent, Calista, and Andrew looked at her. Eudora smiled somewhat smugly.

"You were saving that bit of information as a surprise?" Trent asked.

"Sorry," she said. "Couldn't resist."

60

Trent and Andrew sat at a table in a small neighborhood pub at the end of Frampton Street and watched the front door of Number Six. They were the only customers. The balding proprietor was happy to chat so long as he got paid for his time.

"Aye, there's a lodger at Number Six," he said. "Never comes in here. You won't see him out and about much during the day. Never had a good look at him. He sometimes leaves his house after dark but he goes out the back and through the alley. Good neighbor, though. Never had any trouble at Number Six."

"Does he ever have visitors?" Trent asked.

"Not as far as I know." The proprietor rocked a little on his heels. "Well, except for one night earlier this week. It was after I closed up for the day. I was upstairs with my wife. We were in bed. Heard a hansom stop in the street. My wife was curious to see which of our neighbors was coming home at such a late hour. She went to the window. When she saw the passenger go up the steps to Number Six, she called me."

"Was the visitor male or female?" Andrew asked.

"Male. Carried a black satchel, the sort of bag a doctor carries. He stayed about half an hour or so. When he left he seemed to be in a bit of a hurry. No surprise, I suppose, given the late hour."

"Do you happen to know why the lodger at Number Six needed a doctor late at night?" Trent inquired.

"None at all." The proprietor rocked back and forth a few more times. "Expect he had an accident or maybe came down with a fever. I'll tell you one thing, though. Doctors don't make calls at two in the morning—not unless they're well paid for their services."

"Thank you," Trent said.

He put some coins on the table. The proprietor made the money disappear and went back behind the bar.

Andrew looked at Trent, excitement sparking in his eyes.

"It's him, isn't it?" he said. "The man who attacked you with the knife. He must have summoned a doctor after you whacked him with the wreath stand."

"It seems likely," Trent said. "With luck we will find out for certain later tonight."

"We're going to follow him if he leaves?"

"You are going to follow him at a very discreet, hopefully very safe distance. We are dealing with a killer, Andrew. Our goal is to acquire evidence we can give to the police. Understood?"

"Yes, sir."

"When I get word from you assuring me that Number Six is empty, I'll go in and have a look around."

Andrew nodded wisely. "Good plan. Just the sort of scheme that Clive Stone would concoct."

"What an amazing coincidence." Trent paused. "Listen closely, Andrew. You must make absolutely certain that the lodger in Number Six doesn't see you. But just in case, be sure that you take your revolver with you."

"Of course. I always carry it these days." Andrew patted the pocket of his overcoat and then turned very serious. "Do you mind if I ask you a question, sir?"

"Depends on the question."

"Do you think there might be a future in this line of work?"

"What line?"

"The private inquiry business."

"You call this a business?"

"I am thinking of becoming a private inquiry agent—like Clive Stone."

Trent exhaled slowly. "Stone is a consultant. And he has a private income from some rather vague investments, if you will recall."

"Properties. He invests in properties."

"What I'm trying to say is that I doubt very much that you'd be able to make a good living at the private inquiry business."

"It occurs to me that if I worked by referral—the same way that Calista does—I might be able to attract clients who are willing to pay well for a guarantee of very discreet service."

"It's one thing to make discreet inquiries into the backgrounds of your sister's clients," Trent said. "It would be quite another to set yourself up as a consultant who is willing to get involved with missing persons or situations such as the one we are in at the moment."

"The thing is, I rather like discovering secrets."

"I suspect that it would be a rather dangerous career path. In my experience everyone has secrets. Some will go to extreme lengths to protect those secrets. If you will recall we have turned up a number of dead people in our own investigation, and at this very moment we are sitting in a pub a few doors down from a man who quite possibly enjoys cutting ladies' throats."

Andrew gave that some brief consideration. "I admit I don't like the fact that Calista is in danger. But when this case is resolved and she is safe, I think I might see about going into the private inquiry line. It's not like I haven't had some experience."

Clearly the prospect of danger was not going to be a deterrent. Trent considered his options. There were not a lot of them.

"I doubt if your sister would approve of your career plans," he ventured.

"I'm sure I can convince her that I would be successful. I told you, I will be very careful when it comes to taking on clients."

"Andrew, your future is none of my affair; however, I feel an obligation to advise you. I am a few years older than you and I've had some experience. Believe me when I tell you that—"

"Enough about my future. What about your future with Calista? I think it is time I inquired into your plans."

Trent looked at him. "What?"

"It's obvious that the two of you are involved in a romantic relationship, sir. I'm all the family that Calista has. It is my duty to see to her best interests." Andrew squared his shoulders and elevated his chin. "I want to know your intentions."

There was a little steel in his voice and more in his eyes.

"My intentions," Trent repeated.

"Yes."

"An excellent question," Trent said. "All I can tell you at the moment is that my intentions will depend entirely on Calista's intentions."

Andrew's brows scrunched together. "What the devil is that supposed to mean?"

Trent got to his feet. "It means that, although I respect your desire to protect your sister, in the end she will make her own decisions. Meanwhile, we must tend to the matter at hand. I'm going to leave you here to keep an eye on Number Six. Send word immediately if our suspect leaves the house. That will be my cue to commit another act of burglary."

61

"M R. TAZEWELL EXPRESSED an interest in a tour of my conservatory," Eudora said. "He said he may be able to offer some advice on the heating system. I have been having problems with it lately. The pipes are old and so is the furnace."

Calista sipped some tea and glanced at the clock. She and Eudora were forcing themselves to make casual conversation. Neither of them wanted to be alone and neither of them wanted to talk about their fears.

Andrew had been gone all afternoon and evening. He had sent a street urchin to the back door of Cranleigh Hall a short time ago with a message informing Trent that the knifeman had left Number Six. Andrew was following him.

Trent had immediately left the mansion with a lock pick in his pocket.

"What about Mr. Tazewell's two daughters?" Calista asked.

"As I told you, Edward wants them to have a modern education,"

Eudora said. "He seems to think that I might be a good influence on the girls. It has occurred to me that I might make a very good teacher. In fact, I am considering the possibility of opening a small day school for girls. What do you think?"

Calista smiled. "I think it is a brilliant idea."

62

THE HANSOM CARRYING the knifeman halted at the far end of a quiet street. The passenger descended to the pavement and almost immediately faded into the shadows.

Andrew opened the trapdoor in the roof of his cab.

"Driver, what street is this?" he asked.

"Blanchford Street, sir."

Alarm jolted through Andrew. He had heard the name somewhere. Then it struck him. Florence Tapp, the medium, lived in Blanchford Street. It was possible that the knifeman planned to attend a séance but it seemed unlikely. It was Friday night, the evening of the appointment that Anna Kettering had scheduled with the medium—the appointment that, in her haste to disappear, she had neglected to cancel.

"Do you know of a medium in this street?" he asked.

"Aye, sir. Number Twelve. But she usually holds séances on Wednesday evenings, not Fridays."

The knifeman would have no way of knowing that Anna Kettering did not intend to keep her appointment. Perhaps he had come here to murder her. If Mrs. Kettering died in Blanchford Street the finger of blame would point to the medium.

There was no way to know why the knifeman might want to murder Anna Kettering, but if he was mentally unbalanced, as everyone seemed to believe, no logical reason was required. There was also no predicting what he would do when he discovered that his target had not arrived for her appointment.

"I understand the medium sometimes books private appointments on other evenings," Andrew said to the driver.

"Couldn't say, sir."

"I'll be back in a few minutes. Wait for me."

"Aye, sir."

Andrew handed some money to the driver and got out of the cab.

The other hansom, now empty, moved off down the street. Evidently the killer had not instructed his driver to wait. There was no way to know what that indicated but it seemed ominous. The knifeman did not want any potential witnesses.

Andrew reached into the pocket of his coat and closed his fingers around the handle of the revolver.

There was no sign of the knifeman on the street but when Andrew got close to Number Twelve a chill shot down his spine. His pulse, already beating quickly, began to pound as he realized what had happened.

The killer had climbed over the railing that surrounded the front area of the house and descended the steps to the kitchen entrance.

The door stood partially open. It squeaked on its hinges.

The killer was already inside.

Andrew clambered quickly over the wrought-iron railing, trying hard not to make any noise, and went down the steps. Holding the revolver in his right hand, he gently pushed the kitchen door. It swung open a little farther.

No one leaped out at him.

He moved cautiously into the darkened kitchen. His nerves were stretched to the limit. He could feel a cold sweat dripping down his sides.

There was just enough light from the low-burning wall sconce to allow him to make out the large kitchen table in the middle of the room and the narrow staircase that led up to the ground floor.

He stood still, listening intently. Somewhere overhead a floorboard squeaked. The killer was prowling through the house. By now he must have realized that Anna Kettering was not there, yet he was still on the premises.

Comprehension slammed through Andrew.

The knifeman had not come for Anna Kettering. He was there to murder the medium.

Unable to think of anything else to do, Andrew went up the stairs into the hall, shouting at the top of his lungs.

"Miss Tapp, there's a killer in the house. Lock your door. *Lock your door.*"

There was a beat of silence overhead and then a woman's scream rent the night. Somewhere a door slammed. Heavy footsteps pounded above.

Andrew paused at the top of the kitchen stairs. The wall sconces illuminated the narrow corridor that led to the front hall and the staircase to the floor above.

The knifeman came down the stairs with frightening speed, spun around at the bottom, and charged toward Andrew. The blade of the knife glinted faintly in the low light.

Andrew pulled the trigger. There was a great roar and a flash of light. The heavy gun kicked up violently in his hand.

He knew at once he had missed but the effect on the knifeman was dramatic. The killer halted abruptly, evidently shocked. Andrew braced himself for another shot. He could not afford to miss a second time. If he did, all would be lost.

But the knifeman whirled around and ran for the front door. He got it open and disappeared out into the street.

Andrew lurched forward, rushed down the hall, and moved cautiously out onto the front step. He was in time to see the killer fleeing toward the single hansom left in the street.

The hansom driver, evidently concluding that he would be better off trolling for fares in another neighborhood, had already whipped his horse into a panicked gallop. The vehicle raced away from the scene.

A constable appeared, blowing mightily on his whistle. Bedroom windows were thrown open up and down Blanchford Street. Overhead, Florence Tapp leaned out of her window and continued to scream.

Andrew scanned the street. There was no sign of the man with the knife.

63

Trent opened the alley gate, crossed the barren patch of ground that had been intended to serve as a garden, and let himself into the killer's house by way of the kitchen door.

He stopped just inside the hall and held aloft the shielded lantern he had brought with him.

There was no way to know how much time he had, so he moved quickly. The kitchen yielded a wedge of cheese and a partially eaten loaf of bread. With the exception of a kettle, there were no cooking utensils. Evidently the killer purchased most of his meals from street vendors.

He went upstairs and made a sweep of the three small bedrooms. They were all empty of furniture save one. It contained a pallet that was clearly serving as a bed.

The wardrobe, however, was surprisingly well stocked with clean, neatly folded shirts and undergarments. There were also expensively tailored trousers and a coat. All of the clothing was of excellent quality.

What sort of man lived like a monk in a nearly empty house while going about his murderous business in fashionable clothes? Trent wondered.

He was about to leave the bedroom when he noticed that the foot of the neatly made pallet was slightly elevated, as though someone had tucked an object underneath it.

He went back across the room, raised the end of the pallet, and saw a small box and a little leather-bound book. He removed the lid from the box and saw three jet-and-crystal locket rings. There was a twist of hair inside each.

The small book looked like a diary.

He put both the box of rings and the diary into the pocket of his coat.

He left the bedroom and went back downstairs. He did not expect to find anything of note in the parlor. According to the proprietor of the pub at the end of the street, the knifeman never had visitors, aside from the doctor who had called late one night.

When he arrived in the doorway he saw that he was only partly correct—there were no furnishings. There was, however, what appeared to be a small altar in one corner.

An unlit candle was positioned on top of the altar. But it was the framed photograph of an ethereally beautiful lady that filled Trent with a gut-wrenching fear.

He had got it wrong right from the start and now it might be too late.

He ran for the door.

64

"THE TEA HAS grown cold," Calista said. She glanced at the clock. "It looks like we will be up awhile longer."

It was well past midnight and there had been no word from Trent or Andrew. She and Eudora were both doing their best to conceal their growing anxiety from each other. But really, she thought, one could only discuss efficient filing techniques and cross-referencing for so long.

"I'll ask Mrs. Sykes to bring us another pot," she said. She rose and tugged on the bellpull. "It will give her something to do. She and Mr. Sykes are as anxious as we are."

"What can possibly be detaining Trent and Andrew?" Eudora said.

Calista looked at the coffin bell sitting on the desk. The steel chain attached to it was neatly, tightly coiled. Like a snake, she thought.

"I have been telling myself that the traffic may have made it difficult to find cabs," she said.

Eudora gave her a worried look. "But you don't believe that, do you?"

"No." Calista made herself look away from the coffin bell. "I'm quite terrified."

"So am I," Eudora said. "We should never have let them go through with their dangerous plans."

"I do not think we could have stopped them."

"No, I suppose not," Eudora said. "They are both quite stubborn, aren't they?"

"I suppose they would say the same about us."

"Yes."

Eudora rose from her chair and went to the hearth. Picking up a brass poker, she prodded the dying fire.

Calista moved to stand beside her. She put her hand on Eudora's shoulder.

"They will find something that will constitute evidence against the killer," she said, trying desperately to convince herself. "Perhaps the reason they have been delayed is because they are even now explaining the situation to the police."

"Perhaps." Eudora hesitated. "I wonder what Mr. Tazewell will say when I tell him about this strange adventure. I expect he will be quite shocked. Appalled or even repelled, perhaps."

"Surprised, no doubt, but not appalled or repelled," Calista said.

"Let us be honest, Calista. We both know that very few gentlemen would approve of a lady who becomes embroiled in an investigation involving murder. Edward Tazewell will likely think me a bad influence on his two little girls."

"You said that he was very keen on providing a modern education for his daughters."

Eudora managed a weak laugh. "I doubt that he had this sort of an education in mind."

"When this is finished there will be no need to tell him what we have been about. You have a right to your secrets, Eudora."

"That is true, but I do not want to keep secrets from the man I marry. I want a true partner, one who will accept me for who I am."

"I understand."

"I know you do."

The two of them stood in silence for a time.

"I meet a great many people in my profession," Calista said after a while, "and there are some I call friends, but in truth they are acquaintances. You and Trent are in a different category. I trust both of you in ways that I have never been able to trust anyone except Andrew in a very long time."

"I, too, value our friendship, Calista. But I think that what you feel for my brother is something more. Love, perhaps?"

"Yes, but I'm not at all certain that is what he feels for me."

"How can you doubt it?"

"I do not wish to bring up the unhappiness of your past," Calista said, "but surely you are aware that for years Trent has blamed himself for failing to save your mother from the horrid man she married and for very nearly failing to save you and Harry."

Eudora closed her eyes. "I have been afraid of that. We never talked about it, but somehow I knew."

"And you blame yourself because you think you are the reason that Trent was scarred."

"It's all very complicated, isn't it?"

"The three of you have carried the heavy burden of guilt for some time now. Perhaps you should all set it down and move on with your lives."

Eudora opened her eyes. "You fear that Trent has developed warm emotions for you because he sees you as a lady to be rescued. He blames himself for what happened in the past and he is desperate not to fail a second time."

"Yes, that is why I cannot be certain of his true feelings for me.

Like you, I want to know that I am loved for myself, not because Trent sees me as a lady to be saved."

"When it comes to love, you and I both demand a great deal."

Calista looked down into the fire. "That is probably the reason why neither of us has ever married."

"Perhaps."

"Have you ever stopped to think that the reasons your brother never married might be similar to our own?"

Startled, Eudora considered that while she set the poker back in the brass stand. "I see what you mean. I have never considered that men might have their dreams, just as women do. One thinks of them as being driven by more elemental emotions: physical desire, practicality, the wish to secure an inheritance—those sorts of things."

"All of which have their place, I'm sure. But I think that Trent is also very much a romantic at heart."

"An interesting thought." Eudora smiled. "Perhaps that explains Clive Stone's great interest in Wilhelmina Preston."

"We can speculate all we like. Trent is the only one who knows how he truly feels." Calista straightened her shoulders. "Speaking for myself, I feel the need for some more tea. As there has been no sign of Mrs. Sykes, I think we can deduce that she and Mr. Sykes did go to bed, after all. I'll go to the kitchen and put the kettle on."

"I'll come with you. I do not want to be alone tonight."

"Nor do I."

Eudora paused at the end table and glanced at the Kettering journal of financial accounts. "Trent was right about one thing. It's amazing how much one can learn about a person from a record of his personal expenditures. I must say, Kettering did not stint when it came to his tailors."

"Or memento mori items," Calista said grimly. "He must have been as mad as that killer he hired. It is unnerving to know that he was able to conceal his true nature so well."

"I suppose that is why evil is so dangerous. It can so easily be masked behind an attractive façade." Eudora moved toward the door. "I must say, Kettering kept excellent accounts, though, and in a very neat hand."

A shiver of uncertainty iced Calista's neck. She was at the door, about to open it and go out into the hall. Instead, she paused and glanced back at the Kettering journal.

Her intuition whispered to her.

"Did you say that Nestor Kettering had a very neat hand?" she asked.

"Yes. Why do you ask?"

Calista turned away from the door and went to the end table. She stared at the journal for a few seconds before she picked it up.

For the first time, she opened it and studied the pages of neatly penned entries.

"Because this is not how I remember his handwriting," she said quietly.

"What?"

Calista carried the journal to the desk and set it down. She opened a drawer with shaking fingers.

"What are you looking for?" Eudora asked.

"Back at the start of this affair, Nestor sent me two bouquets of flowers before he made the appointment to meet with me."

"He was trying to woo you. What of it?"

"I instructed Mrs. Sykes to toss the flowers into the rubbish but I kept one of the cards."

"Why?"

"Mostly because it infuriated me. I wanted a reminder that I could never again trust him."

"As if you needed such a reminder," Eudora said. "But why do you want to see the card now?"

"Because I have just had a very odd thought."

She sat down at her desk and riffled through her personal correspondence until she found the elegant white card that had accompanied the second bouquet of flowers.

She removed it from the file and placed it on the desk. Then she
opened the journal of household accounts that Trent had brought out
of the Kettering residence.

Another jolt of awareness nearly shattered her nerves. She stared
at the card and then at the last page of the journal of accounts.

"Dear heaven," she whispered.

Eudora leaned over the desk and read the card aloud.

> *I have known only loneliness since we parted. Please tell me*
> *that you have some feelings for me. Together we shall find*
> *true happiness on the metaphysical plane.*

> *Yours,*
> *N. Kettering*

For a moment Eudora simply stared at the short note. Then she,
too, studied the last page of the journal.

Calista watched her, hardly daring to speak in case she was wrong
in her conclusion.

But when Eudora looked up there was shocked comprehension in
her eyes.

"The handwriting does not match," she whispered. "The card and
the journal were written by two different people."

"Nestor Kettering wrote the note that accompanied the bouquet.
But he is not the one who kept the journal of accounts."

"A secretary, perhaps? Many wealthy families employ one."

"Andrew never mentioned a secretary. I'm sure he would have
done so."

Eudora put a hand to her throat. "We've been looking at this affair from the wrong perspective all along."

"Yes." Calista leaped to her feet, rounded the desk, hoisted her skirts, and ran for the door. "Come, we must wake Mr. and Mrs. Sykes."

Eudora hurried after her. "What are we going to do? Send for the police?"

"The first order of business is to get a message to Trent, assuming he is still at the knifeman's house. There is no telling where Andrew is at this hour. No way to warn him."

"Surely Andrew is safe," Eudora said. "Trent gave him stern instructions not to let the killer see him."

"I pray my brother has the good sense to follow those instructions," Calista said. "I just hope we are not too late."

She rushed down the hall to the kitchen and swept into the room. She came to a halt so abruptly that Eudora nearly collided with her.

"Sorry," Eudora said, stepping back quickly.

But Calista did not respond. She stood, transfixed with shock, at the sight of the ghastly tableau assembled around the kitchen table.

Mr. Sykes was crumpled on the floor, one hand flung out to the side as if he had made a desperate effort to ward off a blow. An overturned coffee cup was on the floor next to his hand. It was impossible to tell if he was dead or alive.

Mrs. Sykes was slumped over the table. She did not move.

Anna Kettering stood over her, a large meat cleaver in her elegantly gloved hand. The sharp edge of the blade was poised above Mrs. Sykes's neck.

"There you are," Anna said in the bright, charming tones of a lady welcoming guests to a garden party. "When I heard the service bell ring a short time ago, I thought you might eventually come to the kitchen to see what was keeping your housekeeper and butler. Really, one cannot rely on anyone in service these days, can one?"

65

"I T WAS YOU all along, wasn't it?" Calista said.

A strange, eerie sense of detachment settled on her. She was amazed by her own unnaturally calm voice. But she knew she needed to maintain that cool, controlled edge because she and Eudora were dealing with a madwoman. The smallest spark might ignite Anna's fevered brain.

"Yes, of course it was me," Anna said.

"You were the one who hunted all of us—the three governesses and me. How many other women did you torment with your little game?"

"There were only the four of you this past year," Anna said. Her voice abruptly tightened with rage. *"And it wasn't a game.* I punished my husband's whores because they seduced him and turned him away from me. He loved me back at the start, you see. He thought I was beautiful. He *wanted* me. But after our honeymoon he took up with that first governess."

"Elizabeth Dunsforth," Eudora said.

"She was nothing," Anna said. *"Nothing.* Just a governess. But she made Nestor desire her. I had to teach her a lesson."

313

"You sent her the memento mori gifts from Mrs. Fulton's shop and when you finished terrifying her you sent someone to murder her," Calista said. "Then you paid for a very fine safety coffin."

Anna snickered. "I knew she would never ring the bell. None of them ever rang the bell. It was a little joke, you see."

"You controlled the household accounts," Eudora said. "You made all of the purchases from Mrs. Fulton's shop."

"The money is mine." Anna got very fierce for a moment. "Papa left it to me. But as it happens, Nestor was content to let me deal with the household accounts. He didn't want to be bothered with the details of managing a fortune. As long as he had everything he wanted, he was happy."

"So you paid all his bills," Calista said. "And you began to realize that some of the money you gave Nestor was being spent on other women."

"Really, I don't know how he expected to hide that from me. But that was the thing, you see. He didn't even care enough about my feelings to conceal his affairs. He flaunted them."

"I noticed that you gave yourself a rather generous allowance," Eudora said.

Anna frowned. "How did you know about that? Well, I don't suppose it matters. Yes, I gave myself an allowance."

"Why not just pay your own bills?" Eudora asked. "You just said that Nestor never questioned the household accounts."

Anna giggled. "I was afraid that if he ever did examine the records he would become suspicious of some of my expenses. I did not want to have to explain them so I simply paid them out of my allowance."

"But not the house in Frampton Street," Calista said. "You bought that outright, didn't you?"

Anna looked startled. "You know about that, too? Yes, the house was a major purchase. I couldn't cover it out of my allowance. But Nestor never even noticed. He was obsessed with his other women."

"He was *obsessed* with them?" Calista repeated.

"Yes, I'm afraid Nestor was cursed with an obsessive personality. I tried to cure him."

"By destroying the objects of his obsessions," Eudora said, "the other women."

Anna gave her an approving smile. "Precisely. Sooner or later Nestor always tired of his whores—usually sooner. When he was done with them I sent them the memento mori gifts. They thought the presents were coming from Nestor, you see. They became quite unnerved."

"And finally you sent your hired killer to murder each of the women," Calista said. "But I rejected Nestor. Why hunt me?"

*"Because he wanted you before he married me,"* Anna said, the rage seething again in her voice. "And then, a few weeks ago, he wanted you *again*. He sent you *flowers*—flowers purchased with my money. He never wanted me the way he wanted you. All he cared about was my inheritance."

The atmosphere in the kitchen was charged with an ominous tension. Calista struggled to find some means of distracting Anna. She knew Eudora was also searching for a way to buy some time—time for Trent and Andrew to return.

"You seem to know a great deal about obsessions and how to cure them," Calista said. "How did that come about?"

"I have studied the science of psychology since I was a girl of twelve, Miss Langley. Indeed, I am an expert."

"An unusual subject for a lady," Eudora said.

"I had an excellent teacher." Anna smiled. "Dr. Morris Ashwell."

"Who is he?" Calista asked.

"The doctor who tried to cure me of my obsession with death. I tried to explain to dear Papa that the emotions associated with the great transition from this world to the next are the strongest of all the passions. Papa did not understand. When I turned thirteen he sent me to Dr. Ashwell."

"Evidently Ashwell was unable to rid you of your fixation," Calista said.

"Quite the opposite." Anna chuckled. "He became obsessed with me, you see. Amusing when you think about it—the doctor developing a great passion for his patient. I was just thirteen at the time but quite pretty, if I do say so."

"How old was Dr. Ashwell?" Eudora asked.

Anna grimaced. "Old enough to be my grandfather. Not at all pleasant to look upon, I must say. I hated the feel of his beard and his thick body disgusted me."

Eudora took a sharp, shocked breath.

Calista was stunned. "He assaulted you? You were just a girl."

Anna gave her a serene smile. "No need to feel sorry for me, Miss Langley. I assure you, I soon realized that his obsession with me gave me a great deal of power over him. And in the end I used that power to escape."

"From where?" Eudora said.

"Brightstone Manor," Anna said impatiently. "I hated that place. I was locked up every night. We all were."

"Dr. Ashwell ran a private asylum," Calista said, comprehending at last. "Your father had you committed."

*"For nearly three years,"* Anna shrieked. "That bastard, Ashwell, conducted experiments on us. He told Papa that it was necessary to keep me in Brightstone Manor because I was a danger to myself and others. But every night Ashwell came to my room. Every night I pretended that I was dead. I got rather good at it."

"How did you escape?" Eudora asked.

An artificial calm settled on Anna. She smiled her angelic smile. "My brave knight in shining armor slew the monster and rescued me. And then we burned Brightstone Manor to the ground."

"The man with the knife who tried to murder Mr. Hastings and me that night in Mrs. Fulton's coffin display room," Calista said. "He's your knight, isn't he?"

"Oliver is devoted to me. He is obsessed with me also, but not like Ashwell. Oliver lives a strict, celibate life. He is purifying himself by serving his lady."

"You," Calista said.

"Yes. I saved him. He had been locked away in Dr. Ashwell's asylum for years. Oliver was born a gentleman and educated as one but his family signed commitment papers when he was seventeen years old."

"Given his habit of slitting throats, that is not terribly surprising," Calista said. "So he murdered Dr. Ashwell for you, the pair of you escaped, and you burned down the asylum."

"Yes."

"What about the other inmates in the asylum?" Eudora ventured. "There must have been some besides you and Oliver."

"A dozen, perhaps. I've forgotten. Why?"

"You didn't rescue the other inmates, did you?" Calista asked. "You left them to die in the inferno."

"They were all quite mad. I'm sure their families were relieved not to have to pay Ashwell's fees any longer."

"You shot Nestor, didn't you?" Calista said.

"Yes. I waited for him in his dressing room. He never saw me until I put the gun to his head. And by then it was too late, of course."

"And then you had Oliver carry his body into that locked chamber," Eudora concluded.

"I hadn't planned to get rid of Nestor that evening," Anna said. "I wanted a more suitable death for him. But I was forced to take action."

"What constitutes a more suitable death?" Calista asked.

"I wanted him to die much more slowly." Anna's eyes heated with a dangerous fire. "I wanted to watch Oliver slit Nestor's throat. I wanted to see the blood flow slowly but surely from the wound. I wanted Nestor to know that I was watching him die. But I had just discovered that he intended to try to have me committed again. I had to move quickly."

"Having you committed would have violated the terms of your father's will," Eudora said.

"Nestor conspired with his friend Dolan Birch. They were going to make it appear that I had gone away for an extended stay in the country and that I had put Nestor in charge of my financial affairs. No one would have questioned the papers. Everyone is accustomed to the notion of the husband dealing with such matters."

"They planned to send you to an asylum that disguises itself as a hotel and spa outside a village named Seacliff," Calista said.

"You know everything, don't you? I don't understand, but I suppose it doesn't matter now."

"How did you discover that Nestor was conspiring to have you locked up again?" Eudora asked.

"That was a matter of sheer luck," Anna said. She shuddered. The blade of the meat cleaver dipped lower toward Mrs. Sykes's neck. "Oliver followed Nestor everywhere, but Nestor never paid any attention to him. Recently Oliver overheard Nestor and Birch discussing the plan to get rid of me. They were quarreling. Evidently Nestor had not yet fulfilled his part of the bargain. It seemed he still owed Birch."

"What did he owe him?" Calista asked. But she was quite certain she knew the answer.

Anna laughed. "Nestor claimed that he could deliver access to your client files to Birch. Amusing, isn't it? Just think, if it hadn't been for you, I might have been locked away in another asylum by now."

"Why did your father marry you off to a fortune hunter?" Calista asked.

"I *chose* Nestor." Anna's voice rose again, this time on a thin, fragile note. "I met him while he was visiting at a nearby country estate. There was a party and all of the local gentry were invited. Nestor danced with me and I thought him the handsomest man in the world. I fell in love with him that night. He told me that he loved me and I believed him."

"He lied to you."

"At the start he truly did love me," Anna insisted. "He was quite passionate. But partway through our honeymoon he developed a profound disgust for my person. He said that making love to me was like making love to a corpse. I didn't understand. Dr. Ashwell liked it when I pretended to be dead."

"Why have you come here tonight?" Calista asked. "You are safe now. Nestor can no longer hurt you. What's more, you have full control of your money."

"I came here to punish you, just as I did his other whores," Anna said. "You were the one he wanted most of all."

"I told you, I rejected him," Calista said. "I did nothing to encourage him."

"That doesn't change anything," Anna wailed. "He didn't want me but he desired you, a woman who is operating a business that is only one step above a brothel."

It would take very little now to shatter whatever weak forces were holding Anna together.

"You say you came here to punish me," Calista said. She took a step forward, one hand outstretched. "I understand. But please leave my housekeeper and my butler out of this. They had nothing to do with any of it."

"Stop or I'll kill the housekeeper right now," Anna warned.

Calista stopped but Anna was trembling with rage.

319

"I am curious about why you waited so long to murder Nestor," Eudora said in a conversational tone. "Why wait until you found out he was planning to have you committed?"

"Until that point I was sure that if I could rid Nestor of his obsessions he would realize how beautiful I am. I was sure he would come to love me again. But when I discovered his plans I had to face reality."

That last comment would have been almost amusing in other circumstances, Calista thought. It was highly unlikely that Anna had ever grasped the concept of reality in her life.

"Before you do whatever you intend to do this evening, I have a message for you from your father," Calista said.

Anna stared at her. "Papa? But that's impossible. Papa is dead."

"He is in the spirit world. Florence Tapp, the medium, was able to summon him so that I could speak to him."

"You're lying. Florence Tapp is a fraud. I sent Oliver to her house to kill her because she tried to deceive me."

"She was not a fraud," Calista said. "I saw your father. He was wearing a dark suit, a white shirt with a turndown collar, and a necktie."

Anna was transfixed by that information. "I gave him a necktie for his last birthday."

"He said that he wears it every day because it makes him think of you."

"You must be lying," Anna said. But she was uncertain now. "Why would he appear to you but not to me?"

"He said that he wanted you to see him but that your troubled state of mind made it difficult. He appeared to me because he wanted me to give you a message."

"What message?"

Calista took a chance. "He said to tell you that he loved you."

"Now I know for certain that you're lying. Papa never really loved me. He only pretended to love me. In truth he was frightened of me. That is why he sent me to Dr. Ashwell."

The claim that her father had loved her had been a serious misstep, Calista thought. Frantically she tried to recover.

"No, he said you did not understand," she said gently. "He was frightened *for* you. He was afraid of what would happen to you if you were not cured of your obsession. But you were his daughter. Of course he loved you. Ask him yourself."

"What are you talking about?"

"He's here, right behind you in the pantry doorway. He is trying to reach you through the veil. His hand is stretching out to touch you."

"Yes," Eudora said quickly. "I can see him, too. He is trying so hard to reach you. He is just inside the pantry."

Anna turned quickly to face the open door of the pantry. "Papa? Are you really here? I have missed you so. Did you really love me?"

It was now or never, Calista thought. She looked at Eudora and motioned toward the long wooden table. Understanding sparked in Eudora's eyes.

They rushed toward the table. Each grabbed an end. Together they managed to overturn it. There was a thundering crash as it fell on its side.

The unconscious Mrs. Sykes slipped off her chair and toppled to the floor, landing next to her husband.

Anna swung back around, confusion and then fury coloring her pretty face. She raised the meat cleaver but her target was now on the floor. She started to bend down to slash Mrs. Sykes's throat.

"No," Calista shouted.

She grabbed a heavy mixing bowl and hurled it at Anna, who reflexively put up a hand and tried to dodge.

The bowl caught her on the shoulder and smashed on the floor.

Eudora seized plates one by one from a sideboard and hurled them at Anna.

Calista grabbed a frying pan off a wall hook and sent it sailing across the overturned table.

Faced with a barrage of crockery, cookware, spice containers, tins of cocoa powder and oatmeal, Anna screamed and retreated through the nearest doorway—the entrance to the pantry. Her muffled footsteps could be heard as she rushed up the back stairs to the next floor.

Calista ran forward and slammed the stairwell door shut. She grabbed a wooden kitchen chair and wedged it under the knob.

"We can't chase her through the house," Eudora said, breathless from the frantic battle. "It's too big. She could wait for us behind any door or inside one of the rooms, and what do we do if we catch her? She's still got that damned cleaver."

Calista tried to catch her breath. Her heart was pounding. "We have to get out of here and summon a constable but I'm afraid to leave Mr. and Mrs. Sykes alone. What if that madwoman comes down the main staircase and returns to the kitchen?"

"We'll have to drag them outside into the gardens and then summon a constable."

"Mrs. Sykes first." Calista reached down and grasped one of the housekeeper's wrists. "We'll get her outside and then we'll come back for Mr. Sykes."

"Right." Eudora grabbed Mrs. Sykes's other wrist in both hands.

The housekeeper was not a large woman but in her unconscious state she was surprisingly heavy. Once they maneuvered her out into the uncarpeted hall, however, it proved easier to slide her across the polished floorboards.

They were almost to the library door with their burden when the sound of crashing glass and splintering wood startled them into dropping Mrs. Sykes's wrists.

"The library," Calista said. "Someone's in there."

Oliver loomed in the doorway. The blade gleamed in his hand. For a split second he paused to take in the scene in the hallway.

"Run," Calista shouted to Eudora. "The garden door."

But she knew that, hampered by their skirts and petticoats, neither of them could hope to outrun the big man. Only one of them stood a chance. She moved to step in front of the man with the knife.

"Oliver, listen to me. Anna needs you," she said. "Can't you hear her? Your lady is calling to you. Hurry. You must go to her. She is upstairs. Listen."

At that moment there came another thud and a scream of rage from the floor above.

Oliver looked up toward the ceiling, dazed.

"My lady," he whispered.

Then he switched his burning gaze back to Calista. He raised the knife for a killing strike. She tried to retreat but she stumbled over Mrs. Sykes's prone body and went down.

Eudora screamed and tried to haul Calista out of reach.

Oliver moved out of the doorway and into the hall.

Calista saw an object fly out of the library. Light gleamed on metal. There came a sickening crunch as the missile struck Oliver's skull.

A nightmarish bell tolled, the dark notes echoing throughout the house.

Fresh blood sprayed from Oliver's bandaged head, splashing on Calista's skirts.

Oliver staggered under the force of the blow. He fell to his knees in front of Calista, still clutching the knife.

"My lady," he whispered.

She caught a glimpse of the madness in his eyes, and then Eudora helped her scramble out of the way.

Oliver pitched forward and fell, facedown. The floorboards shuddered beneath the impact. His hand opened, releasing the blade.

The library doorway darkened. Calista looked up.

"Trent," she whispered.

"Thank heavens," Eudora said.

"We have to get out of here." Trent kicked the knife out of the way and hauled Calista to her feet. "Where is Mr. Sykes?"

"Unconscious in the kitchen," Calista said. "I think he's still alive."

"I'll get him." He went swiftly down the hall. "You two take Mrs. Sykes. Go out the front door. There's a constable on his way here."

"Anna Kettering is still in the house," Eudora called after him.

"I know." Trent disappeared into the kitchen. He reappeared a moment later with Sykes draped across his shoulders. "She set fire to the place. Can't you smell the smoke?"

66

H E WAS NOT too late.
A crashing tide of relief swept through Trent. He followed
Calista and Eudora through the front door and out into the night.

It had been a very near thing but Calista and Eudora were both
unharmed. In that moment that was all that mattered.

Somewhere in the distance a fire bell clanged. The constable arrived,
breathing hard, just as Calista and Eudora got Mrs. Sykes onto the
front steps.

"'Ere, I'll take her," the young man said.

He picked up Mrs. Sykes and carried her down the steps, into the
garden.

"Get away from the house," Trent said.

Calista and Eudora hoisted their skirts and hurried through the
darkened gardens. He followed and set Sykes down on the grass. The
constable put Mrs. Sykes next to her husband and looked at Trent.

"You said something about a madwoman and a man with a knife, sir?"

"They're both inside," he said. "I'm quite sure the man with the knife is in no condition to escape. But the woman may flee through the back entrance. If she escapes, there's no telling—"

A shrill, anguished scream—rage and grief and madness blended into a tormented, despairing cry—rose above the scene. Trent looked up. So did Calista and Eudora and the constable.

Flames poured out of the upstairs windows.

Anna appeared on one of the small, ornamental balconies. Her gown was ablaze.

She seemed to hover there for a few seconds. Trent was almost certain that she was glorying in the destruction she had created.

And then she jumped.

Her fiery skirts fluttered around her as she fell to earth, a desperate, dying moth in flames.

"Dear heaven," Calista whispered.

She turned away from the firelit spectacle. Trent wrapped one arm around her and pulled her close.

"Andrew?" she asked, sounding as if she were skating on the thin ice of panic.

"I don't know," Trent said.

"Do you think—?" She could not finish the question.

He steeled himself for the honest answer.

"I don't know," he said again.

A hansom turned into the long drive. The horse was in full gallop.

"There he is," Eudora said.

The hansom slowed to a halt and Andrew leaped out of the cab.

"Calista?" He came to a halt. "Are you all right?"

"I am now," she said. "Everyone is all right."

"Can't say the same for your lovely house," Eudora said. "I'm afraid it will be gone by morning."

Andrew exhaled deeply and turned to watch the blaze. "You know, I never did like the place."

"Neither did I," Calista admitted. "However, I would remind you that it is—was—our home. Everything we possess is inside that damned house. Not to mention my business. Oh, heavens, my files."

"You need not worry," Trent said. He tightened his arm around her. "You have friends."

Eudora moved closer to Calista. "My brother is right."

Calista smiled. In the fiery light Trent could see tears glittering on her cheeks.

"Yes," she said. "We have friends. That is all we need."

67

THE FOLLOWING AFTERNOON they gathered for tea at the house Trent and Eudora shared. Harry and Rebecca Hastings joined them. Eudora's housekeeper served tea with professional skill and efficiency.

Mr. and Mrs. Sykes were at the home of a nephew, recovering from the drugged coffee. Calista and Trent had called on them earlier in the day. They were talking about retiring to the village where their son and his wife lived.

Calista looked around the small group assembled in Trent's library, aware that, in spite of the nearly disastrous night, she was experiencing an unfamiliar sense of optimism.

They were all seated, except for Trent, who was propped against his desk, arms folded across his chest, and Andrew, who was inspecting the tray of sandwiches and tea cakes.

"You saved Florence Tapp," Trent said. He acknowledged Andrew with an approving man-to-man look. "The medium would be dead if not for your quick action."

Harry nodded. "Excellent work."

Calista could have sworn that Andrew blushed. He was obviously pleased by the praise. He inserted a small sandwich into his mouth and brushed crumbs from his hands.

"I don't mind telling you, I've never been so terrified in my life," he said around the mouthful of sandwich. He managed to swallow quickly. "I missed my shot, you see. Wasn't sure I'd get a second chance. I was relieved at first when the villain ran off but then I started to worry about where he would go and what he would do next. I headed for his address, fearing that you were still inside, sir. When I saw that you were gone, I didn't know what to think but at least there was no blood."

"Always a good sign," Trent said.

"Yes, but then I thought about Calista and Eudora and got a terrible premonition."

"You were right to conclude that we were in jeopardy," Eudora said.

"Overturning the kitchen table was brilliant," Rebecca Hastings said. "You were dealing with a madwoman. Distraction was your best strategy."

"It was all I could think of at the time," Calista said. She shivered at the memory. "But it would have been for naught if Trent had not arrived when he did and dealt with that man with the knife."

"That man with the knife now has a name." Trent picked up the diary that he had found. "Oliver Saxby. And he was truly mad. He murdered his parents when he was just seventeen. Used a kitchen knife. An uncle was left to deal with the boy. Oliver was committed to an asylum. The killings were hushed up, of course."

"No one wants rumors of a possible taint of madness in the bloodline," Harry said. He shook his head. "That sort of thing can destroy a family, especially a high-ranking clan."

"Yes," Trent said. He flipped through some of the pages in the diary. "According to this, Saxby was given books to read because they kept him quiet. Evidently he treasured the legends of King Arthur and the Knights of the Round Table. In his madness he came to believe that he inhabited a bizarre, fictional world. He perceived himself to be a knight-errant."

"But the knights of old were said to be honorable, upright men who slew dragons and served their noble ladies," Eudora pointed out.

"I doubt if Saxby slew any dragons, but he did find a lady to serve," Trent said.

Calista had been about to take a sip of tea. She paused. "Anna Kettering."

"Precisely." Trent set the diary on the desk. "Anna was equally mad but quite brilliant in her own way. It's clear from Saxby's notes that she manipulated him to further her own ends. She convinced him that the reason he had been locked up was because he had committed a grave offense against the knightly code."

Andrew lowered a half-eaten sandwich. "In other words, he had dishonored himself."

"Anna offered him a way to remove the stain on his honor?" Harry asked, intrigued. "Yes, that would have worked, given what we know of Saxby's delusions."

"She made him think that he could purify himself by murdering innocent women?" Eudora asked. "That makes no sense."

"In his demented state of mind, they were not innocent," Trent explained. He tapped the diary. "Anna convinced him that the women he killed were evil sorceresses. By the way, Saxby's diary answers one other question."

"What?" Andrew asked.

"I have been wondering who wrote the notes that accompanied the memento mori gifts and the coffin bells," Trent said. "The handwriting matches that in Saxby's diary."

"Anna sent him out to murder people she wanted to kill," Calista said. "Those three governesses and, eventually, me—all women she believed had seduced her husband. Nestor Kettering evidently had affairs with the poor governesses. But I rejected him."

"That didn't matter," Trent said. "The problem was that Nestor appeared to want you. And for the second time."

"She no doubt believed that her husband was more obsessed with you than with the others precisely because he couldn't have you," Harry said.

"Anna spent nearly three years in an asylum run by a man who raped her on a regular basis," Rebecca said. "She no doubt learned a great deal about the nature of obsession."

"She told herself that she could cure her husband's obsession with other women by removing the objects of his obsession," Calista said. "But first she tried to satisfy her own obsessive nature by punishing Nestor's paramours with the memento mori gifts. They were meant to induce fear. When the ritual was concluded, she sent her knight-errant to murder them."

"And then she celebrated by providing her victims with an expensive funeral," Harry concluded.

"But why did she kill her husband?" Andrew asked. "He was the object of her obsession."

Harry pondered that briefly. "I'm speculating here because there is no way I can question the patient, herself. But I suspect that when Anna discovered that her husband was planning to have her committed, she finally realized she could never win his love. She killed him to save herself from an asylum but I think there was another reason, as well. In the end she tried to cure herself of her own obsession using the same therapy she had employed to cure Nestor. She destroyed the object of her obsession."

Eudora looked at Calista. "I've been meaning to ask you how you came up with the clever notion of holding a séance right there in your kitchen. Pretending to summon the spirit of Anna's father was brilliant."

"I remembered what Trent said about séances being theater—just another way of telling a story," Calista said. "He pointed out that, in the case of a séance, the medium has a huge advantage."

"The audience wants, above all else, to believe," Trent said.

68

"LISTEN TO THIS," Calista said.

She pushed her plate of eggs and toast aside, picked up the morning edition of the *Flying Intelligencer*, and read the story aloud to the others gathered at the table.

Andrew listened with rapt attention, as did Eudora. Trent, however, calmly continued to eat his breakfast.

> A great house fire occurred in Cranleigh Square two nights ago. The blaze was set by a madman armed with a knife. He broke into the house with the evident intention of outraging the two respectable ladies who were in residence at the time. Both women were rescued, unharmed, by Mr. Trent Hastings, the well-known author of the Clive Stone novels, who arrived in time to subdue the madman.
>
> Thanks to Mr. Hastings's heroic actions, not only were the two ladies saved, but also a pair of elderly servants. Many of those at the scene observed that Mr. Hastings appeared to be a real-life version of his fictional character, Clive Stone.

Unfortunately, a third person, a recently widowed lady who had called at Cranleigh Hall earlier that evening, was trapped upstairs by the flames and leaped to her death. The intruder was also killed by the inferno.

Eudora sniffed. "Well, the correspondent got part of the story correct. There was, indeed, a great fire. But most of the rest is nonsense. That dreadful man with the knife, Saxby, did not intend to outrage us—he came to murder you, Calista. And it was Anna Kettering, the *recently widowed lady*, who set the fire."

Andrew set aside the paper he had been reading and gestured toward it with his fork. "Same mistakes in the other accounts. I suppose it is too much to expect the press to get the facts right."

Calista smiled. "The reporter was correct on one point—Mr. Trent Hastings, well-known author of the Clive Stone novels, did indeed arrive at a most opportune moment. I suspect that the accounts of the incident in the press will sell a few more copies of the author's books."

"One can only hope," Trent said. He got up and went to the sideboard to help himself to more eggs. "But I believe you are all overlooking the most important aspect of the newspaper stories."

"What is that?" Calista asked.

Trent heaped the eggs onto his plate and turned to face the table.

"None of the reports in the press mentions your introductions agency," he said. "That means you don't have to be concerned that the public will form any unfortunate opinions about the precise nature of your business."

Eudora brightened. "Trent is right. There will be no misunderstandings, Calista. You can relax."

"I don't think so," Calista said. "In case it has escaped your notice, my business burned to the ground."

Eudora sighed. "There is that aspect of the situation."

Calista drummed her fingers on the tablecloth, thinking.

"I can reconstruct some of my files," she said finally. "And I expect that, when they learn of the disaster, many of my clients will get in touch to see if I intend to continue my services."

Andrew met her eyes. "I can help you. I remember a great deal about the research I did for you. I still have some of my recent notes on your clients. They are in the same notebook that I was using to track Kettering."

"My conservatory," Eudora said suddenly.

They all looked at her.

"What about it?" Trent asked.

"It would make a perfect setting for a salon. You are most welcome to use it as often as you like, Calista. Trent can lock himself in his study. Isn't that right, Trent?"

"Certainly," Trent said. He sat down and started to eat. "So long as none of Calista's guests expects me to pretend to be interested in their detailed critiques of my novels, I have no objection."

Andrew laughed.

Calista's eyes filled with tears.

"I don't know how to thank you and Eudora, Trent," she said.

"No thanks are necessary," Eudora said. "You have changed my life for the better, Calista, by introducing me to Mr. Tazewell. Providing you a place to hold your salons is the least I can do. Isn't that right, Trent?"

Trent looked at Calista.

"The very least," he agreed.

69

THE RUINS OF the great house smoldered and smoked under a dull gray sky and a steady drizzle of rain. The stone chimneys still stood and so did portions of the outer walls but there was no salvaging the structure.

Calista contemplated the scene from beneath the shelter of the umbrella that Trent held. Andrew stood nearby.

"No point trying to rebuild," Trent said. "The world is changing and so is the market for grand houses like Cranleigh Hall. Costs too much to keep them staffed and in good repair."

"I agree," Calista said. "But I must admit that Cranleigh Hall served a purpose when it came to my business. I could not have established my introductions agency without it."

"Your clients are the most important aspect of your business," Trent said. "You've still got them."

"And more where they came from," Andrew added cheerfully. "There's no lack of lonely people who want to meet other people for purposes of friendship, love, and matrimony."

"True," Calista agreed. "But I would remind you that you and I own that pile of smoldering rubble. What on earth are we going to do with it?"

"If I might make a suggestion," Trent said.

"Of course," Calista said.

"The property has considerable value," Trent said. "It is large and well situated in a good neighborhood. It could be used to build some very fine town houses, the sale of which would bring a handsome profit."

Andrew's eyes lit with enthusiasm. "Excellent notion. We could make a small fortune if we build elegant town houses."

"But it takes money to build houses," Calista pointed out. "We would have to convince someone to loan us the funds. I think the best thing to do is sell the property outright to an investor."

Andrew grimaced. "Won't make nearly as much money that way."

"Yes, but an outright sale would give us a nice profit and we will be able to invest the money in other ways," Calista said.

Trent cleared his throat. "I would remind both of you that I have something of a knack for investing."

"I could not ask you to undertake such a commitment," Calista said. "You and your sister have done so much for us. It would not be right."

"Rest assured that I consider this an excellent investment, not just a favor to you and Andrew. There is money to be made here. I see no reason why the six of us should not take the profits."

"The *six* of us?" Andrew asked.

"Eudora and Harry will want to invest in the town houses, as well," Trent said. "And then there is Mr. Pell. I do believe we will all come out of this quite nicely."

Andrew grinned. "In that case, I trust you will both excuse me. I have an appointment with my first client."

Calista looked at him, startled. "You have a client for your detective services?"

"Rebecca Hastings referred her to me," Andrew said. "Her name is Mrs. Foster. Evidently, her housekeeper has gone missing. Everyone is saying that the woman left for a post that paid better. But Mrs. Foster is convinced that the housekeeper would not leave without giving notice."

"Congratulations," Trent said. "You have a talent for detective work."

"For heaven's sake, be careful," Calista said.

"I will," Andrew promised. "And don't worry, I will always be available to research the backgrounds of your prospective clients."

"I am glad to know that."

Andrew loped off to a waiting hansom and jumped up into the cab. Calista watched the vehicle move off down the street. A wistful sensation—a mix of sadness and joy and understanding—swept through her. She smiled a little.

"It's time, isn't it?" she said.

"For your brother to find his place in the world?" Trent watched the hansom disappear around a corner. "Yes. A young man needs to maintain his own lodgings, make a few mistakes, and find his footing in life. But do not fear. He will never be alone because he has a sister he loves and who loves him."

"I know. We do not need to share a home to be a family."

"True."

"I suspect that I am not the only one who will be learning to live without a family member under the same roof," Calista said. "Eudora and Mr. Tazewell are developing what appears to be a very serious relationship. I would not be the least bit surprised if they announce plans to marry in the near future."

"About time Eudora got a household of her own to manage."

He sounded quite pleased, Calista thought.

"It seems we have fulfilled our responsibilities to our siblings at last," she said. "We can both take comfort in that knowledge."

Trent contemplated the smoking ruins of the house. "In that case, I think we are free to turn our attention to our own situation."

"Are you afraid that you might be lonely once your sister has left your house?"

Trent turned to face her. "Not if you will do me the honor of consenting to marry me."

She was suddenly breathless. "Are you asking me to marry you because you do not want either of us to be lonely?"

"No," he said. "I am asking you to marry me because I love you."

"Trent." Her heart was suddenly overflowing with an intoxicating emotion.

"I am aware that I am not ideal husband material," he continued. "I do not consider myself moody, but Eudora is right—I do tend to retreat into my study for long periods of time when I am working on a book, which is frequently. I keep odd hours, especially when I am nearing the completion of a manuscript. I am not inclined to be sociable, especially when I am writing. And some of my friends are, as my sister has pointed out, not the sort one invites to tea. But if you think you can put up with my eccentricities I would be the happiest man on earth."

"I love you, Trent. Looking back, I'm quite sure that I fell in love with you that very first afternoon when I mistook you for a potential client. I will be happy to tolerate your eccentricities because you have proven that you will be tolerant of mine. Of course I will marry you."

His eyes heated.

"Calista," he said. "I promise you that I will love you until—"

She stopped him by putting one gloved finger on his lips.

"Hush," she said. "I will marry you, but please do not say that you will love me until death do us part. You are a writer, sir. Find other words that suit the occasion."

He smiled slowly, caught her hand in his, and drew her into his arms.

"I was going to say that I would love you until the end of time. Always and forever."

"Always and forever." A glorious, effervescent sense of certainty sparkled through her. "Yes, I believe that will work very well, indeed."

70

Fʀᴏᴍ ᴛʜᴇ ʟᴀsᴛ chapter of *Clive Stone and the Affair of the Missing Bride* . . .

*Clive Stone propped his heels on the hassock and contemplated the fire while he savored his brandy. "It would appear that together we have successfully solved this rather odd case, Miss Preston."*

*"Indeed, we have, Mr. Stone." Wilhelmina took a sip of the sherry that Mrs. Button had poured for her. "The young lady is safely home with her new husband and all is well."*

*"Thanks to your scientific analysis of the drug that Charlotte Bliss was using to keep the poor woman in a trance. You were the one who deduced that Bliss required a certain type of herb to concoct the poison."*

*"Which enabled you to identify the apothecary who sold the herb to Bliss."*

*Stone drank a little more of his brandy. "It occurs to me that we might work together again on another case. We are entering a new era*

341

*in crime detection, one in which science will play a major role. Your skills and knowledge would be invaluable."*

*"I would enjoy consulting for you again, Mr. Stone. I find your investigation business quite fascinating."*

*"And I find you quite fascinating, Miss Preston."*

*Wilhelmina smiled.*

*It occurred to Stone that before the affair of the missing bride, he had been in danger of sinking into a state of ennui. That was no longer true. Now his future promised to be extremely interesting.*

"An excellent ending," Calista said. She tossed the copy of the *Flying Intelligencer* onto the nightstand and watched Trent come toward the bed. "You have set the stage for an intriguing relationship between Clive Stone and Wilhelmina Preston."

"Unfortunately, not all of my readers will agree with you."

"There will always be critics, of course, but you will ignore them."

He stopped beside the bed and smiled down at her. "Will I?"

"Certainly. Just think of all the readers who will enjoy this ending."

"I'll try to remember that when the editor forwards the complaints that will surely arrive in his office."

She opened her arms. "Never fear, I will console you."

He took off his dressing gown, pulled aside the covers, and got into bed.

"How, exactly, will you do that, Mrs. Hastings?" he asked.

She smiled and put her arms around his neck, pulling him down so that she could kiss him.

"Like this, Mr. Hastings."

"Yes," he said after a while. "That will work very well."